ERLE STANLEY GARDNER

- Cited by the Guinness Book of World Records as the #1 best-selling writer of all time!

- Author of more than 100 clever, authentic, and sophisticated mystery novels!

- Creator of the amazing Perry Mason, the savvy Della Street, and dynamite detective Paul Drake!

- THE ONLY AUTHOR WHO OUT-SELLS AGATHA CHRISTIE, HAROLD ROBBINS, BARBARA CARTLAND, AND LOUIS L'AMOUR *COMBINED!*

Why?

Because he writes the best, most fascinating whodunits of all!

You'll want to read every one of them, coming soon from
BALLANTINE BOOKS

By Erle Stanley Gardner
Published by Ballantine Books:

The Case of the
Haunted Husband

Erle Stanley Gardner

BALLANTINE BOOKS • NEW YORK

Copyright © 1941 by Erle Stanley Gardner
Copyright renewed © 1969 by Erle Stanley Gardner

All rights reserved under International and Pan-American Copyright Conventions. Published in the United States by Ballantine Books, a division of Random House, Inc., New York, and simultaneously in Canada by Random House of Canada Limited, Toronto.

http://www.randomhouse.com

Library of Congress Catalog Card Number: 96-96430

ISBN 0-345-33495-7

This edition published by arrangement with William Morrow & Company, Inc.

Manufactured in the United States of America

First Ballantine Books Edition: August 1981

10 9 8 7 6 5 4 3 2 1

Cast of Characters

STEPHANE CLAIRE—Ex hat-check girl who hopefully hitch-hikes her way to Hollywood

FIRST DRIVER—Possessed of paternalistic instincts, he guides her carefully from San Francisco to Bakersfield

SECOND DRIVER—Provides the nonstop flight from Bakersfield to Los Angeles

HORTENSE ZITKOUSKY—Stephane's well-upholstered, ever-loyal friend

DELLA STREET—The one-in-a-million secretary, who plies her trade with

PERRY MASON—Lawyer-detective extraordinary

PAUL DRAKE—Supersleuth who knows an angle when he sees one

L. C. SPINNEY—Elusive tenant who pounds a typewriter, makes telephone calls and mails letters, but is never seen

MRS. LOIS WARFIELD—Who does a fancy feminine trick with a compact

JULES HOMAN—Camera-shy Hollywood producer who works in seclusion

HORACE HOMAN—Playboy brother of movie magnate Jules

MAX OLGER—Stephane's over-solicitous uncle

JACKSON STERNE—Stephane's self-effacing suitor

LIEUTENANT TRAGG—Homicide Squad expert who sticks his neck out for Mason

ADLER GREELEY—Whose business duties required frequent trips to San Francisco

DAPHNE GREELEY—His wife, who believes a clever woman can turn a man's head but not his heart

FRANK CORVIS—Traffic officer, who found lipstick on the steering wheel

EDITH LIONS—Accident witness, who saw a woman and a middle-aged man in the coupe

ERNEST TANNER—Homan's chauffeur, who is interested in mileage and speedometer figures

1

STEPHANE OLGER gripped the counter over which hats were checked by the patrons of Zander's Tropical Shack. She could feel the skin drawn tight across her knuckles, could feel blood pounding in her cheeks as she watched the departing back of the manager.

Back of her, Emily Carr, a poker-faced brunette with swiftly competent fingers and thin lips, went quietly about the job of straightening coats on the hangers.

"Well," Stephane said, without taking her eyes from the manager's back, *"that* was crude."

"He isn't noted for finesse," Emily Carr observed, smoothing a flap over a pocket. "Funny how much a man will try to get in one overcoat pocket—no, pardon me all to hell—how much he *will* get into an overcoat pocket. . . . What are you going to do?"

"Walk out—under my own power," Stephane Olger said.

Emily Carr turned away from the rack of coats to survey Stephane's blonde beauty. "It won't work, Stephane. He's plenty smart. You've been high-hat with him. He isn't accustomed to that and he doesn't like it. So what? He gets a couple of patrons to put marked dollar bills in the tips. You check out the coin. The tips aren't there. Where does that leave you?"

"Emily, I don't know what happened to that money. I distinctly remember both tips. I put them in the drawer, and . . ."

"And were called away?" Emily asked.

"Yes, why?"

"Oh, nothing. He lifted 'em out himself while you were gone—and left all the rest of the money. Then he checks up. You're responsible. You've been knocking down on tips. What are you going to do? You'll do as *he* says now."

"I wish I'd slapped his face. I'll do it yet."

1

"He'll blacklist you for dishonesty. Tip chiseling is the one thing they won't stand for in this business."

"Emily, *you* never have trouble like that. I have plenty. What's wrong with me?"

"You leave yourself wide open."

"What's a girl supposed to do with a man who takes advantage of his position?"

"Laugh him off," Emily Carr said easily, "before he gets funny ideas."

"I didn't notice any preliminaries."

"I did. Not today, but yesterday, the day before, and most of last week. I went with a fighter once. He told me never to let the other man get set. He said to keep 'em off balance. Whenever the other man gets set, you're going to get jarred. Don't let 'em do it."

Stephane said, "Well, I'm tired of checking hats. I'm going after something else. I've got a friend in Hollywood. You remember Horty?"

Emily shook her head.

"The girl who came to call on me when she was on her vacation. I brought her in here. . . ."

"The girl with the upholstered curves?" Emily interrupted.

"That's the one."

"I'll bet nothing gets *her* goat," Emily Carr said.

"You're right. She'd take something like this right in her stride."

"Listen, Stephane, use your brains. Don't get all worked up because . . ."

"I'm fired?" Stephane asked.

"That's what he *said,*" Emily agreed. "Those were the words he used, but he doesn't mean it that way. He means that you're to come to him filled with tears and humility while you try to convince him someone else got the dough. I told you he wasn't noted for finesse."

Stephane looked at her watch. "Think you can handle it alone, Emily?" she asked.

"If you want it that way."

"I do. If he comes back here looking for me, tell him I've decided to— Tell him I've decided to look for a new *proposition.*"

Emily Carr's sensitive mouth twisted into a quick smile. "He'd appreciate that."

"Yes, I suppose he would."

"Need any dough?"

"No. I'll hitchhike."

"What's your middle name, Stephane?"

"Claire. Why?"

"All right, drop the Olger. It sounds hard, and with your complexion it sounds sort of Russian. Make it Stephane Claire. That'll take. You can't tell, babe, you just might get a break in Hollywood. And if you get a break, you'll make good. You're not like those yellow blondes that fade fast. You've got that white-gold touch. You're metal, the kind of metal that takes a temper and holds it."

"Thanks," Stephane said, and put on her coat and hat.

"You're different from most of us in this game—and you're running away from something. What is it, a husband?"

Stephane said, wearily, "No, from money with strings tied to it."

"What money, and what strings?"

"A rich uncle. He thought he could dictate to me—even pick out the man I was to marry."

Emily studied her. "Better go back, kid."

"Not me. I'm headed for Hollywood. You can't tell, I might bust into pictures."

"You might at that. Tell Sam Goldwyn hello for me. Tell Clark Gable I sent my love. Any messages you want to leave for the manager?"

"Yes, one."

Emily's eyes twinkled. "I'll try and convey it to him so he'll understand. 'By, kid."

" 'By."

"Luck."

"Thanks."

2

THE MAN SAID, "That's Bakersfield ahead. I'm sorry I'm not going through."

"How far to Los Angeles?"

"A little over a hundred miles. You can make it in a little over two hours' driving time. I wish you wouldn't insist on going through tonight."

"Oh, I'll be all right. I have a friend in Los Angeles. I can stay with her."

"I'll be glad to . . . to get you a cabin. There's a very fine auto hotel here."

"No, thanks. Don't bother."

"It's rather late, and . . ."

Stephane smiled. "Listen, I can take care of myself. I've done this before."

"Well, here's the traffic circle. Los Angeles traffic goes around. . . . Tell you what I'll do. I'll run you out to a boulevard stop. It's in a well-lighted district. That'll help you catch a ride."

"Oh, don't bother. I can get a ride anywhere."

"It's only a short distance."

"You live here?" Stephane asked.

"No. I'm stopping over on business."

Stephane opened the door. "All right," she said, smiling, "I'm getting out. Quit worrying about me."

"I wish you'd let me take you down to the boulevard stop, and . . ."

"No. This is fine. Thanks a lot. I appreciate the ride and everything. You were—nice."

She gave him her hand. He held it for a moment, a man in the late forties who looked on a girl of twenty-four as a mere infant. His solicitude was flattering but annoying. "I'll get along all right," she repeated, withdrawing her hand, smiling and closing the car door.

He didn't drive on at once, but sat watching, as though

4

waiting to size up the person with whom Stephane was going to ride.

She came back to him, laughing. "Listen, you can't do that. It looks like a racket. Motorists won't stop when they see you parked here keeping an eye on me. I'm sorry," she added at the expression on his face.

He started the car. "Try and pick a woman driver. It's late, you know."

Stephane, holding her handbag in her left hand, watched the tail light out of sight, then looked hopefully up the highway. It was only a little after ten. She should be in Los Angeles by one o'clock.

For the space of nearly a minute, there were no cars, then they came in a bunch, four of them in a procession of blinding headlights. Stephane knew that cars in a string seldom stop. Each driver is too intent on jockeying for position and getting past the others to bother with hitch-hikers. She stepped back a few paces.

The cars bore down on her. White, blazing headlights dazzled her eyes. The first car roared past. The air currents sucking in behind the car whipped her skirts. She automatically raised a hand to her hat. The second, third, and fourth cars whizzed by. A fifth car was almost on her when she opened her eyes. It came on with a smooth hiss of power, a mere whisper of speed as it rocketed past, intent upon overtaking and passing the four cars ahead. Then the rear blazed into red light, weaved slightly as the brakes slowed the big car to a stop.

Stephane glanced behind her to make certain the road was clear, and started to run.

That running was a gesture. She hoped the driver would back up; but he didn't, and when Stephane drew abreast of the car, she realized he was the sort who wouldn't.

He matched the arrogant luxury of the car in every way, a man in the early thirties with dark, impudent eyes which shifted from her face to her legs as she climbed in beside him. He was wearing a dinner jacket, under a light-weight black topcoat. The hand on the gearshift lever was soft-skinned. The nails were well manicured. A diamond ring glittered on the fourth finger, and Stephane's nostrils caught the faint but unmistakable reek of whiskey. He had a short, black mustache, and drink-red eyes.

But the man seemed competent. The car was a big modern machine geared for speed, totally different from the car in which she'd made the long trip from San Francisco to Bakersfield.

The man shifted through the gears. The motor noise became a reassuring whisper as the car sped forward.

"Los Angeles?" he asked casually as he made the boulevard stop.

"Yes. Are you going that far?"

"Uh huh. Cold?"

She knew what was coming, so she smiled, despite the chill which had been gripping her ankles ever since sunset, and said, "No, I'm fine, thank you."

"Flask in that glove compartment. Nice stuff."

"I'm fine."

"Better take a drink. It'll warm you up."

"No, thanks."

He turned to look at her, dark eyes glittering with assurance. "You aren't going to go puritan on me, are you?"

She laughed. "I'm not puritan. I'm just me."

"All right, have it your own way. We'll stop up the road a ways. I need a short one. Get out of some of this traffic first."

For a few minutes he devoted his attention to driving. The car slid smoothly past the string of four cars which had been ahead of them. The wheels seemed to lift up the cement miles, roll them through the speedometer, and toss them scornfully behind. Stephane thought they must be doing sixty. She glanced at the needle of the speedometer. It was holding steady at eighty-five.

"You don't believe in speed laws, do you?" she asked with a light laugh, making conversation.

"No."

By the time they reached Lebec, Stephane knew her man like a book. She took one short drink from the flask, listened to him gurgle down a good jolt of the whiskey.

The man evidently had money. He seemed to take intimacy for granted. He had a quick, cynical mind. Back of his complacent assurance there was a cold savage something—a contempt for women. Here was a man, Stephane decided, whose attitude and temperament would appeal to but one type of woman—and because his experience had been confined to that selfish, vacuous-minded fringe, he judged the entire sex by those standards.

But there was a cold wind blowing up on the ridge. The car had a heater which sent a current of warm air caressing her cold ankles, thawing out the numbness of her feet. The man was a good driver, and within a little more than an hour they should be in Los Angeles. She'd kid him along and go on through in this car.

Stephane played up to him as little as she could, just enough to keep him from putting her out on the road, a maneuver of which he seemed thoroughly capable.

After the second drink, he screwed the cap back on the flask, tossed it into the glove compartment. His hand patted her back, slid along her shoulder, down her arm, touched her leg briefly.

"Okay, baby," he said, "let's get to L.A. And when I get there, I've got a job to do . . . a . . . oh, well, what the hell?"

He crowded the car into speed. A gust of wind hurtled against it, swaying it on its springs. The night was cold and intensely clear. The headlights streamed down the pavement in a brilliant fan of illumination. Oncoming motorists blinked their lights repeatedly, but that was all the good it did them. This driver wasn't one to bother with roadside courtesies. His own lights were bright enough to minimize the glare of lights from other machines.

They were going faster now. Stephane could feel the car, despite its low center of gravity, swaying on the curves. She realized that that last drink he had taken had been pretty heavy. He was stealing glances at her now, glances which were frankly appraising. She pretended to be very much preoccupied, looking at the scenery through the right window so she wouldn't have to meet his eyes. Thank heavens, the front seat was wide enough so he couldn't . . .

"Come on over here, baby."

She looked at him in surprise.

"Come on. Don't be so standoffish."

She laughed. "I always did like to sit in a corner."

"Well, forget it, and come on over here."

She slid over a few inches.

"Hell, that's not *over.*"

"You need room for driving."

"You can drive this bus with one finger. Come on. . . . Say, what's the matter with you? You aren't an old-fashioned stick-in-the-mud, are you? . . . Oh, come on *over.* . . . Here. . . ."

His right arm circled her neck, dragged her over toward

him. He gave one quick glance at the road, then, still holding the wheel with his left hand, forced her chin up.

She saw his eyes, felt the touch of his lips. The reek of liquor was in her nostrils. She fought free, not worried so much about the embrace as about the careening course of the car. Her gloved hand shot to the steering wheel. "Watch where you're going," she cried sharply.

He laughed and caught the wheel from her hands. The big car had swerved across to the left side of the highway. Now it came screeching back to the right, as an indignant motorist shot past, his palm pressed against the horn.

"What are you trying to do, kill us both?" Stephane asked.

"When I want something, I want it."

She moved back toward the far corner of the seat. She was trembling.

"All right, stop the car. I'll take a transfer."

"No chance, sister. This is a nonstop flight."

She was frightened, but wasn't going to show it. She calmly opened her purse, took out her compact and lipstick. She took off her right glove, placed lipstick on the tip of her little finger.

He said, "We aren't finished yet."

She turned calmly toward him. "I am."

"Think you're going to pull that stuff with me?"

"If you'll stop the car, I'll get out."

He said, "There's the door."

A ring of keys dangled down from the switch. She reached forward quickly, turned off the ignition, and jerked out the keys. She popped the keys into her purse, snapped it shut.

"You little devil," he said; and lunged.

She fought him back, pushing out with her right hand. The lipstick on her little finger left a long red streak down the front of his shirt. He grabbed her wrist. The car, with the ignition shut off, was slowing from eighty-five to seventy, from seventy to sixty. He was trying to wrench the purse from her left hand. As her grip resisted his efforts, he took his left hand from the steering wheel. Her lips pressed against his shirt.

She raised her knee to push back against his body, twisting to look through the windshield.

"Look out," she screamed and quit struggling.

He paused for one pawing familiarity at her surrender, then whirled back to grab the steering wheel.

The car had swerved far to the left. The pavement was three lanes wide. Two cars directly ahead blocked the right lane. A big truck and trailer were coming toward them in the left lane. Headlights in the middle lane blazed through the windshield.

The man swung the wheel hard to the right, automatically stepped on the throttle, then, as there was no response from the dead motor, tried the brakes.

A slight jarring impact came from the rear as the car swerved under the sudden application of the brakes.

There were headlights directly ahead. They grew larger. They bored directly into Stephane's face. She screamed— And the headlights seemed to pounce on her. She had never realized headlights could be so widely separated, so bright— so close.

A great wave of blackness submerged everything, headlights, cars, highway. There was a high-pitched tinkle of sound which persisted after that final crash. It was strange, she thought, that the sound of falling fragments of shattered glass would be so enduring. What had happened to the light? The wave of darkness had engulfed the road, why hadn't—and then the darkness flowed over all sound and submerged it, and flowed over her as well.

3

STEPHANE WAS CONSCIOUS of a flickering light—a light which came and went. There was pain in her chest, the sound of some liquid gurgling.

Lights again, this time stabbing into her eyes. She raised her lids with an effort. The beam seemed to pierce her brain.

A man's voice said, "She's alive. Her eye moved."

She felt the thing which was beneath and on her left sway, as though waves were rocking it. A man said, "We can lift her through."

Again she opened her eyes. This time her senses had cleared so she could see, and could understand what she saw.

She was behind the steering wheel of the big car. Her gloved left hand and her bare right hand were holding firmly to the perimeter of the wheel. The car was over on its side, balanced precariously on a steep bank. Water was running out of the radiator, oil from the crankcase. The lights were off, and the motor was dead.

Someone turned the flashlight toward her again. She saw the windshield interspersed with myriad cracks, saw broken glass glittering on the seat.

There were people above her. Arms reached down through the wide window in the car. Fingers circled her wrists, were pulling her up. A man's voice said, "Give me a hand here. This thing may catch fire. Hurry up. Can you use your legs, sister?"

She tried to struggle. Her legs seemed twisted and useless. She felt herself falling. Only the inexorable pressure on her wrists held her up. Then there were other hands under her armpits, on her body, and she was being lifted smoothly up.

Darkness again, the feeling that she was being carried. . . . Voices, voices engaged in meaningless conversation. She could hear the sounds, and knew they were words, but they conveyed no meaning to her mind. . . . Blood-red lights on the road. . . . Screaming of tires. . . . "Hurry, there's been an accident." . . . "Over there." . . . "I think he's dead." . . . "Right here." . . . "Beg pardon, Madam, there's been an accident." . . . Screaming tires. . . . Sirens.

The darkness of oblivion

Pain stung her into consciousness, short, sharp road jolts which came from tires hitting expansion joints on the concrete pavement at great speed. The steady sound of a siren, the clanging of a bell. . . . She was in traffic now. She could hear the sound of traffic signals, of horns, the rumble of streetcars. But the ambulance went right ahead, its siren clearing a right of way. Stephane could feel the short, sharp jolt of streetcar tracks, feel the sway of the big car as the driver spun the wheel first to one side then to another, avoiding obstructions as the ambulance raced through the frozen traffic.

She felt the touch of hands. A man's voice said, "Take it easy." She heard the sound of rollers, then she was being lifted on a stretcher. She caught the smell of ether, opened her eyes, and saw the walls of a white corridor flowing past. She was on wheels . . . bright lights in her eyes, skilled fingers exploring her body. . . . She felt a twinge of pain, heard a man's voice whisper, heard the rustle of stiffly starched garments, then the jab of a hypodermic needle. . . . She was having difficulty with her breathing. She tried to fight something off her face, trying to get fresh air. A nurse said, "Don't fight. Breathe deeply. . . ." A long deep breath. . . .

4

HORTY LOOKED DOWN at Stephane's blonde hair spilled out on the pillow. "You're a mess," she said.

Stephane smiled. "I feel it. I ache everywhere."

"You're lucky nothing's broken. Some bad bruises and a few stitches in your leg. A cut on your shoulder, but it's all patched up nicely."

"Any scars?"

"Not where they'll show, unless you take up fan dancing."

"I might at that," Stephane said. "My mouth feels like a hotel room after a salesmen's convention has moved out. What happened?"

"You're in a jam," Horty said.

"I'll say I am. I came down here to get a job, and here I am laid up. How long will it be before I can get out, Horty? Give me the real low-down."

Horty was in the late twenties, and weighed a hundred and fifty. Her figure didn't bulge. She carried her weight in comfortable curves which attracted the masculine eye. There was bubbling good nature in her eyes, a smile always twisting the corners of her lips. She perpetually found something in life to laugh at. The broad-minded tolerance of her outlook enabled her to see humor in any situation. She was never insulted, never shocked, never annoyed. She took life in her stride, ate what she wanted when she wanted, and never worried. "Sure, men like slender, willowy figures," she said. "They also like good nature. Good nature goes with upholstery. And I like food. So there you are." And Horty never suffered for any lack of men friends. Men were always taking her out, starting in as good pals and winding up in the grip of fascination which made other women seem insipid.

"Come on, Horty," Stephane said. "How long?"

Horty looked down at her. The smile quit trembling at the corners of her mouth, but her eyes still showed humor. "You must have been pretty high," she said.

"What do you mean?"

"Stealing the guy's car."

"Stealing a car! What are you talking about?"

"Didn't you grab the buzz buggy?" Horty asked.

"Good heavens, no. I was riding . . ."

"There was liquor on your breath."

"Yes, he kept after me until I took a drink."

"But you were driving the car."

"I was doing no such thing, Hortense Zitkousky."

Horty's eyes became grave. "You wouldn't kid an old friend, would you?"

"Of course not."

Horty looked around the room, lowered her voice. "It's okay, Stephane. The nurse is out."

"I tell you I *wasn't* driving that car."

"When they found you, you were behind the wheel."

Sudden realization came to Stephane's mind. "I was, at that," she admitted. "I remember that much. What happened to the man?"

"What man?"

"The man who was with me—who was driving the car."

Horty shook her head.

"Anybody hurt?" Stephane asked.

"Lots of people. Some of them bad. You sideswiped into a car on the right, went directly toward a car coming in your direction, raked across its front, and sent it over into the other line of traffic. It was a hit head-on. Then you went on down the bank, turned over four or five times, and came to rest right on the edge of a sheer drop. It's a wonder you didn't burn to a crisp."

"But I *wasn't* driving that car. Who owns it?"

"Some big shot in Hollywood. It was stolen yesterday afternoon."

"Yesterday. . . . What day is this?"

"Thursday."

"It was really stolen, Horty?"

"Uh huh."

Stephane tried to sit up, then, as she felt the soreness in her muscles, dropped back to the pillows. "What a mess," she moaned.

Horty said, "Oh, it's not so bad. They can't hook you for stealing the car, *if* you stick to your story. They can't prove you were intoxicated. Reckless driving is the worst they can pin on you—unless—look here, Stephane, you didn't *really* get high and don't-careish and steal that car, did you?"

"Don't be silly. I was thumbing my way down from San Francisco. I can prove I was in San Francisco yesterday morning. I picked up this ride in Bakersfield."

"The fellow had been drinking?"

"Yes."

"How much?"

"Not too little, not too much."

"Pawing?"

"Uh huh. He was trying to. That's what made the trouble."

"Look here, Stephane, you wouldn't kid me. You didn't think he was drunk, and get him to let you drive? It isn't someone you're protecting?"

"No, honest Injun."

Horty's eyes lost their twinkle. "Well," she said, "it looks like *you're* going to need a lawyer."

5

DELLA STREET, Perry Mason's secretary, listened to Horty's story, said apologetically, "Mr. Mason doesn't have time to handle many small cases and . . ."

"And I'm just a working girl," Horty interrupted. "I've got a little money saved up. I'm willing to put that into the kitty. What's more, I'm making a fair salary. I'm a secretary myself. Working for a nearsighted man," she added with bubbling laughter. "I'm not supposed to be an office ornament, so I can eat three times a day. Tell Mr. Mason I'll raise some money on a salary loan and . . ."

"I don't think that will be necessary," Della Street said with a smile. "Mr. Mason is usually very fair about fees. It's a question of whether he has the time to take on these small cases. Just a moment, please."

She walked through the law library to Mason's private office.

Perry Mason, seated in his comfortable, creaking swivel chair, was studying a bill of exceptions. The desk was piled with transcripts and leather-backed law books.

He looked up. "What's it?"

She said, "The case isn't anything you'd be interested in, but the woman is."

"What woman?"

"The one who's brought it in."

"Tell me," Mason said, pushing the swivel chair out from the desk, spinning around, and propping his feet on an open drawer. "Give me a cigarette out of that humidor, and tell me what it's all about."

Della Street handed him the cigarette. Mason snapped flame from the end of a match, and lit up.

"Well, it seems she's Polish. I guess the Poles hang together. She has a friend, a Stephane Claire Olger, whom she says is beautiful, and has decided to go by the name of Stephane Claire and . . ."

14

"Which one is out there?" Mason interrupted.

"Hortense Zitkousky. Apparently everyone calls her Horty. You'd get a kick out of her. She's got a full-of-curves figure, lots of good nature, lots of loyalty—about twenty-six, I'd judge. She says she's working in a secretarial position for a nearsighted man so she doesn't have to be an office ornament."

"What's the case?"

"Stephane Claire was hitchhiking down from San Francisco. She picked up a ride. A man was driving. He'd been drinking. There was a smash, and when she came to, she was behind the steering wheel. There was no sign of the man. The car belongs to a man by the name of Homan, some big-shot producer out in Hollywood. It was stolen yesterday afternoon."

"What time was the smash-up?"

"Around quarter past eleven last night."

"Where's Miss Claire?"

"Emergency Hospital, bruised, torn ligaments, cuts and a few stitches. The accident was pretty bad. I understand one of the men isn't expected to live. Three cars were involved. There's evidence the girl had been drinking. She admits she took one drink. She claims it was with the man who was driving the car. The police don't think there was any man. They think she stole the car—think it had been stolen twice, in fact."

"How come?" Mason asked.

"Apparently, the car was stolen from Hollywood yesterday afternoon. Someone drove it to Bakersfield, and abandoned it. This girl was hitchhiking down from San Francisco. She'd been fired up there for knocking down on tips. She saw the car with its doors unlocked and the key in the ignition, saw it was from Hollywood, and decided to drive it back."

"What does Miss Zitkousky say to that?"

"She says it's absurd—only she uses more colorful language."

"No one saw anything of a man in the wreck?"

"No."

Mason frowned, said, "Let's talk with this girl, and see what she looks like. Send her in."

Della Street brought Hortense Zitkousky into Mason's private office. Mason listened attentively to her story, said,

"I like your loyalty to your friend. Perhaps later on there'll be something I can do. I doubt if there is now. What you need is a good detective. The Drake Detective Agency has offices on this same floor. Ask for Paul Drake personally. Tell him I sent you, and tell him not to overcharge you. Let him see if he can find out a little more about that car. If he can find the man who was operating it, your friend will be in the clear. Even if he can find some witness who will swear there were two persons in the front seat, it will be enough. Surely someone involved in that smash must have seen two people in the car."

Horty said dubiously, "Yes, you'd think so."

"Tell Drake to report to me," Mason said, "and I'll see what I can do."

"That'll be swell, Mr. Mason. About a fee, I . . ." She opened her purse.

Mason waved the money aside with a gesture. "Forget it. I won't put in that much time on it. Drake will need some money for expenses. I wouldn't pay for having an operative on the case more than two or three days. I think that's all you'll need. Hope so, anyway."

Hortense said, "That's awfully white of you, Mr. Mason. Her girl friend in San Francisco knew she was planning to hitchhike down. Would her statement help?"

"Not much. As I understand it, the police claim your friend picked up the car in Bakersfield. Tell Drake to concentrate on that end of it. If she can show what time she got to Bakersfield, it would have some bearing. Police would hardly claim she stole the car unless they thought she was in Bakersfield for some time. Possibly the man who took her as far as Bakersfield can help."

"That's right," Horty said. "I'll ask her about him. She said he was perfectly swell. We can probably get hold of him. He may know something."

"That's the idea. Drake will know what to do. What you need right now is to get the facts. If you get them, you won't need a lawyer. If you don't have them, a lawyer won't do you any good. Tell Drake to report to me. Goodby."

When she had left, Mason picked up the telephone, got Drake on the line and said, "Sending you a girl and a case, Paul. I think it's something I may be interested in, but don't tell her so. Get the facts and then let me know."

6

PAUL DRAKE sprawled his tall figure crosswise in the big leather client's chair. "That auto-smash case, Perry," he said, pulling a notebook from his pocket.

"You mean the girl with the curves?"

"That's the one."

"Get anything on it?"

"Worked a couple of days and don't know what to do next. Had a couple of *good* operatives on it here, and an associate in San Francisco."

Mason said, "Okay, Paul, let's hear it."

"To begin with, Perry, every time I get to fooling around with it, I smell something fishy. That Stephane Claire is a good egg. She had a fight with an uncle, took out for herself, and learned how to light on her feet. Incidentally, Perry, she's a raving beauty, the platinum blonde type."

"What's wrong with Horty?" Mason asked.

Drake grinned. "If you'd take about thirty pounds off of her, Perry, you'd . . ."

"Ruin her disposition," Mason interrupted.

"There's something to that," Drake admitted. "She certainly is comfortable, that girl. Feels comfortable herself, and makes you feel comfortable. Miss Claire tells me that the boy friends who talk to Horty talk matrimony."

"Bet she's a good cook."

"I'll bet. Well, here's the dope on this thing, Perry. The D.A.'s office is showing lots of activity. That man who was injured died. That means they're going to put a manslaughter charge against the girl."

"Are they investigating her story?"

"Not the D.A.'s office. They're sold on the idea she was driving the car. The way they put it together, the girl got a lift as far as Bakersfield all right, just as she says. But they think the man who gave her the ride had a bottle and that Stephane Claire wasn't at all unwilling to help him

17

empty it. By the time she got to Bakersfield, she was pretty high. She blundered into this car, which another thief had abandoned, saw that its home was Hollywood, climbed in, and started going places."

"Sounds goofy," Mason said.

"No more goofy than her story. Well, anyway, here's the point, Perry. The car belongs to Jules Carne Homan. He's a big-shot Hollywood producer. Probably about half as big as he thinks he is, which still makes him draw quite a bit of water. He had a fight with his insurance company a couple of years ago, and decided to carry his own car insurance. Now get this, Perry. *If* that car was being driven with his permission, expressed or implied, he's stuck for damages up to ten thousand dollars. If Stephane Claire was driving that car, he's going to claim he isn't responsible for anything because the car wasn't being operated with his implied permission. *If* the car was being used by an agent of his—someone who was working for him or doing something for him at his request—he's stuck for the whole hog. So you can see what it means to Homan. On one theory, it costs him nothing. On another theory, it costs him ten thousand. If the person who was driving the car was on business for him, it might cost him plenty—and then some."

Mason narrowed his eyes. "Why do you talk about the car being driven by someone on business for him, Paul?"

"Because I think there's a darn good chance that's what happened."

"Let's have it."

"Well, I went out to see Homan. I didn't get anywhere. He was nasty nice, in an insulting way. Something about Homan didn't register. His story about how the car happened to be taken in the first place didn't click. It was all right from his viewpoint, but when I put myself in the position of a car thief and looked at it from that angle it sounded phony. If the car wasn't stolen he must have known who the driver was. What's more, the car was stolen around the middle of the day. According to Claire, the driver was wearing a tuxedo. Car thieves don't wear tuxedos when they walk out to swipe parked cars in the middle of the day.

"So I did a little detective work based on the theory that Homan might be lying. I had a man go down to the telephone office, say he was Homan's butler, that there was something wrong with the long-distance bill, and Homan wasn't going to pay some of the charges. I was looking for telephone calls from or to Bakersfield. Of course, the telephone office told him Homan was stuck if the calls had been placed from that phone. My man got in an argument and finally got to see the telephone bills.

"There was nothing to or from Bakersfield, but the day before the accident, Homan had been calling San Francisco, and San Francisco had been calling him, collect."

"You got the numbers?" Mason asked.

"Sure."

"What were they?"

"They all came from a cheap rooming house. The phone's listed in the name of L. C. Spinney—and there's lots of mystery about Spinney."

Mason's eyes showed interest. "Go ahead, Paul."

"Spinney has a cheap room in a cheap house in a cheap district. He has a telephone. It's a single line with an unlisted number. Spinney shows up about once a month. He has a portable typewriter. He bats out letters and mails them. He puts in calls to numbers we haven't been able to trace as yet, but other tenants in the building hear him talking. It sounds like a long-distance conversation. They hear him putting through long-distance calls, always station-to-station. They hear him tapping away on his typewriter. Spinney gets mail once or twice a month. He shows up to get that mail at irregular intervals. Sometimes the letters stay in his mailbox two or three weeks before they're taken out.

"But, get this, Perry—no one has ever seen Spinney."

"What?"

"It's a fact. He rented the room one night by sending a taxi driver in with some money and hand baggage. He has a room with a private outside entrance. He comes at night and he goes at night. No one knows whether he'll come in tonight and leave tomorrow before daylight, or come three weeks from now, stay a half hour while he bats out some stuff on his typewriter, and then vanish again.

"Of course, people have had glimpses of him, but not close enough to get stuff that would give me a description. He's a man. He's between twenty and fifty. He's not very thin and not very fat. He wears an overcoat and a felt hat —and quite frequently he's seen wearing evening clothes. Get it? A man in a cheap rooming house wearing evening clothes?"

Mason's eyes were partially closed in concentration.

"One of these letters is in his mailbox now," Drake went on. "My operative was afraid to steam it open, but he held the envelope up in front of a powerful light. He was able to see there was a money order in it and a letter. We managed to photograph that letter without opening the envelope."

"How?" Mason asked.

"Oh, it's a simple dodge. You put a piece of film in front of the envelope, clamp it firmly, turn on the light, and develop the film. Because the letter is folded, you get a scramble of slanting lines, but with a little care you can make out what's in the letter. This one said, 'I'm sending fifteen dollars which is all I can possibly spare this month. I wish he could write to me. Tell him I carry on somehow, but if he'd only write, it would make me so much happier.' "

"How was the letter signed?"

"Just 'Lois.' "

"Who's the money order from?"

"Lois Warfield."

"Check on her?" Mason asked.

"Sure. What do you think they're paying me for?"

"Darned if I know. Go ahead."

She was frightened to death when my New Orleans correspondent contacted her. She wouldn't talk. She's working in a cafeteria. One of the girls in the cafeteria gave my correspondent a little dope. Mrs. Warfield's only been in New Orleans a short time. Her husband left her a couple of years ago—some trouble over his thinking she was going to have a baby—and then she didn't. They were estranged for over a year, then she told him she still loved him and was saving money to come out and join him. He was supposed to be in Hollywood. Next thing she got a letter from one of the husband's friends saying something had happened, that Warfield was in a jam, couldn't even communicate with her himself. Evidently he was dodging cops and was afraid they'd watch her mail. She was in Ridgefield, Connecticut, then. She wrote this friend she was coming west to see if she could help, and started working her way across the country. When she hit New Orleans, she got a letter saying her husband was in jail. He'd done something so reprehensible, he wanted her to forget him. But she stuck. So she keeps herself broke sending money to pay for a lawyer who is going to try to get the husband's sentence shortened to ten years, or something like that. My operative had to get it second-hand. Mrs. Warfield wouldn't talk."

"How much does Homan make in salary?" Mason asked.

"Probably three or four thousand a week, perhaps more, perhaps less. You can't tell. Those Hollywood salaries are one thing for the publicity releases, and another for the income tax."

Mason pushed back his swivel chair, got up, and started pacing the floor.

"I hated to go as strong on it as I did," Drake apologized. "This girl with the upholstery hasn't got a lot of jack. Wires and that stuff cost money."

"You can't trace Spinney?"

"Not with anything I've been able to do so far. He comes and he goes. When he goes, he disappears. He got a wire a few days ago."

"Can't you get a copy of that wire?"

"It's illegal to . . ."

"Phooey! Are you arranging to get a copy?"

"If I can, yes."

"Think you can?"

"I don't know. It isn't easy. Someone will have to go into the telegraph office, say he's Spinney, and . . ."

Della Street tapped on the door from the law library, opened it, said, "Hi, Paul. Hope I'm not intruding. I have a message, just came from your office."

She handed Drake a folded sheet of paper. Drake opened it, read it, passed it over to Mason. "Copy of the telegram," he said.

Mason read, "HAVE LANDED JOB IN RIGLEY'S CAFETERIA LOS ANGELES WANT TO BE NEAR HIM WILL EXPLAIN WHEN I SEE YOU CAN HITCHHIKE ALL THE WAY—LOIS."

Mason tore the paper into small pieces, dropped them into his wastebasket, looked up at Della Street, and said, "Get me the person in charge of employment at Rigley's Cafeteria, Della. Tell him it's important."

Della Street nodded, stepped into her own office to put through the call.

Drake said, "Taken by and large, Perry, I hate to see this girl railroaded on a manslaughter charge."

Mason grinned. "You've sold me, Paul."

"Going to handle her case?"

"I'm going to see she isn't railroaded as the fall guy for some Hollywood producer."

"Might be a good idea for you to run out and have a chat with her, Perry. She's pretty low, and she doesn't look like the sort who's accustomed to being down in the dumps."

"They haven't made a formal charge yet?"

"They're filing one today. She's being held in the hospital. The D.A.'s office is going at it hammer and tongs. I can't understand their eagerness—unless something's behind it."

Della Street said, "Here's your party on the line, a Mr. Kimball."

Mason picked up the telephone, said suavely, "Mr. Kimball, this is Perry Mason, the lawyer. I'm interested in getting some information about a girl you've promised a job to."

Kimball became vocally cordial. "Yes, indeed, Mr. Mason, I'll be glad to give you anything I can. I heard you in court on that dog case. That was a masterly presentation. What can I do for you?"

"I want to find out about a Mrs. Warfield who is coming on from New Orleans," Mason said.

"Oh."

"What's the matter?"

Kimball laughed apologetically. "I'm not certain I can help you much there, Mr. Mason. She has a friend working here. The friend tried to get her a job, and I—well, I said I thought it would be all right."

"When's she arriving in town?"

"She isn't coming."

"No?"

"No."

"Why?"

"I—well, I changed my mind."

"Can you tell me why?"

Kimball's voice sounded strained and embarrassed. "I'm sorry you asked me that, Mr. Mason. Almost anything else I could tell you, but this I don't feel at liberty to discuss. I—well, the vacancy that I expected would occur didn't materialize, and I had to tell her friend that it was no go. Would you mind telling me what *your* interest in the matter is?"

Mason laughed. "I'm more embarrassed at your question than you are at mine. I can't discuss the affairs of a client. Is that all you can tell me about it?"

"I'm sorry, Mr. Mason. That's all."

"Something you found out about her that made you change your mind?"

"No. . . . I think we'll have to let it go at that, Mr. Mason. The vacancy didn't materialize."

"All right, thanks," Mason said, and hung up.

"No go?" Drake asked.

"No. Something happened, and he decided to drop her like a hot potato."

"Wonder," Drake said, "if that something could have been a little whisper from Hollywood."

Mason said, "You're either reading my mind or making a damn good stab at it." He walked over to the closet, picked up his hat and coat. "Come on, Della," he said. "Let's go out and take a look at Stephane Claire. I want to see how you react."

"She's all wool," Drake said, and then added after a moment, "and her friend's a yard wide."

Della Street brushed aside Drake's comment. "Don't take him too seriously. She's a platinum blonde," she said, "and you know Paul."

Mason grinned.

Drake said, "Honestly, Della, she's a *good* kid."

"*I'll* take a look," Della Street said laconically.

Mason said to Drake, "You've got an opening in your office, Paul, for a receptionist."

"*I* have?"

"Uh huh."

"What are you talking about? My receptionist . . ."

"Needs an assistant," Mason interrupted, "temporarily, at any rate. Have your New Orleans correspondent tell Lois Warfield to come on out to the Coast and he can get her a job. Advance her bus fare. I have enough hitchhiking troubles on my hands for the present. I want to be sure she gets here in one piece."

"You're taking over," Drake asked, "—financially?"

"I'm taking over," Mason said, "and Hollywood's going to pay for it."

"This Horty girl is about at the bottom of her war chest."

"I'm just at the top of mine," Mason said. "With a setup like this, if I can't make *someone* in Hollywood pay for it, I'd better quit practicing law."

Drake sighed. "I was hoping you'd look at it that way," he said, and jackknifed up out of the chair.

Mason, putting on his coat, said, "I think it would be a swell idea, Paul, to pick up a photograph of Jules Carne Homan."

"So do I," Drake said. "I've been trying to for the last twenty-four hours. It can't be done."

Mason stood by the door of the closet, staring at the detective. "You mean to say a Hollywood producer hasn't pictures of himself draped all over Hollywood?"

"That's right. Homan is one of the boys who's camera-shy."

"Go out to *Photoplay*. They've got one of the best photographers in the business. There isn't any such thing as hiding from his lens—not if he wants a picture badly enough, and he wants everyone who is anyone."

"That's an idea," Drake said.

Mason nodded to Della Street. "Come on, Della. Let's go pat the bunny."

7

THE BIG TRANSCONTINENTAL bus rumbled into the terminal. Travel-weary passengers came out through the door and walked into the depot to await the distribution of baggage.

Drake, with the skill of a professional detective, carefully scrutinized each face without seeming to pay the slightest attention to any of them.

"Okay, Perry," he said out of the side of his mouth, "this will be the one we want, the one with the tan coat and the brown hat."

Mason studied the woman as she walked toward him. She was, he saw, around thirty years old. She was very slender, not with a skinny angularity of figure, but small-boned and light-muscled. Her cheekbones were a little too prominent. The skin across her forehead seemed stretched tight, and her eyes were tired. Her hair was a dark chestnut, and evidently it had been some time since it had received the services of a professional hairdresser. It seemed stringy and thick with travel dust as it curled out from the sides of a small hat.

"What's the move?" Drake asked, looking at the cigar stand.

"Cold turkey," Mason said.

"Okay, you want me in on it?"

"Yes."

Mrs. Warfield was looking around her now, as though rather expecting someone to meet her.

Drake said, "She'd be a good-looking gal if she had the glad rags and a couple of hours in a beauty shop."

Mason said, "She wouldn't be bad looking right now if she'd get her shoulders back. She's pretty tired. Okay, Paul, here we go. She's looking at us."

Mason walked forward, ostentatiously studying every person in the bus terminal. He let his eyes rest on Lois Warfield, turned away, then suddenly stopped, turned back, looked dubious, and after a moment tentatively raised his hat.

She smiled.

Mason moved toward her. "Are you Mrs. Warfield?" he asked.

She nodded, her tired, bluish-gray eyes showing a quick sparkle of animation.

"Are you the man who was—who has the job for me?"

"Perhaps."

There was swift disappointment on her face. "Why, I thought it was thoroughly understood."

Mason's smile was reassuring. "Don't wory, Mrs. Warfield. I think it's all right. If it isn't, I'll pay your expenses back on the bus."

"But I don't want to go back. I gave up my job there to come out here. I need the work. I can't afford to stop working for a minute. I have obligations."

Mason said, "I want you to meet Mr. Drake. . . . Oh, Paul! Here she is."

Drake turned toward them, raised his hat, bowed, and muttered an acknowledgment of the introduction.

"Had dinner?" Mason asked abruptly.

"I . . . er . . ."

Mason laughed. "Come on. We can eat and talk at the same time."

She hesitated for a moment, then smiled and said, "Very well. There's a counter in here."

' Mason grinned across at Paul Drake. "We long-legged men need more room than that. I can't enjoy food when my knees are pressing up against the side of a lunch counter. Know some place around here, Paul?"

"Yes. There's one in the block."

"You don't mind walking a block?"

She laughed. "Good heavens, I'm on my feet all day. I'll bet I walk miles."

They walked down to the restaurant. When they were seated in a curtained booth, Mason said, "I'm the one who suggested the job to Mr. Drake."

"What sort of a job is it? I understand I was to be a receptionist in an office."

"That's right."

Her face lighted. "And the salary was eighty dollars?" she asked eagerly.

Mason slowly shook his head. "No. I'm afraid you misunderstood that."

There was a flash of anger in her eyes, then bitter disappointment. "I see," she said wearily in the voice of one who is accustomed to being imposed upon. "However, I distinctly understood—well, never mind. Just tell me what you're willing to pay."

"The salary," Mason said, watching her, "is a hundred dollars. Drake wants his receptionist to dress well. She couldn't do it on a salary of eighty dollars."

Mrs. Warfield was staring at him.

"We'd have to know something about your background," Mason went on.

"But I thought you understood all that."

"Only that you were attractive, willing, and wanted a job on the Coast. You're married, of course?"

"Yes."

"Husband living?"

She hesitated a moment, then said, "Yes."

"You're divorced?"

"No."

"Just separated?"

"Well, we're not together—temporarily."

Mason looked at Drake. Drake pursed his lips and said, "That's not so good. I thought you were either a widow or divorced. Husbands sometimes make trouble."

"My husband won't make any trouble."

"Well, you know how it is," Mason said. "Suppose you have to work late at night, and . . ."

"Anything that the job calls for, I'll do," she interrupted.

Mason said, "You'd have to get a bond, of course, and the bonding company would want to know something about your husband."

"What would *he* have to do with *my* bond?"

Mason's laugh was cheery. "Darned if I know, but they certainly do stick their noses into your private business."

Drake said, "When you come right down to it, Perry, they *do* have a crust. What difference does it make where the woman's hubsand is or what he does?"

Mason said, "Well, I suppose it would make a difference under certain circumstances. You know, he might have a criminal record somewhere. Where *is* your husband, Mrs. Warfield?"

The waitress came to take their orders. "Cocktail?" Mason asked Mrs. Warfield.

She hesitated.

"I think she wants one," Mason said. "Three dry martinis, and put lots of authority in them."

The waitress nodded and left.

"Well?" Mason asked.

"Oh, my husband?"

"That's right."

"He . . . he's . . . Look here, I don't think he'd care to have it known where he was."

Mason's face showed disappointment and certain reproach. "We're taking *you* pretty much on trust," he said. "Our friend in New Orleans seemed anxious to get the job for you and recommended you so highly we decided to . . ."

"Oh, I'm sorry," she interrupted. "I—I *can't* very well explain."

Mason's voice was cold. "Well, of course, if you wish to adopt that attitude, Mrs. Warfield."

"Oh, but I don't. Can't you understand? It's . . . it's something that I can't very well tell you."

"Just as you please," Mason said with formal politeness, lighting a cigarette. "Would you care for one, Mrs. Warfield?"

She blinked back sudden tears, shook her head. "No, thank you."

Drake's eyes were sympathetic. Mason frowned at him.

There was a moment of uncomfortable silence, then Mrs. Warfield said, "And I suppose that costs me the job?"

Mason glanced at Paul Drake, made a little motion with his shoulders, and went on smoking.

"All right," she said suddenly with feeling in her voice, "have it your own way. I'm sick and tired to death of the whole lousy business. Every time I work for anyone, I give him value received, but any time I try to get a job, the person acts as though it's charity or something. It isn't charity. It's a business transaction. I w-w-work for a man, and I draw a s-s-salary, and the man makes a p-p-profit on what I do. All right, *keep* your job!"

She pushed back her chair.

The waitress came in with the cocktails.

Mason said, "No reason why we can't buy you a dinner, Mrs. Warfield. Have a cocktail. It'll make you feel better."

"No, thanks."

"Better wait," Mason said. "I'm very sorry this happened. And there's the matter of your return transportation, you know."

The waitress looked from one to the other, then quietly placed the cocktails on the table. Mrs. Warfield hesitated, reached for hers, and gulped it down, not pausing to taste it.

Mason said, "I'm sorry it has to be that way. I think I could have worked you into something out here."

She turned toward him, blinking back indignant tears. "All right, my husband's a convict. He's in a penitentiary. I don't even know which penitentiary. He won't let me know. He wants me to get a divorce, says he's unworthy of me. He won't have any communication with me except through a friend. *That's* why I couldn't tell you. You can see what a fat chance I'd have of getting a bond if I told that to the bonding company."

"That's the truth?" Mason asked.

She nodded.

Mason exchanged glances with Paul Drake, gave his head an almost imperceptible nod. Drake promptly pulled a billfold from his pocket. "Well, Mrs. Warfield, *that* makes the situation entirely different. I'm certain *you* can't be held responsible for something your husband has done, and I think your efforts to carry on are very commendable."

She stared at him, too incredulous for words.

Drake took two hundred dollars from his wallet. "The

vacancy I want you to fill hasn't developed yet, but I think it will within a week. I'm putting you on a salary. Here's two weeks' wages."

Mason said abruptly, "Say, I bet your husband was the Warfield who was sent up for kiting checks in San Francisco."

"I don't know what he was sent up for," she said. "He'd never tell me, just a letter from him saying that he was in trouble and that he couldn't have any direct communication with me for a long while, that I'd have to keep in touch with him through a friend. He gave me the address of a friend in San Francisco—a Mr. Spinney."

Mason said, "Why, of course, that must have been the Warfield that was sent up on that check-kiting charge. Personally, I always felt they convicted him on a frameup. Did he say anything about that to you?"

"He never even mentioned what it was." She took a compact from her purse, surveyed her eyes, put powder on her nose.

Mason reached into his brief case. "As it happens," he said, "I'm doing some work on that very case. I'm a lawyer, Mrs. Warfield. I wouldn't doubt if your husband was out of the penitentiary within another thirty days—if my facts are right.—Tell me, is this your husband?"

Mason whipped out a photograph of Jules Carne Homan. The photograph had originally included some of the more notable movie stars, and had borne the caption, "Producer and cast discuss new play over champagne at Hollywood night spot."

Mason had cut out the center of the photograph so that the caption was eliminated, and all that remained was Homan's likeness smiling up at the camera.

Mrs. Warfield said, "Oh, I'm so glad you're working to help him. I always knew . . ." She stopped in mid-sentence.

"What is it?" Mason asked.

She said, "I never saw this man in my life."

Mason studied her intently. There was no evidence of acting on her face, merely the numbed expression of one who has received a bitter disappointment. But she held the photograph in her right hand, the compact in her left for several seconds, then she passed the picture back to Mason.

"Perhaps," Mason said, "this is Spinney's picture."

"I've never seen Mr. Spinney."

"Your husband wrote you about him?"

"Yes. Mervin said not to try to write direct, that I could trust Spinney with my life. I can't understand," she went on wistfully, "why Mervin won't let me know where he is. Can't a person in the penitentiary receive letters, Mr. Mason?"

"Yes, subject to certain rules. Perhaps your husband didn't want you to know he was actually in the penitentiary."

"No. He had this friend write me that he was in trouble, and I wrote the friend and demanded particulars, and he finally told me that Mervin had been sent to the penitentiary. I thought it was somewhere in California. I wrote him at both Folsom and San Quentin, but the letters came back."

"Why did you think it was in California?" Mason asked.

"Because the friend . . . I'm sorry, but I think I'd better quit talking about it."

"Might be a good idea at that," Mason said. "It will spoil your appetite, and here comes your seafood cocktail."

During the dinner, Mrs. Warfield tried to find out something about her duties and where she would work. Drake parried her questions. His receptionist, he explained, was getting married. She had intended to be married on the twentieth of the month, but circumstances had made it necessary for her to postpone it a few days. She wanted to work until the very last minute.

Mason suggested that Mrs. Warfield should go to the Gateview Hotel, stay there overnight, and in the morning look for a place to live. He suggested she might find someone who would like to share expenses, and by living together, the two could get a better apartment at a lower rental. After dinner the two men drove her to the Gateview Hotel, registered her, and secured a comfortable room.

"And how will I let you know where I am?"

Drake said, "Better not communicate with the office, because my receptionist would probably quit right now if she thought I had someone on a salary ready to take the job. She doesn't want to quit until she has to, but she's been with me for years, and I want her to stay on as long as she can. Tell you what you do. As soon as you've found a place to live, leave a message here for me. Just write a note to Paul Drake, put it in an envelope and leave it with the clerk. I'll pick it up and let you know just as soon as the job is open."

She gave him her hand. "You've been very, very kind to me, Mr. Drake."

"Forget it," Paul said, avoiding her eyes.

They wished her good night, and walked out to the car. "I feel like a heel," Drake said.

"Doing it for her own good," Mason pointed out.

"But how about that job?"

"Stall her along. Pay her salary, and let her rest. The rest will do her good. She looks worn out. Tell her to go down to the beach and lie around in the sun for a while, take sort of a vacation."

"How long are you going to keep shelling out expenses for her?"

"Why, until we get her a job," Mason said.

Drake's face showed his relief. "Well, *that's* damn white."

Mason ignored the comment. "Do you think she was lying about that picture, Paul?"

"No. I'm darned if I do, Perry. She acted too disappointed."

Mason said, "I wish we'd had Della Street there. I'm not certain but what she knew what was coming the moment I reached in my brief case."

"You think she was lying?"

Mason said, "Everything points to Homan. Look at the way this case is being handled. Look at the way that cafeteria suddenly decided to drop her like a hot brick. I tell you, Paul, there's influence back of this thing, and influence in this town that can make the district attorney's office jump through a hoop and then go down into a cafeteria and dictate who shall be employed, can come only from one source."

"Hollywood?" Drake asked.

"Hollywood."

Drake said, "Of course, Perry, if her husband had been convicted here in California, we could run down the records and . . ."

Mason said, "Remember she's already tried San Quentin and Folsom. Don't kid yourself, Paul. Let's say that Warfield came out to the Coast. He got a job—probably in pictures. He began to draw good money. He had a chance to meet beautiful women. To get anywhere in the picture business, even in the clerical jobs, a woman has to have a personality that makes her alive and vital. You don't find any women who hang around the movie offices who are washed-out automatons going through life making motions. They're right up on their toes. Well, naturally, Warfield fell in love. He probably played around a while first, and then he found his big moment. He wanted to get married. He wanted to have his wife divorce him. He didn't dare try to divorce her because she was too much in love with him to let him go. If she'd ever found out where he was, she'd have joined him. He was a big shot now—and he was haunted by a past he didn't dare disclose to anyone.

"He tried to solve the problem by pretending he'd got in a jam and had gone to the pen. He told his wife not to come out to California because she couldn't see him. Moreover, to make certain she didn't try, he got her to send him every spare cent of money she could scrape up."

"You think he was heel enough to do that?" Paul Drake asked.

"Sure, he was," Mason said. "That's the reason he had her sending money to Spinney."

"Well, how do we know the husband is Homan?"

Mason said, "Spinney is an intermediary. He's someone the husband can trust. He goes to San Francisco. Naturally, he gets mail there, and if anything happens, he's supposed to communicate with the husband in Los Angeles."

"That's reasonable."

"All right, Spinney's communicating with Homan."

"Darn it," Drake said. "When you look at it that way, it's mathematical. Homan has to be Warfield. Of course, there's Homan's younger brother who's living in the house with him—but he was away the day of the accident and also the day before."

"We'd better check a little more on him," Mason said. "Tell me about him."

"His name's Horace. He's seven or eight years younger than Jules. He's an enthusiastic fisherman and golfer. Quite a playboy."

"How does he work?"

"How does everybody in Hollywood work?" Drake asked. "By fits and starts. Jules gets him jobs here and there as a writer. He's trying to build the brother up. Jules has a small yacht, a saddle horse, a golf club membership, and all the things that go with Hollywood prosperity. Horace works for a while on a job, then puts in his time using his brother's playthings, going fishing, playing golf, and . . ."

"Wait a minute," Mason interrupted. "Horace wasn't in Hollywood the day of the accident?"

"No. He was out on the yacht on a fishing trip."

Mason said, *"He* might be Spinney."

"He might at that."

"Or Horace might be the husband, and Jules could be protecting him."

Drake frowned. "I'd never thought of that. But Jules is the one who has the big-time job. The brother is just a hanger-on. He could write her a letter and say, 'Look, babe, I'm out in Hollywood, but I'm not doing so good. I'm getting by because my brother is standing back of me, but he's going to chuck me out on my ear if he finds out I have a wife. What say we call it off? I'll send you a little dough, and you can get back into circulation.' "

Mason thought over Paul Drake's observation. "I can't get over the casual way she acted when I showed her Homan's picture. You're sure it's his photo, Paul?"

"Yes. I've talked with him. It's his photo all right, and a good one."

"We'll sleep on it," Mason announced. I'm seeing Stephane Claire again tonight. I told her I thought I'd have good news for her. I hate to tell her it's a flop."

"Can't you stall her off?"

Mason said, "Not that girl. Think I'll have a go at Homan, Paul."

"He'll be hard to see at this time of night."

"He'll be just as hard to see during the daytime, won't he?" Mason asked.

"I suppose so."

"Where does he live?"

"A castle out in Beverly Hills."

"His phone's unlisted?"

"Oh, sure."

"But you must have had the number when you made the kick to the telephone company."

Drake nodded, fished in his pocket, pulled out a notebook and passed it across to Mason. The lawyer copied the telephone number.

"It's queer this man Spinney, living in a cheap San Francisco rooming house, would have the unlisted number of a movie magnate," Mason said.

"He ain't a magnate, Percy, just a poor three-thousand-a-week wage slave . . . has to pay social security 'n' everything."

Mason grinned. "Well, I'm going to talk with him."

"You won't find out much," Drake warned. "He plays 'em close to his chest."

"Unless I'm badly mistaken, Paul, he's haunted by the ghost of a former life. That's going to make him jittery—and I'm not going to do his nerves any good."

8

STREET LIGHTS illuminated the front of the Spanish-type white stucco house. The red tile of the roof showed up almost black in the indistinct light.

A Filipino boy in a white coat answered Mason's ring.

"I telephoned Mr. Homan," Mason said. "I'm . . ."

"Yes, Mr. Mason," the boy said. "This way, please. Your hat and coat, please?"

Mason slipped out of his coat, handed it and the hat to the boy, followed him along a corridor floored with waxed red tiles, across the huge living room, mellow with indirect lighting, to a study which opened on a patio. Homan was seated at a desk, frowning intently over a typewritten script, the pages embellished with penciled alterations. He looked up as Mason came in, held the pencil poised over the page, and said, "Sit down. Don't speak please."

Mason stood, amused antagonism in his eyes, staring down at the figure at the desk. After a moment, he sat down in one of the deeply cushioned chairs, watching his man as a big game hunter studies his quarry.

Drapes had been drawn back from the plate-glass windows to disclose the patio with its palms, its fountain illuminated by colored lights, and behind that its swimming pool. The house fairly oozed prosperity, a house which had been designed not only to be lived in but to be looked at. It had been built and decorated by a showman and for showmen.

Homan bent over the manuscript in what was either a concentration so deep that he was entirely oblivious for the moment of his caller, or in a pose designed to impress that caller with the importance of the man upon whom he was calling.

The man at the desk said, without looking up from the script, "In just a moment I'll have this one scene licked, then we'll talk."

The very lack of expression in his voice made his concentration seem the more genuine.

Homan was evidently a showman. A fringe of close-cropped hair grew around a bald spot on the top of his head. He had made no effort to conceal this bald spot by letting the hair grow and combing it back. A pair of large, tortoise-shell spectacles rested on his nose. The straight brows pressed against his graying temples. He kept his head slightly bowed. His eyes stared in unwinking concentration at the script. Abruptly, he snatched up a soft-leaded pencil from the desk, and swooped down upon the manuscript in a frenzied attack, scratching out words, scribbling inserts and marginal notations. There was not the slightest hesitancy. He seemed to be struggling to make his hand keep up with his thoughts. Under the rush of that attack, the lower half of the page became a veritable patchwork of penciled notations. Then he dropped the pencil as abruptly as he had picked it up, pushed back the script, and turned on Mason a pair of reddish-brown eyes. "Sorry to keep you waiting. Didn't think you'd get here quite this soon. Had to finish with that scene while I was in the mood to take part in it. Your visit is going to throw me all out of gear. That detective was bad enough. You're going to be worse. I hate it, but I'll have to do it and get it over with. All right, what do you want?"

Mason sought to draw him out with a few preliminary remarks. "I didn't realize you'd be working so late."

"I work all the time, the later the better. A man does his best work when those around him are asleep." He waved a short, thick arm in a sweeping gesture which included a quarter circle of generalization. "I mean the people in the city. There's a lot of telepathy, not individual telepathy so much as group telepathy, mind beating on mind, chaining you into a convention of business humdrum. What *do* you want?"

"And I've thrown you out of the mood for further work?" Mason asked.

"Not out of the mood for work. Out of sympathy with the script. Here are characters facing a dramatic moment in their lives. You can't put anything like that across on the screen unless the characters are real. You can't tell whether they're real unless you sympathize with them, unless you open a door and walk right into their lives. That's subjective thought, intuition, telepathy, auto-hypnotism. Call it whatever you want to. Now you're here. You're objective. I've got to talk with you objectively. You pretend you want information. Probably you're trying to lay a trap. I've got to watch myself."

"Why?" Mason asked, seizing the opening. "To keep from committing yourself by some inadvertent statement?"

"No. To keep from saying something you can misconstrue and throw back at me later on."

"I'm not that bad."

"Your detective was. He threw me out of my stride for a whole half day. *What do you want?*"

"You're carrying your own car insurance?"

"Yes—if it's any of your business, which it isn't."

"It makes some difference—this accident."

"How?"

"Your legal liability, whether the automobile was being used with your consent, express or implied."

"It wasn't."

"Nevertheless, you can appreciate the legal difference."

"All right, it makes a legal difference. So what?"

"And," Mason went on, "if the person who was driving that car happened to be an agent of yours . . ."

"I don't have any agents."

"That's what the layman occasionally thinks, but if you ask a man to take your car and run down to the post office to mail a letter, he becomes your agent so far as that trip is concerned."

"I see. Good point. Glad you told me. I'll remember that. What else?"

Mason said, "And if you sent a man to San Francisco to do something for you in your car, he would automatically become your agent for that purpose."

"So what?"

"And if he had an accident while he was driving the car,

you'd be responsible just as though you were driving the car yourself."

"All right, you're leading up to something. Go ahead. What is it?"

Mason said, "I'm an attorney, Mr. Homan. I'm representing Stephane Claire. I'm interested in unearthing any bit of evidence which would clear her of the charge of negligent homicide."

"That's obvious."

"Now then, you're interested in minimizing your legal liability. If someone actually stole the automobile, that's one thing. If someone was driving it with your permission, that's another; and *if* the person who was driving it was actually your agent, that's something else. You're naturally interested in the interpretation of the evidence which will give you the least financial liability."

"That's obvious."

"Therefore, our interests are adverse."

"Naturally. I knew that before you ever got here. Tell me something new."

Mason said, meaningly, "It's occurred to me, Mr. Homan, that you might be penny-wise and pound-foolish."

"How?"

"In an attempt to avoid a few thousand dollars in legal liability, you might expose yourself to a flank attack."

"By whom?"

"By me."

Homan's brown eyes stared at Mason long and searchingly from behind the horn-rimmed spectacles. "Go on," he said, after a few moments. "What's the rest of it?"

Mason said, "I want to prove that Stephane Claire wasn't driving your car. In order to do that, I want to prove who *was* driving it. And in order to do that, I have to pry into your private affairs. When I pry, I make a good job of it."

"Is this blackmail?"

"A warning."

"It's finished?"

"No. I'm just starting."

Homan shifted his position in his swivel chair. "I'm afraid," he said, "this is going to be even worse than I thought," and started drumming nervously on the edge of the desk with short, stubby, but well-manicured fingers. A diamond ring on his right hand caught the light and glinted in scintillating brilliance as he moved his hand.

Mason said, "Obviously, it would be most to my advantage to prove that the car was being operated by some agent of yours."

"You think I'm lying about the car being stolen?"

Mason said, "When I'm representing a client, I like to assume that anyone who tells a story that's opposed to the facts as related by the client is falsifying."

"Can't blame you for that. That's business. Go ahead."

"Now then," Mason said, leaning forward and suddenly pointing his finger directly at Homan, "if there's any reason why you don't want the facts about Mr. Spinney brought out, it'll be to your advantage to say so right now."

Homan's face didn't change expression by so much as the flicker of an eyelash. "Who's Spinney?"

"A gentleman in San Francisco."

"Don't know him. Therefore, I don't care what facts you bring out."

"And if you don't want anything known about a waitress in a New Orleans cafeteria, now would be a good time to say so."

"Threatening me with women?"

"With a woman."

"Go ahead. Bring 'em all in. What the hell do I care? I'm a bachelor. Everyone says I'm a philanderer and a libertine. I don't pretend to be anything else. You can't hurt me by digging up a hundred women. Nothing hurts a man unless he gets caught. People don't feel that you're being caught when you stand right out in the open and . . ."

"You misunderstand me," Mason said. "I'm not referring to some woman with whom you might have been intimate."

"What about her then?"

"Some woman who perhaps was remaining true to a man whom she hadn't seen in some time, some woman whom that man wanted to remain in New Orleans because he didn't want her to know where he was or what he was doing."

"Why?" Homan barked.

"Because," Mason said, "he wanted her to get a divorce."

"Why?"

"Probably because he'd become prosperous and wanted to marry someone else."

Homan's eyes narrowed thoughtfully. "You've got a good idea there, Mason. I think you could develop it. Probably do something with it. Human interest. Self-sacrifice. Drama. All that. Keep your woman meek and good, but don't overdo it or you'll make her a sap. Go ahead, develop it."

"I intend to."

Homan waved his jeweled hand, suddenly laughed. "Scenario stuff," he said. "Pardon me, Mason, I have so many writers come in with ideas, toss them at me, and ask me what I think of them that I get so I look at everything from that angle. For a moment I thought you were asking me about an original. This sounded like a good idea for a scenario."

"I'm talking facts."

"Facts that don't mean anything to me. Got anythng else?"

Mason said, "Yes. You're going to have to go on the witness stand and tell your story. Any falsification will be perjury. Perhaps when you first heard about this, you thought you could keep yourself out of it by telling your story to the police and then going back to work. That's out. You can't do it. You're trying to rush a young woman to jail. If I can catch you in perjury I'll try to send you to jail. Do I make myself clear?"

Homan said, "Sit still for a minute. I want to think that last one over."

Mason sat motionless, watching Homan. The producer stared down at the top of his desk. There was no expression on his face, no motion save the nervous drumming of the fingers of his right hand.

Abruptly the drumming stopped. Homan looked up, said to Mason, "My story stands. I'm telling the truth. There's nothing you can do about it. I've told the police the facts. I'm sorry about the Claire girl. I'm not certain she stole the automobile. I think somebody else stole it first. I don't give a damn about you, Mason. I could get sympathetic about that girl if I put my mind on it. Lying there in the hospital, injured, scarred perhaps, no funds, no job, few friends, facing a trial when she gets well, newspaper notoriety. It's a tough break. I could see the human side of it, the drama, the tragedy. I can't afford to think of it. Right now, my studio's paying me to concentrate on the problem of a man who's fallen in love with a woman who, unfortunately, is married to someone else. Her husband won't let her go. He's hanging on. The intimacy develops, then suddenly the husband catches them. The cruel gloating, the malice, the . . . What I'm concerned with, Mason, is what that would do to a woman's character. Forcing her to live a lie. Forcing her to . . ."

Mason pushed back his chair. "And *I'm* not interested in *your* problems. I'm being paid to keep a girl out of jail, and I'm damned apt to do it."

"Yes, I see *your* problem. I think I'm getting back into the mood for my script now. Good night, Mr. Mason. Try not to come again."

Mason said, "One warning is all I ever give."

"Should be enough. I get it all right." Homan reached for the script, pulled it toward him.

Mason started for the door, then suddenly turned and stepped back toward Homan's desk. "Just as a matter of curiosity," he said, "would you mind telling me the name of the script you're working on? I'd like to see it on the screen and see if my intrusion has left any perceptible . . ."

Homan absently picked up the title page, said, "It's an adaptation from a novel the studio bought a couple of years ago. The title of the book is *Where the Chips Fall*—you know, part of the old adage. 'Hew to the line and let the chips fall where they will.' It's a lousy title. We'll change it. All right for a book perhaps, but too deep for the theater-goer. He wants a title he can understand, something that appeals to him, something that's as dramatic as a newspaper headline, as filled with . . . Say, why the hell am I telling you all this?"

Mason said, "I wouldn't know either," and walked out, gently closing the door behind him.

The white-coated Filipino boy was waiting, in well-trained silent deference, in the hallway, with Mason's hat and coat.

Mason let the boy help him on with his coat, took the hat, then stood for a moment looking toward the massive radio in the living room. The dial was faintly outlined in light, and low strains of organ music reproduced with remarkable clarity, came from the speaking attachment.

Mason glanced from the radio to the Filipino. "Your master lets you turn on the radio?"

White, even teeth gleamed at Mason in a shameless smile. "No, sah. When he works, he hears nothing. I cheat a little bit. I have to wait for you to go out, and this my favorite program."

Mason said, "Is that so?" and walked over toward the

radio. "I'm interested in this type of radio," he said, and stood staring down at it.

The Filipino seemed vaguely uneasy. "Very nice radio," he said. "Please do not turn up loud. Mastah become very angry."

Mason stood in front of the radio listening.

Abruptly, the smooth harmony of deep-throated organ music was disrupted by a rasping rattle followed by a click. Six times this was repeated, the rattle varying in length as someone in the house, using an automatic telephone, dialed a number.

Mason turned at once to the door. "Thank you very much," he said. "Good night."

The Filipino boy stared after him thoughtfully. "I shall tell Mr. Homan, please," he said.

"Tell him what?" Mason asked.

"That you wait to see if he use telephone."

Mason smiled. "Please do," he said.

Mason was within a few inches of the door, conscious of the hostility of the Filipino boy who was about to turn the knob. Quick steps sounded just outside the door, as the Filipino boy swung it open. Mason, starting to go out, all but collided with a deeply bronzed young man who had sprinted up the steps and was about to insert a latchkey into the door.

"Hello," the young man said. "Didn't intend to make a flying tackle. I'm sorry."

Mason noticed deep-set, dark eyes, high ridged features, long sloping forehead, and a wavy profusion of black hair which swept back from the hatless head.

"I say, you didn't come to see me, did you?"

"You're Horace Homan?"

"Yes."

"I'd like a word with you."

"I'm in a devil of a hurry. Could it keep?"

"No. I'm Perry Mason, a lawyer. I'm representing Stephane Claire."

"Oh, my God, another breach-of-promise suit! All right, tell her if she takes it to court, I'll say yes and marry her. That will . . . Oh, wait a minute. Stephane Claire. Oh, I get you now."

"The young woman who is accused of driving your brother's car."

"I get it."

"I understand you were fishing at the time."

"That's right—out on a cruise."

"I was just telling your brother that this is a serious matter, one which he couldn't detour by simply telling a story to the police and then going back to work. He's got to go on the witness stand, and when he gets on the witness stand, I'm going to ask him about anything which I think will clear the matter up."

"Can't blame you. I'll bet Jules didn't like that very much —that is, if he quit working long enough to listen."

"He quit working, and he listened, but I'm not certain his mind was on what I was saying."

The younger brother grinned. "It probably wasn't, at that. However, if you told him, you've done your duty. Don't worry about Jules. He takes care of himself. You won't catch him off first base."

Mason said, "It seems rather foolish for a man to risk something which may mean a great deal to him simply to save himself a damage suit for the negligent operation of his car."

Horace Homan looked at his wrist watch. "Listen, I'm in a hell of a hurry, but I've got five minutes. Let's go talk. Felipe, get the hell out of here."

"Yes, sah. I shall wait beyond earshot to show Mr. Mason out."

"I'll show him out."

"I beg your pahdon, sah, but the Mastah orders, sah."

"Okay, suit yourself, Felipe. I'll call when we're ready. Want to sit down?" he asked Mason.

"Let's not waste any time. Let's just stand here and talk."

"Okay."

"What," Mason asked conversationally, "do you know about Spinney?"

"Spinney?" Homan asked frowning. "Say, I think I've heard that name somewhere. Wait a minute. Spinney. No, I guess not. What else?"

"Or perhaps the woman in New Orleans?"

"New Orleans.—I don't see what that's got to do with it. Look here, you don't look like the type that would just pick up women and throw them at Jules in order to get even with him."

"I'm not."

"As I understand it, it's a question of who was driving the car."

"That's right."

"Boy, oh, boy, am I thanking my lucky stars *I* wasn't behind the wheel. You know how it is, Mason. I make up my mind I'll never drive when I'm drunk. That's when I'm sober. After I've been drinking, I think I'm sober enough to drive, and when I'm so tight that I can't kid myself into thinking I'm sober enough to drive, I'm so tight that I say it's a short life and a merry one, and to hell with the consequences. Wish I could do something about it."

"You might quit drinking," Mason suggested.

"Oh, I meant something practical."

"Why not take out the car keys and mail them to yourself whenever you start drinking?"

"Shucks, I want to *use* the car, not just leave it parked in front of the first nightclub."

Mason laughed. "Afraid I can't help you, and I don't suppose you could help me."

"In what way?"

"I don't think Stephane Claire was driving that car. I don't even think it had been stolen."

"Jules says it was stolen. He's pretty accurate as a rule, but frightfully absent-minded when he's working, and he's working most of the time. I suppose you're going to go after him most on cross-examination?"

Mason nodded.

"I don't think he'll like that. He gets nervous when people cross him. Well, I'm glad I don't know anything about it. . . . Say, Mason, I feel sorry for that girl. I'm going to drop in and see her, not that there's anything I can do about it, but I just want her to know I feel sorry for her and all that. *I* don't think she stole the car."

"Who did?"

"Oh, some bum who happened to be drifting along the street and saw the car where Jules had left it parked."

"Then you could make a guess as to the identity of this party?"

Horace Homan's eyes narrowed. He lowered his voice and said, "Well, if you put it that way . . ." Abruptly he laughed. "Wait a minute. You're the big bad wolf so far as this house is concerned. What big teeth you have, Grandma! No, Mr. Mason, I couldn't even venture a guess, and I've got an appointment with a perfectly swell wren in exactly twenty minutes, and it's going to take me ten to change. Sorry, old boy, but you know how it is. And I'm going to drop in on that Miss Claire. You don't think she'll mind?"

Mason said, "That's all right, if you don't expect to work any information out of her. She'll be under instructions not to tell you anything."

Homan grinned. "Well, I don't know anything that could be fairer. *I* haven't told *you* anything, have I?"

"Not a thing," Mason said.

"Okay, we're quits. Glad I met you."

Lean, brown fingers enclosed Mason's hand. Horace Homan raised his voice and said, "Oh, Felipe, he's ready to go, and the family silver is all intact."

The Filipino boy glided noiselessly from behind a heavy drape across an archway. He had, Mason realized, worked himself up to a position of vantage where he was within earshot. Wordlessly, he held the door open for the lawyer, and silently Mason walked out into the night.

9

A SLENDER, gray-headed man, whose eyes twinkled alertly over a pair of half spectacles, was standing at the hospital desk when Mason entered. Slightly behind him and to one side was a young man in a gray overcoat. Mason had a blurred impression of broad shoulders, coal black hair, and a deeply cleft chin.

The woman at the cashier's desk said to the gray-headed man, "We aren't permitted to let anyone see Miss Claire without permission from the police."

Mason moved toward the barred wicket, keeping unobtrusively in the background.

"You've changed the patient into a private room?" the gray-haired man asked.

"Oh, you're Mr. Olger?"

"That's right."

"Yes, Mr. Olger. We followed your instructions to the

letter. You mentioned over the telephone that you were her uncle."

"That's right."

"As a relative, I think you'll be permitted to see her. I'll find out in just a minute, if you'll wait please."

"And Mr. Sterne too," Olger said. "This gentleman here."

"He's a relative?"

"Well, in a way."

The nurse smiled. "I'm sorry. I'll have to know. Is he or isn't he?"

The young man in the gray overcoat moved uneasily, said, "Max, I don't think I'd better go in."

"Why not?" the older man snapped, biting off the words.

"It's going to upset her. She'll think I'm trying to get to her when she's down and . . . well, I don't know. I think perhaps it would be better . . . I could wait a while."

"Nonsense!"

"I could wait here for a few minutes, and you could see how she feels."

"He's not a relative?" the office nurse asked.

"He's engaged to her," Olger said.

"Oh."

"Was at one . . ."

"Shut up," Olger interrupted the young man, and turned to let his eyes glitter at the nurse. His motions, Mason saw, were birdlike in their swift accuracy. He was a wiry little wisp of a man, perhaps somewhere in the late sixties, but he seemed far more forceful than young Sterne, who had a deep-chested physique, rugged features which would have graced a collar ad, and quite apparently a lack of decision.

The office nurse caught Mason's eye. "Oh, that's all right, Mr. Mason. You may go in. I've received special instructions concerning you."

Mason nodded his thanks, noticed that apparently his name meant nothing to either of the two visitors who stood in front of the wicket watching the nurse as she swiftly dialed a number.

Mason walked on down the linoleum-covered corridor, clean with its smell of antiseptics, and paused at the door of the ward. A nurse in stiffly starched garments rustled past, looked up at him with a smile, and said, "Your patient's just been transferred, Mr. Mason."

"Where?"

"Private room, sixty-two. I'll show you."

Mason said nothing, followed along behind the nurse, his heels thudding the linoleum in contrast to the subdued pad . . . pad . . . pad of the nurse's rubber-soled heels.

She knocked gently at a door. Stephane Claire called, "Come in," and Mason pushed at the door, smiling his thanks at the nurse.

Stephane Claire was sitting up in bed. "Who," she asked, "is Santa Claus? Private room, flowers. . . ."

"When did it happen?" Mason asked.

"Just a few minutes ago. They took me out of the ward, removed my stiff nightgown, brought me this come-hither creation—or do you notice nighties, Mr. Mason?"

Mason smiled down at the lace over her shoulders, at the pale blue of the silk which swelled over the contours of her breasts. "Nice going," he said. "And the flowers?"

"They were delivered just now."

Mason said, "Apparently, Santa Claus is a gentleman by the name of Max Olger. He is now . . ." He broke off at the expression on her face. "What's the trouble?" he asked.

"Uncle Max?" she said. "How in the world did *he* find out?"

"Apparently you overlooked the fact that the story is a natural for headlines: *Car belonging to Hollywood producer involved in accident.* Beautiful blonde accused of theft—claims she was hitchhiking. Mysterious man makes passes at blonde and vanishes. What's your objection to your uncle?"

"Oh, he's all right, but he wants to dominate me. He can't get it through his head that I've grown up."

"When did you see him last?"

"A little over a year ago?"

"Want to tell me about it?"

"No, but I suppose I have to."

Mason sat down on the edge of the bed. "I think he'll be in here at any moment," he said, "so you'd better hurry. He's in the hospital office now."

"Was he—alone?"

Mason regarded her searchingly. "The young gentleman who was with him is the broad-shouldered, masculine type. However, he seemed to have some difficulty making up his mind. . . ."

"That will be Jackson," she interrupted. "It's just like Uncle Max to bring him along."

Mason said, "Let's hear about the uncle first."

"He was my father's brother, quite a lot older. Uncle Max made money. When Dad and Mother died, Uncle Max took me over. My parents didn't leave me anything. I hadn't been accustomed to much. At first, Uncle Max was afraid I was going to think I was a rich girl and go on a spending spree. He wanted to impress upon me that I was living with him merely by sufferance."

"And you didn't like it?"

"I reveled in it," she said. "It was swell while it lasted. I had a job and felt independent, and then Uncle Max got parental complexes, and started being both a father and a mother, as well as an uncle. He began to squander money on me. I was waited on by servants, spent about half of my time being measured for clothes. He talked me into giving up my job because he wanted me with him when he went to Palm Beach. Just a lot of hooey to get me away from work and into the life he thought I should lead."

"And Jackson Sterne?" Mason asked.

"Jacks," she said, and smiled. "Another one of the things Uncle Max thought would be good for me. He . . ."

A knock sounded at the door.

She glanced at Mason, called dubiously, "Come in."

A nurse, crisply efficient in starched blue and white, swung the door back. Max Olger came marching into the room with little springy steps, his eyes beaming over the top of his half spectacles. "Well, well, well, so this is my little runaway!"

"This is it," Stephane announced.

"How are you? You're not permanently injured? You're not . . ."

She said, "I feel absolutely all right. I'm a little stiff and sore. I have some black-and-blue places on me and a little stitching, but I could leave the hospital right now as far as that's concerned."

"Then why are you staying here?"

"A little prescription written by the police," she said. "Uncle Max, this is Perry Mason, the lawyer—my lawyer."

"Mason," Max Olger said, shot forth his right hand, and let his alert, twinkling eyes study the lawyer over the top of the chopped-off spectacles.

Mason shook hands with the nervous little man.

"Don't want to be rude," Max Olger said, "but you're

relieved of your responsibilities right now, Mr. Mason. Send in a bill. I'll make out a check."

"Uncle Max!" Stephane exclaimed.

"What's the idea?" Mason asked.

"If you want to be frank, I'll be frank, Mr. Mason, brutally frank. Stephane is going to have the best money can buy. I know something about lawyers. The lawyer a penniless girl can get . . ."

"Uncle Max, stop! You don't know. You don't understand."

"I understand quite well, Stephane. I'm taking charge. You're too precious to permit any more headstrong . . ."

"Uncle Max, Mr. Mason is famous. He's the highest-priced lawyer in this part of the state."

Max Olger put his head slightly on one side, peered up at Mason, said, "Humph," walked over to the telephone, picked it up, and said, "This is Max Olger. I'll pay all charges. Rush me through a telephone call to Chicago, law firm of Pitcairn, Roxy and Hungerford, and . . . no, wait a minute. The office will be closed. Hadn't thought of that. Get Alexander Pitcairn. . . . Yes, Mr. Pitcairn of that firm at his residence. . . . No one else if he's out."

He dropped the receiver into place.

Stephane Claire said to Mason, "You'll just have to put up with this, Mr. Mason. It takes more energy to argue with him than it does to let him go and put up with the things he does. You won't mind, will you?"

Mason sat down again on the foot of the bed. "Not at all," he said, grinning across at her uncle. "What are you going to do, Olger? Get your own attorney to come out here and handle it?"

"Probably. I don't know how serious it is, but I don't propose to let Stephane get railroaded."

"That would be tough on her," Mason agreed.

"I appreciate what you've done. Don't misunderstand me. I won't be niggardly on fees."

Mason grinned.

"Neither will I."

The little man snapped his head around, "Humph," he retorted. "You can't slip anything over on me, Mason, I warn you."

"Nor you on me. I happen to have taken too much of an interest in this case to let it get butchered by some corporation lawyer."

Olger said, "I happen to be paying the bills and . . ."

"You're not paying *my* bill."

"No? . . . Huh . . . Who is?"

"The man who was driving the car," Mason said, "— when I find him."

Olger's eyes blinked rapidly as he sized Mason up. "You may have something to you at that," he said. "I'll ask Pitcairn. I . . ."

The telephone rang. Olger lifted the receiver. "Hello, Pitcairn. That's good service. Told you I might want you to come out. Can't tell yet. There's a lawyer on the job, man named Mason, Perry Mason, says he won't get off. How do I make him let loose? Stephane won't help me. Can't count on her. She always was headstrong. She . . . What's that? . . . You're certain? . . . Well, that's different . . . What do you mean? Midnight. It's only ten o'clock. . . . Oh, that's right. I forgot. All right, send me a bill for the call. Good-by."

He snapped the receiver into place, beamed across at Mason, and said, "Pitcairn knows about you, says you're considered one of the best cross-examiners in the country. Says you'd make a fortune if you'd quit this criminal work and go in for a decent practice."

"Thank you," Mason said dryly, "I don't care for the decent practice, as Mr. Pitcairn calls it."

"Oh, he didn't use exactly those words. That was his idea."

"Well, I don't care for the idea."

"All right, every man to his taste. Go ahead, get started. You'll want expense money. I've got plenty. Call on me for anything you want. But itemize your expense accounts, Mr. Mason. I want 'em itemized. You understand that?"

Mason said, "I'm not much of a bookkeeper. I . . ."

"Well, you'll have to learn then. I want it itemized, Mr. Mason. I'm sorry to insist, but that's fair. That's . . ."

Stephane Claire said, with what was almost a groan, "There you are, Mr. Mason. Imagine living with that twenty-four hours a day. He squeezes the individuality out of you like apples in a cider press."

"Don't do anything of the sort," Max Olger snapped. "What do you mean, changing your name, Stephane? Had me fooled until I saw your picture. Good photograph. What the devil do you mean taking a job as hatcheck girl in a San Francisco night spot?"

"That's tame compared to some of the things I've done."

"Humph. Should have kept that out of the paper anyway. Looks like the devil. Max Olger's niece a hat-check girl! Humph!"

"Where's Jacks?" she asked.

His head tilted quickly to one side as he stared at her. "How should I know?"

"When did you see him last?" she asked with a significant side glance at the lawyer.

"Well now, let's see. I get all mixed up on time. Can't remember the difference between . . ." He broke off, looked quickly at Mason, pursed his lips, said, "Oh, I suppose he told you. Come to think of it, you weren't surprised to see me. Yes, he heard your name mentioned. Naturally, being your lawyer, he'd have stuck around and listened. I remember seeing him there now. . . . All right, Jacks is outside waiting. He thought it would be better for you and me to have our chat before he came in."

"Did he reach that decision all at once, or a little at a time?"

"Now, Stephane, don't you go making fun of Jacks. He's thinking of your own good. He's cautious."

"He's a conservative, petrified pelican."

"Well, he isn't rushing in where angels fear to tread, and he doesn't go jumping around in the dark. But he's a mighty fine boy, well mannered, good foundation, good bringing up, good character, steady, dependable, reliable. The sort of investment that's proof against inflation."

"Well, he's here," Stephane Claire said. "I may as well see him. Go on down and bring him up. Wait ten minutes, though. I want to talk with Mr. Mason."

Olger's eyes became instantly suspicious. "Something black about this case you're trying to keep away from me? Don't do it. I'll hire detectives. I'll ferret out anything . . ."

"No," she said. "Mr. Mason's time is valuable. He's tired. He's done a lot for me, and I want to have this conference with him and get it over so he can go home."

"I won't interfere. I'll efface myself."

She laughed. "*You* efface yourself! Go on out and tell Jacks I want to see him—but don't make it too cordial."

"He's been upset all the way out here," Olger said. "We came by plane and . . ."

"Yes, I know."

"You can't understand how upset that boy was when he

thought something had happened to you. . . . And when you left, Stephane, you never saw anyone as broken up as that boy. He . . ."

"Yes, I understand."

"You *understand*," Olger said irritably, "but you don't *sympathize*. You don't appreciate what it means to a high-strung boy . . ."

"High-strung, my eye!"

"Well, a boy who thinks as much of you as he does."

"All right, go call him. Let me talk with Mr. Mason."

Olger got up, started for the door with quick, nervous steps, turned, looked at Mason, said, "Sorry about that call to Pitcairn, Mason, but Stephane's going to have the best there is. I had to check up on you. See you later."

He popped through the door and was gone.

Stephane sighed. "Did you ever want to relax and read a paper, with a young Boston bull pup in the room?"

He smiled. "Doesn't he ever quit?"

"Quit, nothing! He doesn't even slow up—but tell me about things."

"What about them?"

She sat up more erect in bed, pulling a light robe around her shoulders. "You said you'd have some news?"

"I thought I might have."

She let her eyes search his face, then turned her glance away hastily. "Oh, well, never mind."

Mason said, "I'm on the right track. I know I'm on the right track, but the road doesn't go where I think it should."

"What's wrong with it?"

"I don't know. Just when I'm sailing right along, I come to a detour sign—ROAD CLOSED—UNDER REPAIRS—and the damn detour never does come back to the road. It just goes wandering away in an entirely different direction."

"How bad is it?"

"It's not exactly encouraging right now, but it's going to get better. I want every single thing you can give me in the line of description—anything that might prove to be a clue. Go back carefully over everything that happened. See if there isn't something you forgot to tell me. You can't remember anything about the name or license number of the man who brought you down to Bakersfield?"

"No. He was in the forties. It was an old Ford—I should say around a thirty-four or thirty-five, somewhere around in there. I don't know the models well enough to tell, but it had had quite a bit of use. It was still running well, but the upholstery was worn, and there were quite a few rattles. The paint job wasn't much."

"He didn't give you his name?"

"Not his last name. He asked me what mine was, and I told him Stephane, so he told me his was Jim, and that's all I know. You know how it is with hitchhikers. A man picks you up. He's never seen you before, and you'll never see him again. It seems foolish to sit in a car and say 'Miss' and 'Mister.' You can't just call each other 'say.' So when a man gives me a lift and asks me what my name is, I give him my first name, and then he gives me his—and usually is pretty much relieved to think that he can be both intimate and partially anonymous."

"Don't they get fresh?"

"Sure. Some of them."

"Not most of them?"

"No. Taken by and large, they're pretty decent. You know how it is whenever a man comes in contact with a woman anywhere. He puts out little conversational feelers. You can usually tell when a man is just exploring for leads and when he's on the make."

"All right, now how about this man who picked you up in Bakersfield?"

"Well, there were four cars coming—all going pretty fast —and this car was coming behind them."

"That was up near the traffic circle?"

"Yes."

"Then you would have said the car didn't come from Bakersfield?"

"I don't think it did, not as I understand the way that traffic circle is laid out."

Mason said, "Homan's pretty apt to be lying. If he is, the thing to trap him on is the time the car was stolen. Tell me again about the man who was driving the car."

"He was around thirty-one or thirty-two. He was—he had a lot of brass. I guess some girls fall for that sort. I never could. He went past me first. I guess he was looking me over, then he stopped and made me come all the way to the car. He didn't back up. He looked at my legs when I got in. He had an air of assurance as though he expected every girl to fall for him. I can't tell you what it is. It's an impudent lack of recognition of decency. A man of that sort goes through life looking . . . Oh, you know the kind."

"I know," Mason said, "but I want more details. I want to know everything about him. Didn't his conversation give you some clue to what he was doing for a living?"

"No. He didn't say. All I know is that he was hell-bent on getting to Los Angeles—he said he had a job to do. His eyes were dark. I don't think they were a complete black, but some dark shade of brown. I didn't get a real good look at them. He had a little black mustache. His hat was brown felt with a little green feather in the band. He wore a dinner jacket under a black topcoat. When he grabbed me the first time he got my lipstick smeared on his face. The next time, when I took the keys, he got a streak of lipstick across his shirt front, a red smear from my little finger, and also my face was pressed against the starched shirt, so my lips must have left a mark too."

"What became of your lipstick pencil?"

"It's back in my purse. You know how a girl puts on lipstick. She touches it to her lips, then applies it with the tip of her finger. A man doesn't like to get smeared up. This fellow was making passes at me, and I was a little afraid of what he might do, so I smeared the lipstick on just as thick as I could. My little finger was all covered with it."

"But you'd put the lipstick back in your purse at the time of the accident?"

"Just before the accident, yes."

"Now, you took the ignition keys out of the car?"

"That's right."

"And what did you do with them?"

"I . . . say, I think I dropped *them* in my purse."

"Where is your purse?" Mason asked.

"They had it for awhile. The nurse brought it back to me yesterday."

"Have you looked in it?"

"Just for some things I wanted, my compact and . . ."

"Where is it?"

"In that dresser drawer."

Mason opened the drawer, took out a worn black purse, and handed it to her. She opened it, groped around in the interior, then, with an exclamation of annoyance, dumped everything out on the counterpane. "Here you are," she said, holding up a key ring.

Mason examined the three keys which were on the ring.

"This one," he said, "is a car key. These two look like house keys."

"That's right."

"None of these keys is yours?"

"No."

"Now, have you told the officers anything about these keys?"

"Not about having them. I told one of the detectives about what had happened, that this man had been making passes at me, and I switched off the ignition, and jerked out the keys."

"Did he ask you where the keys were?"

She laughed. "No, because he didn't believe a word I said. He just listened to me to be listening, that's all."

Mason said, "How good an actress are you?"

"I don't know. Why?"

"If I take those keys now, and turn them in to the police, it's going to look suspicious."

"Why?"

"They'll wonder why you didn't tell them about the keys before."

"My gosh, Mr. Mason, I was pretty badly smashed up."

"I know," Mason said. "Now then, do you suppose if you waited until you were on the witness stand, and I got you to relate the events that had taken place that night and pretended I thought you'd had these keys in your hand at the time of the accident, and they'd been lost somewhere, and asked you casually if that wasn't the case, and you thought for a moment—then do you suppose you could make your face register just the same puzzled concentration which you did just now, and say that you have a vague recollection of having dropped them in your purse? And then I'll ask you about the purse, and you can fish them out in front of a jury?"

"I don't know. I can try. A girl doesn't get by very long in the looks jobs without learning how to put on an act."

"What do you mean, looks jobs?"

"Oh, being a cigar and cigarette girl in a night spot, checking hats, and stuff of that sort. You're an ornament as well as a worker. People feel free to make passes and you kid 'em along."

"Well," Mason said, dropping the keys back in her purse, "we can try one rehearsal when we've a little more time. I don't want to rehearse you so much that it will look staged.

I want you to make it appear spontaneous and natural. Go ahead now. Try and think of something else about that man, something that would be a clue."

"I can't think of anything."

"That dinner jacket," Mason asked, "he didn't mention it to you, where he'd been or anything of that sort, or how he happened to be wearing it?"

"No. I didn't think much of it at the time."

Mason said, "It's a key clue, if we only knew how to interpret it."

"I don't see why. Tuxedos aren't so unusual."

Mason said, "Stop the first five thousand cars going over the Ridge route at ten o'clock in the evening, and see how many drivers are wearing tuxedos."

Her eyelids narrowed as she thought that over. "Yes," she said, "I can see what you mean. It's unusual."

"And that," Mason observed, "is the secret of crime solution. You find the things that are unusual, the things which vary from the normal or average, and, using them as clues, you get away from generalities, and down to specific individual cases."

"I see what you're getting at, but I can't help you. He didn't say a thing about how he happened to be wearing it."

"You must have left Bakersfield at around ten o'clock."

"Yes."

"And you think this man must have come from some place north of Bakersfield."

"I can't be certain. I was watching the other cars. No, he may have swung around that traffic circle."

"Did you notice any baggage in the car?"

"No, I didn't. It might have been there, and I wouldn't have noticed it. And, of course, some might have been in the trunk."

"Do you think there was any baggage in back?"

She frowned. "I don't think there was."

"He could hardly have gone back, opened the trunk, and taken out baggage after the accident. What's more, you have the keys in your purse."

"That's right."

"Did he have any rings on his hands?"

"Yes. There was a diamond ring on his right hand. I remember seeing it when he reached for the gearshift, and his hands were well cared for, pudgy with short, thick fingers, and they were well manicured."

"He wasn't wearing gloves?"

"No."

Knuckles sounded on the outer door. Stephane said, "This will be Uncle Max, and the boy friend," and called, "Come in."

It was Max Olger who pushed the door open. The young man hung back. Stephane called, "Come on in, Jacks. I won't bite."

He walked over to the bed and stood looking down at her. "Hello, kid," he said, and then very diffidently picked up her hand, which was lying on the counterpane, held it for a moment, stroking the back of it with his other hand. "How you feeling?"

"Swell."

"I didn't want you to think I was—following you up. I wanted you to know about that. I'm just here to help you. Your uncle got detectives to try and trace you. I didn't do a thing, not that I didn't want to know where you'd gone, but I knew you went away because you wanted to go, and I didn't want to do anything—well, you know how it is."

"Thanks, Jacks."

"And I came here just to see what I could do to help. That's all. I'm not going to be a nuisance. I told Max I'd stay at a different hotel and . . ."

She withdrew her hand, said, "This is Mr. Mason, my lawyer."

The young man turned. He was as tall as Mason, and thirty pounds heavier, despite a slender waist. His big hand enfolded the lawyer's wiry fingers. "How are you, Mr. Mason? Mr. Olger has been telling me about you. Do the best you can for her. How do things look?"

"I can't tell yet," Mason said, shaking hands.

Stephane Claire said to Mason, "Really now, how *do* they look?"

"Right now, they look black. All cases do at the start."

"This is a long way from the start."

"And a long way from the finish," Mason said. "You gentlemen won't mind if Miss Claire tells you what happened in rather general terms? I don't want her to tell her story so many times it'll sound rehearsed when she gets on the witness stand."

Max Olger nodded vehemently. "Good idea, Mason. That's splendid strategy. I've been in court and heard people tell stories that sounded as though they'd been learned by heart."

"They probably were. Well, I'll be going."

"Can I get her out of here?" Max Olger asked.

"You can, if you want to put up ten thousand dollars cash bail or twenty thousand dollars bond."

Stephane Claire said, "Good heavens, Mr. Mason! Am I as much of a criminal as that? When did all this take place?"

Mason said, "Late this afternoon."

Max Olger said, "I'll put up cash within the next thirty minutes. I didn't know how much would be required, so I carried ten certified checks, each for ten thousand dollars."

"You must have thought bail was going to be high," Mason said.

"No. I simply came prepared in the event it was high."

"You don't want to get out tonight, do you?" Mason asked Stephane Claire.

"I most certainly do. I haven't said anything because there was no use crabbing about something you couldn't help, but this business of being detained has been like a nightmare."

Mason said to Max Olger, "All right, go put up the bail and get her out. Where are you staying?"

"The Adirondack. We'll have a suite there."

Jackson Sterne said, "I'll go to some other hotel, Stephane. I don't want to intrude. Can you tell me some good hotel that's near by, Mr. Mason?"

"Might try the Gateview," Mason said. "It's within three or four blocks of the Adirondack. It's a quiet place, small but comfortable."

Stephane said savagely, "Jacks, if you wouldn't be so damned self-effacing, I'd like you a lot better. Aren't you going to kiss me?"

"Do you really mean it? May I?"

She turned her head away with a jerk. "No!"

Mason tiptoed out of the room, let the door swing shut behind him, and walked rapidly down the hospital corridor. A cold wind had started to blow, and he buttoned up his coat, made certain that he wasn't followed, and dropped into a drugstore at the corner. He called Drake's office. Drake had just come in.

Mason said, "Paul, I've been thinking we may have overlooked a bet."

"On what?"

"On Mrs. Warfield."

"What about her?"

"We didn't put a tail on her."

"Well, I can do it if you want."

"I think we'd better. Put two good men right in the hotel. They can rent a room and take turns watching and sleeping."

"I'll have them there within half an hour."

"Call me back at my apartment," Mason said, "and before they start work, have them find out if Mrs. Warfield is in her room."

"Right."

Mason hung up, drove to his apartment, slipped out of his coat, vest, shirt, and trousers, put on a pair of slacks and a smoking jacket, and was lighting his pipe when the phone rang.

"Drake talking," the detective said. "Everything's okay at the Gateview."

"She's in her room?"

"Uh huh. The light's still on."

"And your men are on the job?"

"That's right. But I've found out something that doesn't look so good."

"What?"

"She went up to her room, then after a few minutes came back down to the lobby. The girl at the newsstand was just closing up. Mrs. Warfield tried to get some back copies of *Photoplay*."

Mason whistled. "Did the girl have any?"

"No."

Mason frowned at the telephone. "That picture of Homan," he asked, "was that published in *Photoplay?*"

"I think it was."

"You don't know when?"

"Some time last summer."

"She didn't ask for any particular number?"

"No, just asked for back copies of *Photoplay*."

"We'll have to raise our sights a couple of notches on Mrs. Lois Warfield."

"You may be right at that," Drake admitted. "It makes my cheeks burn. She didn't act smart. She seemed like a woman who's accustomed to pick up her hand after the deal and find she holds all the low cards."

Mason said, "Scrimping out of her salary to send those monthly remittances to Spinney certainly sounds on the level."

"I'm not so certain, Perry, but what that's just a dodge. If she was sending eighteen dollars a month, it would be two hundred and sixteen dollars a year. That's pretty cheap for a phony build-up."

"Not for a person who's working in a cafeteria in New Orleans," Mason said. "Keep your eye peeled, Paul. I feel that we're walking in the dark, and there are banana peels on the sidewalk."

"Well, I've got two men on the job who aren't exactly simpletons."

"Keep 'em there," Mason said, and hung up.

10

MASON WAS UP at seven-thirty. He closed the windows, turned on the steam heat, glanced through the headlines of the paper, and took a lukewarm shower.

When he had dressed, he went to the bookshelves and selected a large white-backed volume which he spread open on the table in front of the window.

The volume gave much biographical information concerning the prominent men identified with the film industry, and, using it as a reference, Mason checked back against the information which Drake had given him concerning Jules Carne Homan. The producer was thirty-four years old, had had high school education and two years of college. There was a long list of screen originals he had written and plays which had been produced under him. While the volume didn't say so in so many words, it was apparent that Homan's Hollywood activities had occupied a period of but little over two years. He had started as a writer, and, from the meteoric advance, Mason felt certain that there was a story behind the scenes. But there was no inkling as to what that story might be.

Mason zipped open his brief case and stood staring at the photograph of Jules Carne Homan. He turned it over and looked on the back. The words, *"Photoplay Magazine,"* had been stamped on the back. Mason pulled the shades, turned on a desk lamp, and tried holding the photograph at different angles. The words on the back didn't show through the photograph, except when it was held directly in front of a bright light.

Mason was still frowning thoughtfully an hour and fifteen minutes later when he entered the office.

Della Street brought in the morning mail. "How did your interview turn out?" she asked.

"Nothing doing," Mason said.

"She wouldn't talk?"

"Apparently she knew nothing to talk about. But there's an angle I can't get."

"What, for instance?"

Mason handed Della Street the photograph of Homan. "Look at it," he said. "Don't turn it over. Just look at it. How would you know that was taken by a photographer of *Photoplay Magazine?*"

"I wouldn't."

"Well, it was, and she did."

"You're certain?"

"I'm not certain of anything in this case. You follow a blazed trail that looks broad as a boulevard, and all of a sudden it evaporates into thin air and leaves you in the middle of a swamp somewhere. The . . ."

"Wait a minute," Della Street said, staring at the photograph. She held it up to the light.

"No, I've tried that. The paper's too heavy. The light doesn't shine through. Then again, there wasn't any light on the table. She didn't even turn it around, just held it in her right hand, looked at it and then passed it back."

Della Street said, "It's funny she didn't hold it in both hands."

"She was doing some little feminine stunt or other at the time, digging in her bag or something."

Della Street's eyes twinkled. "Not powdering her nose?"

"Yes," Mason said, "I believe she was. Why?"

"Goosey!"

"What's the idea?"

She opened her bag, took out a compact, snapped it open, said, "Hold out the photograph."

Mason held the photograph out in front of her. Della Street tilted her compact. "Get it?" she asked.

"Get what? . . . Oh, my gosh!" Mason exclaimed.

"You should have had me along," Della Street told him reproachfully. "This takes a woman's touch."

Mason said to Della, "I'm just a lawyer, but Paul Drake is supposed to be a detective. Wait until he hears . . ."

A knock sounded on the door. "That's Paul now," she said.

Mason grinned. "Open up for him, Della. This is going to be good."

Drake came swinging into the office, said, "Hello, gang," and sprawled out in the big leather chair.

Mason grinned at him. "How's the great detective this morning?"

Drake cocked a baleful eye in Mason's direction. "This," he said, "has all the earmarks of being the preliminary for a sock right between the eyes."

Mason said, "The trouble with us, Paul, is that we need a guardian. It serves us right for not taking Della along last night."

"What now?"

"Do you remember what Mrs. Warfield was doing when we showed her that photograph last night?"

"Sitting at the table," Drake said.

"Did she look at the back of the photograph?"

"No. I remember she held it for a minute, then passed it back."

"Don't you remember what she was doing when I showed her the photograph?"

"No, hanged if I do. Was it before or after we had the cocktail?"

Mason said, "She was fixing up her face."

"I guess that's right—come to think of it—she was."

Mason said, "Show him, Della."

The lawyer held up the photograph in front of Drake. Della Street snapped open her compact. Drake looked puzzled for a moment, then, as Della Street tilted the mirror to one side and then the other, Drake gave a low whistle.

"So," Mason said, "she may have been dumb enough to send all of her money to the man she loved, but she certainly made us look like a couple of amateurs. Reading the imprint on this photo in her mirror, she had to transpose it in her mind, too. Yet she never so much as squinted."

Drake said, "Well, we won't take it lying down. We'll really give her something to think about this time."

"She's smart," Mason warned.

"She's clever all right. She never let on she had the slightest interest in that photograph—but she made up her mind she'd check the back issues of *Photoplay*, read the 'left to right,' and then wouldn't need to ask any questions."

"Ready to go?" Mason asked.

"Uh huh."

Mason said to Della Street, "Get your things, Della. In dealing with this woman, we need you on the job."

While Della Street was putting on her coat and hat, Mason said to Drake, "One other thing, Paul. Read up on Homan's career in Hollywood. He didn't skyrocket up that far and that fast without having somebody shoving him up the ladder."

"Who?" Drake asked.

Mason grinned, *"I'm* paying *you* money to find out things."

"All ready whenever you are," Della Street said.

"I'll have to stop by my office to get my hat and coat," Drake said. "This is going to be a big relief. I won't feel so darn sympathetic this time. I felt as though I was taking pennies out of the baby's bank last night."

"And all the time the baby was picking our pockets for heavy dough."

"Your car or mine, Perry?"

"Taxicab. It'll save time."

"Okay, let's go."

It took them less than ten minutes to get to the Gateview Hotel. Mason said, "Just to check up, Paul, let's see if there are any messages for you."

"Wait a minute, Perry. I'll talk with my operative first. We'll find out if she's been down to the desk."

Drake moved off to one side. A man who had apparently been completely engrossed in a newspaper lowered the sheet, looked up at Drake, imperceptibly shook his head, changed his position, and went on with his reading.

Drake moved back to Mason. "She's in her room."

Della Street said, "If you want my advice, you won't give her a ring. She isn't expecting you, is she?"

"No."

"Why not take her by surprise?"

Mason looked over at Drake. "Let's go."

"Got the room number?" Mason asked Drake.

"Six-twenty-eight."

Mason looked at his watch. "She may not be dressed," he said. "If she isn't, Della, you'll have to crash the gate and . . ."

"A girl who worked in a New Orleans cafeteria will be up by nine-thirty," she said.

They rode up in the elevator, walked quietly down the carpeted corridor. Mason found the door, tapped on the panel. After a few moments, he knocked again, louder. "Looks like you lose," he said to Della. "She's still asleep."

Mason tried the knob of the door. It was locked. He knocked again, imperatively. There was not so much as a sound from the other side of the door.

Drake turned to Mason. "Gosh, Perry, you don't suppose . . . we didn't get her so frightened or despondent . . . you know, she wouldn't be lying there . . ."

"Give me a leg up," Mason said.

Drake stooped, caught Mason around the knees, lifted him up so he could catch the projection just below the transom. The lawyer pulled himself up and tried to peer through the opening. "Can't make out anything, Paul, except I can see the electric light's on. Come on, let's get the manager."

The manager was inclined to be somewhat distant, and Mason took prompt steps to counteract his suspicions. His sister-in-law, he explained, had come to the city. She was to have been at his office by eight o'clock, and he was to have taken her for an automobile ride. She hadn't shown up. The woman had a heart affliction, and was all alone. There was probably not one chance in a hundred but what she'd simply been detained. However, Mason wanted to make sure.

The assistant manager finally summoned the bellboy. "Go up and take a look in six-twenty-eight," he said, and, as Mason started to follow, said with authority, "You folks might as well wait here."

Drake stepped away from the desk, coughed twice. The man who had been reading the newspaper lowered it. Drake made a signal, motioning toward the bellboy who was waiting at the elevator. The man casually folded his newspaper, tapped ashes from the end of his cigar, stretched, yawned, and got to his feet just as the elevator door opened and the bellboy entered.

"Going *up!*" the man called, and then walked leisurely across the lobby.

Five minutes later, the bellboy was back with a report. "The door's locked from the outside. I used the passkey. There's no one in the room. The bed hasn't been slept in. There's no baggage in the room. The towels haven't been used. The curtains are drawn, and the lights are on."

The assistant manager regarded Mason with cool appraisal. "I believe you said she was your sister-in-law. If there's any trouble about the hotel bill? . . ."

Mason said, "I'll stop by the desk and settle the bill right now. Probably she's had a heart attack in a restaurant, and has been taken to a hospital."

"Sometime during the night," the assistant manager asked pointedly, "before she'd gone to bed?"

Mason said easily, "Yes. She said she was going out to get a cup of tea. Poor girl, I hope she isn't seriously ill. I'll call the hospital. Della, would you mind stepping over to the desk and paying the bill? . . . If she should happen to return, tell her to get in touch with her brother-in-law at once. Will you tell her that, please?"

The assistant manager said, "I'll be only too glad to. But just a moment, please."

He picked up the telephone on his desk, said to the operator, "Get the records on six-twenty-eight. Find out what baggage. I'll hold the line."

He sat with the receiver to his ear. His eyes surveyed his visitors in speculative appraisal while he waited. Then he said into the transmitter, "All right, let me have it. . . . You're certain? Very well."

He dropped the receiver into place and said to Mason, "She checked in with a suitcase and a hat box. They're not in the room now. Would she have taken them to the restaurant?"

Mason became indignant. "Are you insinuating that a relative of mine would leave the hotel to avoid paying her bill?"

The manager's manner became somewhat uneasy. "It's strange," he said. "That's all."

Mason leaned toward him and said, "You're damn right it's strange, and your manner and your insinuations are stranger still. Here's a woman, unsophisticated, inexperienced, staying in a hotel in a large city. She disappears mysteriously. In place of being of any assistance, you start making cracks about her hotel bill. Her bill's been paid. I'm paying it, see? And I'm good for anything she runs up."

The manager said, "I didn't mean it exactly that way. It's a suspicious circumstance, that's all."

"What's suspicious about it?"

"Well, for one thing, she simply couldn't have taken her baggage out through the lobby. The employees are instructed that no guest is permitted to take baggage through the lobby. The bellboy always takes it and goes to the desk. The guest then either checks out or gets an okay from the clerk on duty."

Mason surreptitiously nudged Drake and said, "I fail to see what that has to do with it."

"Was your sister-in-law subject to spells of amnesia?"

"Not that I ever heard of."

"I merely asked," the manager said.

"There's a back way?"

"There's a basement and a baggage room."

"And there's an exit to the alley from those?"

"There is, but it's through a freight elevator, and the freight elevator can't be operated except with the janitor's knowledge. He's under instructions to notify the desk whenever there's any outgoing baggage."

"Then the only way a person could leave is through the lobby?"

The manager coughed deprecatingly. "There's the fire escape," he said.

Mason drew himself up with dignity. "I can hardly imagine my sister-in-law climbing through the window of her room to a fire escape and . . ."

"No, of course not," the manager interrupted, and then added, "I just thought you should know. That's why I asked about the amnesia."

"Thank you," Mason said with frigid dignity. "I believe my secretary has, by this time, paid the hotel bill. Good morning."

The manager was still watching him speculatively as Mason and Drake left his office.

"Just babes in the wood," Mason groaned to the detective as they marched across the lobby.

11

FRANK RUSCELL of the district attorney's office was suave
but insistent. "We'd like to get that Stephane Claire case
on its way, Mason. How about having an arraignment and
setting the preliminary for Friday?"

"You haven't got any case against her," Mason said.

Ruscell refused to be drawn into argument. "I don't
know very much about it. I'm not going to handle it myself. The office thinks there's a case. How about Friday at
ten o'clock?"

Mason hesitated.

"Of course, we *could* go ahead and take her into court
and let the judge fix the time. I understand she's been
admitted to bail. If she's going to object to a prompt hearing, we'd want the bail increased."

"All right," Mason conceded, "Friday at ten. We can
have the whole thing handled at that time by stipulation
and go right ahead with the preliminary."

Ruscell said, "Thank you," with the smug courtesy of a
deputy district attorney who thinks all defense lawyers are
crooks, and hung up.

Mason dropped the phone into place and said to Della
Street, "I'm damned if they're going to send her to the
pen to cover up for some Hollywood big shot."

"Any ideas?" she asked.

Mason pushed the books over to one side of the desk
and sat on the space he had cleared away. His brows were
level. "I think that dinner jacket has something to do with
it, Della."

"I don't get you."

"A man doesn't put on evening clothes to drive an
automobile. This man either expected to arrive in Los
Angeles and attend some party, or else he had some reason
for dressing up before he left. Now look at the time. He'd
have got in *here* sometime after midnight. He'd have hardly

gone to a party then. On the other hand, he left Bakersfield around ten. There's some question whether he came from Bakersfield or down the San Francisco highway. Gatherings for which people go to the trouble of putting on formal or semi-formal clothes don't usually break up that early in the evening."

"Stay with it," Della Street said. "You're doing fine."

"Bakersfield isn't so large but what we should be able to check with the society editors of the papers and find out anything unusual which would have called for evening clothes. Then we might check a list of the guests and see if someone left early."

"Swell," Della Street said.

"Make a note of it. We'll get Paul Drake working on it."

"Any other ideas?" she asked, making pot hooks in her notebook.

"There's some influence back of Homan," Mason said. "He's gone up like a skyrocket."

"Don't people do that occasionally in Hollywood?"

"Occasionally. When it happens, there's usually someone back of them, someone who knows the ropes. You know how it is out in Hollywood. Joe Doakes can go begging for years. Then someone mentions at a Hollywood party that MGM is trying to sign him up on a long-term contract. Within twenty-four hours, Joe Doakes will have four or five telephone calls."

"But what difference does it make about Homan unless you can prove something about the car? He wasn't driving it himself, was he?"

"No, apparently not. He doesn't even answer the description."

"I don't see how the secret back of his Hollywood success is going to help you."

"Neither do I," Mason admitted, "—not yet. But I want to learn more about him, get all of the different angles on his character and personality. Then I'll have something to work on. Of course, the man I want is Spinney. It looks as though I'd have to reach Spinney through Homan, and Spinney is being kept under cover. If I could only find some way of smoking him out in the open . . ."

Mason became silent, staring down at the carpet.

"Look," Della Street said, "I have an idea."

"Shoot."

"If your theory is correct, Spinney is a yes-man, a fixer who cleans things up for Homan, takes care of Homan's dirty linen and all that stuff."

"Uh huh."

"And Homan knows you're looking for Spinney."

"He probably doesn't know exactly how much we have on Spinney, but he knows enough to keep Spinney out of sight for a while."

"But if Homan got in a jam, he'd call on Spinney, wouldn't he?"

"He might. Why?"

Della Street's eyes were twinkling. "Why shouldn't we . . ."

"We couldn't even worry him, Della," Mason interrupted. "He'd have to be faced with something bigger than anything we could frame up to bring Spinney out into the open."

"Well, can't you think up something?"

"Let's try looking at it from Homan's angle. He must be worried. Somewhere, somehow, it must be possible to associate Spinney with him. He must be afraid of that."

"How about Mrs. Warfield? What do you think happened to her?"

"She must have left under her own power. They all say she couldn't have got out of the hotel and taken her baggage with her without being stopped. It sounds reasonable, too. If a person could leave a hotel and take his baggage without going through the lobby, a lot of people simply wouldn't bother to pay hotel bills. So somewhere in there is a factor we've missed."

Della Street said, "She didn't stay, yet she couldn't have left. She . . ."

Mason, jumping from the desk, exclaimed, "You've got it, Della! You've got it!"

"What have I got?" she asked, puzzled.

"The solution. Don't you see? You've got the whole thing."

"Oh, yes. Clear as mud. Pardon me if I don't share your enthusiasm."

"Get Drake," Mason said excitedly. "Don't bother with the telephone. Beat it down the corridor. By gosh, we've got it! We've got the whole thing. This time, Homan has stuck his neck out, and we're going to . . . Get started, Della."

"On my way," she said. "World's record in the fifty-yard dash. Hold the stop watch, Chief."

She dashed through the door, and Mason could hear her running steps in the corridor.

The lawyer paced the floor, nervously impatient, snapping his fingers from time to time. Occasionally he nodded his head.

Drake, accompanying a breathless Della Street, entered the office and said, "What's the excitement, Perry?"

"Della gave me the solution to that hotel disappearance."

"This," Della Street explained to Paul Drake, "is the way you give something you haven't got. It's the way bankrupt nations finance armaments."

"It's so damn simple and so damn daring," Mason went on.

"Go ahead, Perry. What is it?"

"Don't you see, Paul? Your men were in the lobby. She *couldn't* have checked out. She didn't even come down to the lobby to talk with anyone—not even the clerk. Her baggage is missing. The manager says she couldn't possibly have got out the back way, particularly with her baggage. He mentioned the fire escape, but she couldn't have carried her baggage down it."

"Well?" Drake asked.

"She's still in the hotel. Don't you get it?"

"No," Drake said. "I'm damned if I do. They searched her room. My man says they . . ."

"Don't you see? She's in another room."

Drake thought for a moment, then frowned and shook his head. "No, she'd have had to go down to the desk to get another room. She didn't . . ."

"Wake up, Paul," Mason said. "We were tailed to that hotel. Someone else was following every move we made. After we got her placed in a room, that someone simply checked into the hotel and got a room. After he was in his room, he went down to Mrs. Warfield's room—and he must have gone there very shortly after we left. Now he was able to say something to her which meant more to her than the job you'd offered, something which made her decide to double-cross you and go with him."

"You mean she left her room?"

"That's right, and went to his room. She simply moved her baggage down there."

Drake whistled a few bars from a popular tune. "You're right! It's so obvious we overlooked it."

"And it worked," Mason said. "That's the beauty of the scheme—its direct simplicity."

Drake said, "I wish you'd kick me, Perry. If we'd only thought of it last night—and I blame myself for it. *I'm* the detective. I'm supposed to keep a line of what's happening. To think I could have been followed . . ."

"The streets were crowded about that time. A dozen people could have followed us," Mason said.

"Well, if I'd only had the sense to figure out what had happened this morning, when we first went there, we still might have found out something."

"We can still find out."

"What do you mean?"

Mason said, "Mrs. Warfield left that room. She was either lured away from it and into another room, or she went voluntarily. Let's suppose she went voluntarily. There are only two persons who could have done the job, her husband and Spinney. Her husband is keeping out of her way. He's either in a penitentiary or has gone to a lot of trouble to impress her with the idea that he is in a penitentiary. Therefore, the man is Spinney."

Drake said, "You're ringing the bell every time you pull the trigger, Perry. Keep shooting."

"Now then," Mason went on, "we come to the involuntary phase of it. Suppose *she* didn't move her baggage. Suppose that someone went to her room, knocked on the door, told her there was a message for her, asked her to go with him, and took her into another room. She didn't come out. Afterwards, the man went back, got her baggage, put it in that other room, locked the door, and went out."

Drake looked pained. "The more I think of it, Perry, the more *that* theory sounds like the one we'll have to pay off on. The fact that the towels weren't used. . . . I don't like it."

Mason said, "All right, Paul, here's what we've got to do. We've got to find out who followed us to that hotel. We've got to check everyone who registered there after we got that room. Remember, we didn't even know ourselves what hotel we were going to select, so it had to be someone who came in *immediately* after we did."

"I don't get that immediately part," Drake said. "Why couldn't . . ."

"Don't you see, Paul? It was done too fast. The towels weren't used. She wasn't in that room ten minutes—probably not five minutes. . . . She waited until we'd left, then went down to the newsstand to ask for back issues of *Photoplay*. Then she went back to . . ."

"I get you," Drake interrupted. "Okay, Perry, my operatives are still there in the hotel. They had their room already paid for, and when I took them off the case, they decided to grab a few hours' shuteye. I can telephone them, get them on the job, and . . ."

"Well, what the hell are you waiting for?" Mason asked. "Get busy."

"I'll do it from my office," Drake said. "I can . . ."

"Okay, get going. Seconds are precious. I want that information, and I want it fast. On your way."

Drake was back within ten minutes. "Okay, Perry," he said, "we've got him."

"Nice work, Paul. How did you get it through so fast?"

"It turned out my operative hadn't gone to bed. He was standing in the lobby chatting with the clerk when I called him. We've got this man on two counts. First, he registered within five minutes after Mrs. Warfield went up to her room, and there were only two people who registered within the first hour after she went to her room. One of them was this man, and the other was a woman who registered right after he did, then there was no one for an hour. Then a couple, and after that . . ."

"Didn't you use the description of the driver?"

"Yes. I'm coming to that. We've got him on both counts. We . . ."

"To hell with all that stuff," Mason said impatiently. "Where is he *now?*"

Drake grinned triumphantly. "In his room."

"You're certain?"

"Absolutely. He registered as Walter Lossten of Los Angeles, said he'd been having a directors' meeting, and had decided to stay downtown overnight. He didn't have any baggage. He paid for his room in advance and went up . . ."

"What room?"

"Five-twenty-one."

"What makes you think he's still there?"

"There's a 'Don't Disturb' sign on the door."

"You didn't try giving him a ring?"

"No. I told my operative just to look the situation over."

Mason stood for a moment with his hands pushed down in his trousers pockets, his legs spread apart, his head thrust forward. "By Jove, Paul," he said, "I don't like it. That 'Don't Disturb' sign is a danger signal."

"I don't get it."

Mason said, "Mrs. Warfield is in that room. There's a 'Don't Disturb' sign on the door. She hasn't communicated with us. That sign means something, Paul. It *may* mean murder."

Drake thought the situation over. "Shucks, it does look bad."

Mason said, "You go on down to the hotel, Paul. I'm going to get Lieutenant Tragg on the job. We've discovered too many corpses as it is."

"Wait a minute, Perry. You can't get Tragg to go down there without letting him think . . ."

"Leave it to me," Mason said. "I'll take care of Tragg. I'll hand him a line that'll get him down there. Remember, it may be all right, Paul, and if it is all right, we're going to find who Spinney is and who the driver of that car was."

"Do you think they're the same?"

"Looks like it."

Drake said, "You're going to have a hard time with Tragg. Remember *we* got Mrs. Warfield that room in the hotel. If she's . . ."

"Forget it," Mason said. "Leave Tragg to me. You beat it down there."

12

LIEUTENANT TRAGG looked up, saw who was calling, nodded a greeting, and dismissed the detective who was making a report.

"Hello, Mason. This is an unexpected pleasure."

The two men shook hands. Tragg was about Mason's age, an inch or two shorter, a pound or two lighter, but there was a certain similarity about the men which would impress a close observer. Tragg's high forehead, wavy black hair, clean-cut features, and thoughtful eyes were at sharp variance with the bull-necked beef of Sergeant Holcomb whose place on the Homicide Squad he had taken.

"Found any more bodies?" Tragg asked.

Mason grinned. "You're always claiming I play a lone hand and don't take the police into my confidence. This time I'm going to let you in on the ground floor."

"Okay, sit down and confide."

Mason dropped into a seat beside Tragg's desk, lit up a cigarette.

"This Stephane Claire manslaughter case."

"Oh, yes. I don't know too much about it. One of the other boys has been handling it. I understand the D.A.'s ready to go ahead. It's a county case."

"Preliminary's on Friday," Mason said.

"Well, it's out of my hands."

"Not necessarily. You're interested in seeing justice done, aren't you?"

Tragg's smile was somewhat whimsical. "Well, Mason, I am and I'm not. The department has its own ideas of what constitutes justice. If we could uncover some evidence which would bolster the D.A.'s case, that would be justice. If we uncovered some evidence that wouldn't . . . well, you know how it is."

"Suppose you could find evidence that would pin the guilt on some other party?"

Tragg rubbed his hand across his forehead, up over his hair, and down to the back of his neck. His fingertips rubbed the base of his skull. "Lovely weather we're having," he said, "—for this time of year."

"Mason said, "All right, here's the dope. Stephane Claire wasn't driving that automobile. A man was. He's registered at the Gateview Hotel right now under the name of Walter Lossten. I'm going out to see him. I'm going to charge him with driving that car. I think I have enough dope on him so he'll admit that he was the driver."

"Well," Lieutenant Tragg said, "you could subpoena him to appear at the preliminary. If you could make him confess, that would be all there was to it. It's in the D.A.'s hands now."

"You're not interested?"

Tragg said, warily, "Oh, I wouldn't say that I wasn't interested, Mason. I'm always interested, but you understand I've got a lot of irons in the fire. This is really out of my jurisdiction. There are several unsolved homicides I'm working on. I don't think the department would care to have me . . . well, you know how it is."

Mason pushed back his chair. "All right, you're always crabbing that I take short cuts on the police and don't give you an opportunity to cooperate."

Tragg ran his hand over his hair once more, scratched around the base of his ears, seemed somewhat uncomfortable. "That Stephane Claire seems a nice kid," he said.

"She is."

"Somehow," Tragg went on, "I can't figure her as a girl who would steal a car, and . . . This man's there now at the Gateview?"

"Yes. What's more, I have a witness there, a Mrs. Warfield. I think she'll identify this Lossten as a man by the name of Spinney, and I think the San Francisco police are interested in Spinney."

Tragg impulsively pushed back his chair. "I may catch hell for this, Mason," he said, "but I'm going to give you a play. You understand, after the D.A.'s office charges someone with a crime, it's up to the D.A.'s office to get a conviction, and up to us to help them. They won't take too kindly to the idea of me running around with the lawyer for the defendant trying to get a confession from some other party. You understand that."

"I can appreciate how a prosecutor might feel," Mason admitted.

"All right, just understand it. I'm going to stick my neck out. If you can make a case, I'll do something about it, but it's up to you to make it."

Mason said, "I have a cab waiting."

"Cab, hell," Tragg said with a grin, "we can get there in half the time a cab would take. My car's outside."

Tragg led the way to his coupe, equipped with red light and siren. "Hop in," he said to Mason. "Hold your hat."

The lieutenant switched the motor into action, warmed it up for a few seconds, then swung away from the curb, and out into traffic. He made a left turn at a corner, waiting for the signal. Then, as he gathered speed and charged down on the next intersection, he kicked on the red light and siren, screamed through a closed traffic signal with gathering momentum, and shifted into high in the middle of the next block.

Mason settled back in the seat.

Tragg sent the machine whizzing through the frozen traffic, handling it with the deft skill of an artist. His hands didn't grip the wheel, but caressed it. It seemed that something flowed from his fingertips down through the steering post to guide the car, as though car and driver were one indivisible unit.

It was less than four minutes from the time he had turned on the siren until he was slowing to a stop in front of the Gateview Hotel.

"Remember," he said, as he opened the door and got out, "this is your show. I'm a spectator."

"Okay," Mason told him.

Drake and one of Drake's operatives were waiting in the lobby.

"Still up there?" Mason asked.

Drake's face showed relief. "Yes. It seemed like you'd never get here."

"Hello Drake," Tragg said. "I couldn't have come any faster without tearing up the pavement."

"It seemed like a long time," Drake said, and introduced his operative.

"Well, let's go on up," Mason said.

The clerk was looking at them curiously. "Please remember, gentlemen, that the hotel has tried to cooperate. If . . ." He looked significantly at Tragg. "We'd understood this was purely a private matter."

"That's all right," Mason said. "Tragg's just the audience. Come on, boys. Let's go."

The quartet stopped in front of the door from the knob of which hung the usual sign "Don't Disturb." Mason said, "I think this is the man who was driving Homan's car at the time of the accident, Tragg. If you'd ask the questions, we might get more than . . ."

"Nothing doing," Tragg interrupted. "I'm listening. As far as I'm concerned, the case is closed. It's the D.A.'s baby."

Mason said, "Have it your way, but be sure you listen."

"What the hell do you think I brought my ears along for? Go ahead."

Mason knocked on the door. When there was no answer, he knocked again, more loudly.

Lieutenant Tragg said, "This isn't a runaround, is it, Mason?"

Mason glanced at Drake.

Drake shook his head. "He's here—unless, of course . . ."

Mason said, "All right, let's get the manager with a passkey. I think it's a stall myself."

Tragg took a leather key container from his pocket. "We might save ourselves a trip down to the lobby," he said. "I think one of these will do the work—unofficially, of course."

He inserted a passkey, manipulated it for a moment without success. He tried the second passkey and the latch clicked smoothly back. Mason pushed open the door, started into the room, then suddenly stopped.

Drake, looking over his shoulder, said, "Oh-oh!"

Tragg, who had been holding back, said, "What's the matter in here?" and Mason and Drake stepped quickly to one side, disclosing the body of a man, lying face down on the counterpane of the hotel bed.

Tragg whirled to Mason indignantly. "Dammit, Mason," he said, "if this was a plant . . ."

"Don't be silly," Mason interrupted. "I had no idea this *man* was dead. I wanted you to hear him confess."

Tragg said grimly, "I'm inclined to believe you. And I'm the only one in the department who will."

He walked over to the bed, circled it, studying the position of the figure. "Don't you guys touch anything," he said irritably. "Better get out there in the corridor and wait."

Neither Mason nor Drake made any move, but Drake's operative stepped back into the corridor.

The man lay face down on the bed. His shoes were on. The double-breasted coat seemed to be buttoned. The counterpane had not been drawn back but still covered the bed and one of the pillows. The other pillow lay on the floor. The man was stretched diagonally across the bed, his right arm dangling over the edge. On the fourth finger of the hand was a diamond ring. There was a dark patch at the base of his skull, and a sinister dark trickle which had seeped down his neck across the collar of his coat to stain the bed. There had, however, been but little bleeding.

Tragg stooped to examine the hole. "Small caliber bullet," he said, as though thinking aloud. "Gun held close. Powder burns. The tattooed type. Used that pillow on the floor to muffle the sound of the shot. Powder stains on it, too."

"Going to turn him over?" Mason asked.

Tragg said irritably, "I'm not going to touch a damn thing until the coroner gets here. You two get out of here. Go on down to the lobby and wait. And be damned sure you don't leave. There's going to be a stink over this."

"I tell you I had no idea this man was dead," Mason said. "In fact, *I* thought . . ."

"The newspaper boys aren't going to think so," Tragg interrupted, "and the chief isn't going to think so. It looks as though you'd made the department a cat's-paw so you wouldn't discover any more bodies."

"What's the use?" Mason said to Drake. "Let's go."

"While you're down in the lobby," Tragg said, "telephone headquarters, tell them I'm here, tell them to send out the Homicide car. And don't go away, Mason. I want to ask you some questions."

Mason and Drake picked up Drake's operative in the corridor. Mason said significantly, "Paul, wouldn't it be a good idea for your man to see if he couldn't get chummy with the telephone operator and find out if Lossten had any calls last night?"

Drake said, "Shucks, Perry, you know he didn't have any calls. He got that room, went immediately to . . ."

Mason nudged him with his elbow, and, as the dectective ceased talking, Mason went on smoothly, "Well, you know, Paul, he might have done some telephoning, and those telephone calls would be on his bill. After Tragg gets the Homicide Squad here, he'll sew everything up, and we won't be able to get any information at all."

"I get you," Drake said, and then to the operative, "You understand what's required?"

"Uh huh. It's not going to be so easy, because the telephone operator who's on now won't be the one who was on last night."

"Well, see what you can do," Mason said, "and you'd better go on down in the elevator a few minutes before we do. We'll give you a chance for a head start before we show up. And telephone Tragg's message to headquarters. Don't give out any information to anyone except the police."

"I won't."

When the elevator door had closed on Drake's operative,

Mason said in a low voice, "Thought we'd better get rid of him while we talk. What he doesn't know won't hurt him."

Drake said, "Shucks, Perry, we're in the clear on this."

"That shows all you know about it."

"What's wrong with it?"

"In the first place, the baggage. Did you notice the baggage over in the corner of the room?"

"No."

"A suitcase and a hatbox," Mason said. "Mrs. Warfield's. Tragg, of course, thought it was the dead man's baggage. The coroner will open it, and then . . ."

"Oh-oh!"

"We've got to tell Tragg what we were doing here. We've been altogether too prominent around the place, what with Mrs. Warfield's disappearance and all that."

"I suppose so," Drake admitted gloomily, "but he can't . . ."

"Well, there was Mrs. Warfield's baggage over in the corner of the room."

"Why the devil didn't she get it away from there?" Drake asked irritably.

"Take it easy," Mason said. "We've got to reason this thing out. That Warfield woman certainly played *us* for a couple of suckers."

"What do you think happened?"

"This man followed us to the hotel, went down to her room, told her he had a message from her husband, or else told her that he was Spinney. He told her she was sticking her neck out, playing with the wrong crowd, that you were a private detective, and I was a lawyer, and that her husband would have a fit if he found out what she was doing. He told her to grab her baggage and come down to his room."

"So far so good," Drake said, "but I can't figure the play after that."

Mason said, "There's only one thing that could have happened."

"What's that?"

"She found out Spinney was double-crossing her, that her husband was double-crossing her. And the only way she could have found that out was by having seen Homan's picture with the *Photoplay* stamp on it. Don't you get it? She knew then that he was in pictures. Get the sketch?"

Drake pursed his lips, "Damn it, yes."

"Now, then," Mason went on in a low voice, "look at it from Tragg's viewpoint. He'll think I'm protecting Mrs. Warfield, that I advised her to beat it, and that the story we handed the hotel manager about her disappearance was merely a runaround."

Drake's face twisted. "Damn!" he said.

"So watch your step," Mason warned. "And now let's go to the lobby."

They went down in the elevator. Drake's operative came bustling toward them. "That Mrs. Warfield you wanted. She was in the hotel all the time."

"What?"

"The clerk was just telling me," the man said, "that she walked out not over ten minutes after Mr. Mason had paid the bill. The clerk spotted her in the lobby, and asked her to wait a minute. He said the manager wanted to see her, that he had a message for her from her brother-in-law."

"And what happened?"

"The natural and obvious thing. The clerk stepped back to call the manager. Mrs. Warfield stuck her chin up in the air, told them she wasn't Mrs. Warfield, that she had no brother-in-law, and if they tried to detain her, she'd sue the hotel for damages, and with that she swept out of the lobby."

Mason and Drake exchanged glances.

"You know how it was," Drake's man went on. "The manager wasn't going to run out and grab her. Her bill was paid. He just let her walk out."

"Well," Mason said, "if you think we aren't in a sweet spot now, you just don't know Lieutenant Tragg."

Drake said with feeling, "I'll never fall for one of those tired-eyed, droop-shouldered women again. Remember that handbag she was carrying, Perry, how it bulged, and seemed to be heavy? Well, she was carrying a gun in that."

Mason said, "I don't give a damn who killed him, Paul. That's Tragg's headache. My job is to prove that this man was driving the car. When I've done that, I'm finished."

"Well, can't you have Miss Claire come over and identify him?"

Mason's laugh was scornful. "Sure, *she* can identify him, but how are we going to get any corroboration? He can't betray himself by some inadvertent slip of the tongue. He can't confess. Not now. He's dead. Stephane Claire's word won't be any good. If a woman could get out of a negligent homicide charge by simply pointing to a corpse and saying, 'There's the man who was really driving the car'—well, a good lawyer could always find a likely looking corpse somewhere."

Drake's forehead furrowed in a frown. He stood staring down at the floor.

"Our only hope now," Mason went on, "is to find Mrs. Warfield's husband, and make him kick through with evidence that will show Spinney was driving the car, and that this man is Spinney."

"Some little job," Drake said.

"Uh huh. He . . ."

"Good morning, Mr. Mason."

Mason turned. Jacks Sterne was walking toward him with outstretched hand. "How are things looking this morning?"

Mason took the hand in a perfunctory greeting, turned anxiously toward the elevator, said, "What are *you* doing here?"

"Why, you are the one who suggested that I come here. Remember? I was asking you about a good hotel last night . . ."

Mason said, "Get out and get out fast."

"Why—why, I don't understand."

"You don't have to," Mason told him. "Get up to your room, pack up, check out."

"Well, where shall I go?"

Mason's voice showed his impatience. "Never mind that now. Get out of here and get out right away. Don't stand there arguing. Check out. Go to the Adirondack."

"But Stephane wouldn't . . ."

"Go to the Adirondack. It's the natural place for you to be. Act as though you'd been there all the time."

"But I . . ."

"Beat it," Mason said. "Get packed and get out!"

Sterne seemed somewhat dazed. "I was on my way to see Stephane, Mr. Mason. I had telephoned her . . ."

Mason grabbed the man's arm, pushed him toward the elevator. "Sterne," he said, "the reason I'm not explaining is because I haven't time to explain. Get to your room, get your things packed, get a taxi, go to the Union Depot, wait in the waiting room for half an hour, then call a redcap, get another cab, and go to the Adirondack. Now do you get that?"

"Why, yes, I get it, but . . ."

An elevator stopped at the lobby floor. Mason all but pushed him in. "All right then," he said, "get started. If I'm still here in the lobby when you come down, don't speak to me. Don't look at me."

"But what will I tell Stephane?"

Mason turned his back. A moment later the elevator door clanged. Mason rejoined Paul Drake and the operative.

"Who?" Drake asked.

"Stephane Claire's boy friend," Mason said. "Wanted a quiet place to stay, and I suggested this hotel just because it was close to the Adirondack and . . ."

Drake said, "If Tragg finds out he was here, he'll darn near pin the killing on Stephane Claire."

"Are you telling me?" Mason asked, looking anxiously at his wrist watch. "Come on, Paul. Let's go back up and stand in the corridor. I don't want to be talking with Tragg when this drink-of-water checks out."

"Didn't you tell him not to give you a tumble if . . ."

"I *told* him," Mason said, "but he's just the sort who would walk up and say, 'Mr. Mason, *why* didn't you want me to speak to you when I came out?' "

"You *do* have the nicest friends, Perry."

"Don't I," Mason said. "Come on, let's go up."

It was a good half hour before Tragg sent for Mason.

Members of the Homicide Squad were still at work, developing latent fingerprints, taking photographs of the body, drawing a scaled map of the room.

"I hope," Tragg said with the flicker of a smile at the corners of his eyes, "you've got your story ready."

"I have."

"If you want any more time to think up a *good* one, I'll talk with Drake first. You understand the position I'm in. The chief will think you used me as a cat's-paw."

Mason said, "I get fed up with this. If I co-operate with you, I'm using you as a cat's-paw. If I go ahead on my own, I'm included in the list of suspects."

"The trouble, Mason, is that you find too many bodies."

Mason said, "No. The trouble is that I can't stay in my office and wait for people to come in and see me the way clients are supposed to. I have to get out on the firing line. When you do that, you circulate around quite a bit and . . ."

"And you *still* find too many bodies," Tragg said.

"I was going to add," Mason remarked with some dignity, "that once a man gets a reputation for being a good lawyer in a murder case, murders have a tendency to gravitate in his direction."

Tragg thought that over for a few moments, and said, "Yes. I guess that's so. A person who has committed a murder naturally thinks of Perry Mason. And, by the same token, a person who intends to commit a murder naturally thinks of Perry Mason."

"I'm glad you recognize that fact. It may simplify matters."

"Who is this guy?" Tragg asked, jerking his head toward the bed.

"I don't know," Mason said.

"You don't know! I thought you said you did."

"I know that he's registered here as Walter Lossten. That's all I know about him."

Tragg looked at him suspiciously. "You couldn't see the face when you came in?"

"No."

"Then how do you know that you don't know him?"

"If he's the man I think he must be, I've never met him."

"And who do you think he must be?"

"The man who was driving Homan's car."

Tragg frowned. "Listen, Mason, you keep trying to drag Homan into this thing. Hollywood has a few million dollars invested around this town. A group of the highest-salaried men and women in the world are gathered into a few square miles. Naturally, it's the richest blackmail pasture on earth. The D.A.'s office knows this, and tries to give Hollywood the breaks. You know that as well as I do."

Mason nodded.

"Now, I can't go barging up to Homan the way I would an ordinary citizen. You know that."

Mason said, "You were asking me for facts. I was giving them to you. I take it that you want them?"

"Nuts," Tragg said.

Mason said, "Perhaps I'd better take a look at the body."

"Perhaps you had."

Mason walked over to the bed, stepping over a tape measure with which two of Tragg's assistants were measuring the distance from the bed to the window.

The body had been turned over on its back, and Mason looked down upon features so perfectly in accord with the description Stephane Claire had given him of the man who was driving the car that Mason felt he must have known this man at some time, personally and intimately.

He turned away. Tragg raised his eyebrows.

Mason nodded.

Tragg said to one of the men, "You boys finished with this telephone?"

The man to whom he had spoken said, "Yeah. The fingerprints on it are all pretty badly smudged, and I think they're old. I don't think anyone's used it within the last twenty-four hours."

"All right," Tragg said, picked up the telephone, called headquarters and said, "This is Lieutenant Tragg of Homicide. I'm in five-twenty-one at the Gateview Hotel working on a case. Stephane Claire, who's being held on that automobile accident on the Ridge Route, may know this man. Have a couple of radio officers pick her up and bring her here fast. She's at the Adirondack Hotel." He hung up.

Mason said, "So you know where she is?"

Tragg grinned. "Don't be silly. It's a county case, but when she was released on bail—well, they asked us to cooperate. After all, it's a homicide, you know."

"I didn't know you boys worked together with so much harmony."

"Orders from the chief," Tragg said.

Mason smiled. "Hollywood certainly *does* have a drag!"

Tragg changed the subject.

"You were looking for this man?"

"Naturally. He's the driver of the Homan car."

"What name did you know him by?"

"I tell you I didn't know him."

"What name did he give your client?"

"He didn't give her any. The accident happened before they got that well acquainted."

"Cagey, aren't you?"

"No. Truthful."

"When you wanted me to come out, you said something about a Spinley or Semley, or some such name."

"I don't remember it."

Tragg tried another tack. "How did you happen to look for him in this hotel?"

"Paul Drake's men were making a search. They asked the clerk if a man who answered this description had arrived at the hotel last night and found he had."

Tragg's slight frown showed his irritation. "Very, *very* nice," he said, and then added, after a significant pause, "for you. That is, it would be nice if I believed it."

"You can prove it," Mason said.

"How?"

"By checking with the clerk."

"I'm not doubting that. You're too shrewd to give me a false lead on something that could be checked as easily as that. But what I want to know is how Drake's men happened to pick this particular hotel."

"They were looking for the driver of the car."

"You mean the corpse over here?"

"Yes."

"And why did they happen to look here?"

"They were covering the hotels."

"How many other hotels did they cover?" Tragg asked.

As Mason remained silent, Tragg grinned. "You're a tough customer, Mason. You know your rights, and you'll keep within them, but if I have to I'll get the facts from Paul Drake. Remember, Drake's running a private detective agency. He'd hate to have anything happen to his license."

Mason said, "Drake and I had a witness we were keeping in the hotel. We thought this man might try to reach her."

"That's better. Who was the witness?"

"I'd prefer not to discuss that."

"Doubtless you would, but who was it?"

"I don't think I'll answer that, Tragg."

Tragg said to one of the men, "Get Paul Drake up here."

Mason said, "After all, Tragg, you have no right to inquire into the confidential affairs of a lawyer even if you are trying to clear up a murder case."

Tragg didn't even bother to reply.

Paul Drake appeared in tow of the officer.

Tragg said, "All right, Drake, let's have this straight. Your men located this man here in the hotel. No, don't look at Mason. Just answer the question."

Drake nodded.

"How did they happen to locate him here?"

"They made inquiries of the clerk."

"All right, Drake, I'll be patient with you, but don't carry it too far. How did they happen to make inquiries of the clerk?"

"Mason thought the man might be here."

"And when did Mason get that bright idea?"

"About nine-fifteen or nine-thirty this morning."

"Who was the witness that was here at the hotel?"

"I didn't know there was any."

Tragg's face flushed slightly. "How many times have you been at this hotel within the last twenty-four hours, Drake?"

Mason said, "Go ahead and tell him, Paul. He'll find out from the assistant manager, anyway."

Drake said, "Mason and I brought a woman into the hotel last night. I didn't know she was a witness. I thought she was just going to give Mason . . ."

"What's her name?"

"Mrs. Warfield."

"Where's she from?"

"New Orleans."

"Where did she register?"

"Room six-twenty-eight."

"Well," Tragg exclaimed, "it took us quite a little while to get *that* simple piece of information, didn't it? Where is that woman now?"

"I don't know," Mason said.

"You've been to her room?"

"Been to her room," Mason said, "secured a passkey, gone in, and looked around."

"Indeed, and what did you find?"

"Nothing. She wasn't there."

"The room in the same condition now that it was then?"

"Inasmuch as I was paying the bill," Mason said, "and apparently she had no intention of using the room, I checked out for her."

Tragg's voice became crisply businesslike. "All right, Mason—and you too, Drake, get this straight. We aren't always on the same side of the fence. I can't help that, and you can't help it. You have your living to make. I have my living to make. But, by God, when I ask you fellows a question, I want an answer. Beating around the bush isn't going to get you anyplace. If you don't want to answer and think you can make it stick, simply refuse to answer. But don't try giving me a runaround. Is that straight?"

Mason said, "Watch your questions then. Don't accuse me of giving you a runaround if I don't volunteer information."

"If it's going to be like that," Tragg said, "I can take

care of it. All right, let's go take a look at that room Mrs.
Warfield had."

"Someone else may be in it now," Mason said. "We
checked out."

"Get the manager," Tragg told one of his men.

While the man was getting the manager, a radio officer
escorted Stephane Claire out of the elevator. She seemed
white and frightened. Her eyes glanced appealingly at
Mason.

Mason said, "This is Lieutenant Tragg of Homicide, Miss
Claire. You'll find him very competent, but exceedingly
partisan. I'm afraid you're in for a disagreeable experience. We want you to look at a body."

"At a *body!*"

Mason nodded.

"Here?"

"Yes."

"Why? . . . What? . . ."

Mason said, "The man was mur . . ."

"That'll do," Tragg said to Mason. "I'll do the talking
from now on. Miss Claire, we thought perhaps this might
be the body of a man whom you have known. If you
won't mind stepping this way, please . . ." He took her arm
and escorted her into the hotel bedroom.

There was the unmistakable atmosphere of death in
the room. The body that was sprawled on the bed clothed
the surroundings with the quiet dignity of death. On the
other hand, the men who were working trying to develop
clues, seemed entirely set apart from all solemnity. So far
as they were concerned, the body on the bed might have
been a sack of potatoes. It was merely an inanimate object
to be photographed, measured, and studied in connection
with the other objects in the room.

These men worked skillfully and quickly, with a complete air of detachment. Constant familiarity with death
had in some way made them seem immune to it.

Lieutenant Tragg guided Stephane Claire past these men,
moved around the foot of the bed in such a way that his
body obstructed her vision. Not until she was where she
could look directly down at the man's face did Tragg step
quickly to one side.

"Know this man?" he asked.

Stephane Claire stared down at the still gray features.
For several moments her eyes were held as by some mag-

netic attraction which was stronger than her own volition, then she managed to shift her eyes to Tragg's face. "Yes, I know him. I don't know his name."

"Who is he?"

"He was the one who was driving the car the night of the wreck, the one who picked me up as a hitchhiker."

Tragg made a little bow to Mason. "Very neatly done, Mason," he said sarcastically. "I congratulate you. I suppose that will be your defense."

"Naturally," Mason said.

"Why, it's the truth!" Stephane Claire exclaimed. "Mr. Mason hasn't said a word to me. I haven't seen or heard from him since I left the hospital."

Tragg looked from Stephane Claire to Mason. "Dammit," he said to Mason, "I believe you. And offhand I can mention the names of three thousand eight hundred and seventy-six persons directly and indirectly connected with the police who won't."

The assistant hotel manager was profuse in his expostulations, emphasizing his desire to work with the police, and the high reputation which the hotel enjoyed.

"We want to take a look at Mrs. Warfield's room," Tragg said. "Come on, Mason. You and Drake come along—and you can stay with that officer, Miss Claire." And it was significant that Tragg hadn't even mentioned the baggage which he had found in the room with the corpse.

The little group walked down to the elevator, rode up to the sixth floor, and the manager said, "I understand the room is in the same condition as it was when . . ."

"When the party checked out?" Tragg asked.

"When the bill was paid."

"Who paid it?"

"This gentleman here, her brother-in-law."

"Her brother-in-law!" Tragg exclaimed.

"That's what he said."

Tragg looked at Mason. "Well, well, well, you didn't tell me she was related to you, Mason. And you a brotherless bachelor." He turned to the manager. "I don't suppose you know when this party checked out?"

"I most certainly do," the manager said. "Mr. Mason and this other gentleman appeared and paid the bill. There was a very attractive young woman with them at the time. Mr. Mason said the party in the hotel was his sister-in-law, that she had a weak heart, and that he was afraid something had happened to her. I sent a bellboy up to investigate. We found the room unoccupied. There was no baggage in it."

"No baggage?" Tragg asked.

"No."

"Then she had baggage when she rented the room?"

"She had a suitcase and a hatbox."

Tragg digested that information. Once more he kept silent about the baggage which Mason had seen in the room where the murder had been committed.

"Go on," Tragg said. "What else happened?"

"After Mr. Mason had paid the bill and left, he told me that in case I saw Mrs. Warfield, I was to let her know that her brother-in-law had been looking for her and was very much concerned about her."

"The only catch being that he knew you wouldn't see her," Tragg said.

"On the contrary, I did see her."

"You did?" Tragg stopped abruptly and stared at the manager.

"Yes, Lieutenant, she walked across the lobby not more than fifteen minutes after Mr. Mason had paid the bill. You see, the clerk who was on duty wasn't the one who had checked her in, but we had her description, and he knows most of the regular guests. He called to her and told her he had a message for her. She came to the counter to wait for the message. He called me, and I told her her brother-in-law had been here and wanted her to communicate with him. She insisted that her name was not Warfield, that she had no brother-in-law, that we were impertinent, and started for the door. I tried to detain her, but she was so utterly indignant that I couldn't be certain of my ground. After all, her bill had been paid, and there was no legal ground on which I could hold her, but there are several matters in connection with her stay here which haven't been properly explained."

"She had no baggage with her when she left?"

"No."

Tragg said, "Let's take a look at the room."

The manager opened the door, and Tragg, motioning for the others to wait in the corridor, entered the room. He looked quickly around, then turned swifty to the manager.

"Look here, this room has been made up. You said it was in the same condition as when she left."

The manager shook his head. "I understand it's in exactly the same condition as it was when the bellboy opened it with his passkey."

"What time was that?"

"Perhaps around eight-thirty."

Tragg gently turned back the covers of the bed. "*She* didn't make this bed?" he asked.

"No, sir. The sheets are absolutely clean. The bed hasn't been used."

"The chambermaid didn't change the sheets?"

"The chambermaid hasn't been in here."

"You're certain?"

"Yes."

Mason, standing in the doorway, said, "No towels have been used in the bathroom either, Lieutenant."

Tragg turned to Mason, regarded him speculatively, then devoted his attention once more to a study of the room.

He whirled back to Mason. "What was she doing out here?"

"Looking for work."

"Did she find any?"

"She had a job under consideration."

"What sort of a job?"

"I believe she was told that the vacancy hadn't occurred as yet, but might within the next few days, and that her salary would be kept on while she was waiting."

"Do you believe that's what she was told?"

"Yes."

Tragg's smile became a grin. "All right," he said, "who told her?"

Mason answered his grin. "Paul Drake."

"At whose suggestion?"

"Mine."

Tragg said, "Well, I had to make *those* questions specific enough in order to get an intelligent answer."

"You got the answer, didn't you?"

"Yes."

Tragg said, "Let's see if we can't short-cut some of this a little, fellows. You made Mrs. Warfield that proposition because you wanted her for something—what?"

"We wanted to locate her husband for her."

Tragg said, "Nuts," and walked away to stand in the

door to the bathroom. Then he came back, looked at the drawn shades and the electric light.

He turned again to Mason, "What would I have to do, Mason, to get you to give me the whole dope on this thing—the real low-down?"

"Ask questions," Mason said. "Ask anything you want, and I'll answer it."

"And what would I have to do to get you to give it to me without asking questions?"

"Follow up the leads I was working on."

"You mean Hollywood?"

Mason nodded.

Tragg hesitated a moment, then shook his head. "That's too large an order—yet."

"Then keep on asking questions," Mason said.

"Thanks. I will," Tragg promised grimly. "I'll begin by asking you the name you mentioned when you called on me earlier this morning."

Mason frowned as though perplexed. "Homan?" he asked.

"No, no," Tragg said. "Come on, quit stalling. The one from San Francisco."

"Oh, from San Francisco. I'm not certain that I . . ."

"The one that sounded like Spelley or something of that sort."

Mason frowned. "I don't remember any Spelley."

"Was that name Greeley, Adler Greeley?" Tragg asked.

"No," Mason said.

"Well, what was it?"

"So the dead man's name is Greeley, is it?"

"I'm not answering questions. I'm asking them. I want that name that you mentioned, the one that you said was wanted by the San Francisco police."

"Oh, you must be referring to Spinney," Mason said.

"That's it. What about him?"

"That's all I know about him," Mason said. "The name of Spinney."

"And how did you happen to find that out?"

"One of Drake's men uncovered a lead which made him think Spinney was associated with Homan."

"Homan again," Tragg groaned. "My gosh, why do you always come harping back to him?"

"Because he's the angle I'm working on."

"Well, what made you think he was registered here under the name of Lossten?"

"Because," Mason said patiently, "I thought the man who was registered here was the man who had been driving the car. I thought the man who was driving the car was associated with Homan. I thought that Mr. Spinney was associated with Homan. Therefore, I thought it was a good possibility that the man who was registered here was Mr. Spinney."

"You didn't come here because Miss Claire asked you to?"

"No."

"You didn't look him up on account of anything Mrs. Warfield told you?"

"No."

"And why did you come to my office before you went to call on the gentleman?"

"I told you," Mason said. "I wanted to co-operate."

Tragg bowed. "I certainly appreciate your frankness, Mr. Mason. Don't let me detain you. I know you're a busy man, and while I appreciate the *great* help you're giving me, I can't ask you to sacrifice your practice."

"Meaning that we're free to go?"

"Yes, all except the Claire girl."

"Why can't she go?"

"Because I'm holding her."

"I don't know what grounds you have for holding her."

"So far she's the only one we've found who knew this man. She had every reason not to like him. The man's dead. Under the circumstances, we're going to have to hold her for a while."

"She's just been released from the hospital."

Tragg smiled. "It isn't where she's just been that counts, but where she's just going. And that's the D.A.'s office."

"May I talk with her before she leaves?"

"I'd prefer that you didn't."

"She's my client. I demand the right to talk with her."

Tragg smiled, "I wouldn't want to deprive you of your right to talk wth a client," he said, "but unfortunately she isn't here. A detective is driving her to the D.A.'s office."

Mason said irritably, "Even when we co-operate, we don't seem to be of much help to each other, do we?"

"Are *you*," Tragg said, "telling *me*? However, Mr. Mason, don't worry. I'll start an investigation of Mr. L. C.

Spinney who has been residing at San Francisco, and—shall we say Bakersfield?"

"I don't know why not," Mason said.

Tragg, looking at him, said, "Well, I'll pull that one chestnut out of the fire for you. What did Mrs. Warfield look like?"

"About thirty-one or two, tired looking, blue eyes, light chestnut hair, drooping shoulders, average height, thin. Wearing a blue serge skirt and jacket when we last saw her."

Tragg picked up the telephone, called headquarters, and said, "I want a dragnet out for a Mrs. Warfield who registered at the Gateview Hotel last night as Lois Warfield of New Orleans. She checked out of the hotel within the last hour. Search all the restaurants near by. She's thirty-odd, thin, average height, tired looking, blue eyes, light chestnut hair, blue serge suit. I want her damn bad. Rush it."

He hung up the telephone.

"And do you," Mason said, "want us any more?"

Tragg grinned. "Hell, no!"

Out in the street once more, Mason said, "I thought he'd give us more action going after Spinney if he thought I was trying to keep what I knew about Spinney away from him."

"It *may* work that way," Drake admitted. "Why didn't he mention her baggage in Greeley's room?"

"Trying to trap us," Mason said. "Watch your step, Paul. In the meantime, we'll see if there's an Adler Greeley in the telephone book. If there is, we'll pay a very hurried call. While Tragg's busy unscrambling the leads we've given him, we may manage to steal a march."

13

THE BUILDING was a two-flat affair in a high-priced district. Green palm fronds splashed against the background of white stone.

A colored maid answered the bell.

Mason gave her his card. "I would like to see Mrs. Greeley if she's in," he said. "Please tell her it's very important."

The maid took the card, read it, glanced shrewdly at Mason, said, "Just a moment, please," and climbed the stairs. A few moments later, she returned. "Mrs. Greeley will see you," she said.

Mason was ushered into a living room in which dark massive furniture, deep rugs, and a few carefully selected oil paintings, originals, gave an atmosphere of unpretentious luxury. The photograph over the fireplace was unquestionably that of the man whose body Mason had seen at the Gateview Hotel.

Mrs. Greeley was evidently in the early thirties. She was a woman who could extend every courtesy as a hostess, yet managed to withhold the intimacy of her friendship—a woman who had quite evidently done much entertaining, had been entertained, and who would seldom be at a loss under any circumstances.

Surveying him with frank curiosity, she said, "I've heard of you, Mr. Mason, and I've read about your cases in the papers. Won't you be seated?"

Mason said, "My errand is not very pleasant, Mrs. Greeley. It has to do with your husband."

He paused.

She said, "I'm sorry, Mr. Mason. You can't see him. He's in San Francisco."

"Do you know just when he went to San Francisco?" Mason asked.

"Why, yes. He was called rather unexpectedly yesterday evening."

"Does he go to San Francisco frequently?"

"Yes. His business calls him there regularly. Can you tell me the reason for these questions, Mr. Mason?"

Mason said, "Frankly, Mrs. Greeley, I'm investigating an automobile accident in which your husband was concerned."

"Adler in an automobile accident?"

The lawyer nodded.

"You don't mean last night? Tell me, Mr. Mason, he wasn't hurt? . . ."

"No, not last night. It was several days ago."

"Why, I didn't hear him say a thing about it. There was a bruise . . . Can you tell me just what you have in mind, Mr. Mason?"

"Your husband was in San Francisco last Wednesday?"

"He goes up there frequently."

"And does he drive when he makes the trip?"

"Good heavens, no! Not between here and San Francisco! He takes the plane or the night train, usually the plane. Sometimes he'll go up on the early morning plane and take the night train back."

"One more question. Can you tell me if Mr. Greeley knows a motion picture producer by the name of Homan?"

"Why, yes. Well, now, wait a minute. I don't know whether he's met Mr. Homan personally or just over the telephone. But I know he has handled some business for Mr. Homan. I remember we were at a picture a few nights ago, and Mr. Homan's name was flashed on the screen. Adler told me that Homan was a client of his, and I was quite thrilled."

"Mrs. Greeley, has your husband mentioned that he was in *any* automobile accident recently?"

"No."

"Has he seemed bruised or stiff or sore?"

"Except for a slight . . . Mr. Mason, why do you ask *me* these questions? Adler would be the logical person to answer them."

"Unfortunately, he isn't available."

"His office would know where to reach him. You could get him on the phone."

"His office said they couldn't tell me when I could reach him."

She smiled. "Perhaps they'd tell *you* that, but they'd let *me* know."

"Was he here last night?"

"No. I told you he was called to San Francisco—but he expected to take either the morning train or the night train back."

"Has it ever occurred to you that your husband might change his plans—or might tell you he was in one place when he was really in another?"

She laughed in his face. "Are you trying to ask delicately if it's occurred to me that my husband would deceive me?"

"Yes."

She said, still smiling, "I suppose he would. I think any man would if he happened to be tempted sufficiently. But my husband would always play fair with me, Mr. Mason. There's a difference, you see. And I think, Mr. Mason, that you've said enough now so that Adler should know you're here and what you want."

She opened a compartment in a taboret, took out an extension telephone, dialed a number, and said, "Irma, this is Mrs. Greeley. Let me talk with Mr. Greeley, will you please? . . . Oh, he hasn't. Well, where can I reach him? . . . That's in San Francisco? . . . I see. . . . Well, give me a ring as soon as you hear from him then."

She dropped the receiver into place, said, "He told her he'd either be at the office before noon or give her a ring from San Francisco. She thinks he's on his way by plane."

"So you think if your husband were sufficiently tempted, he might . . ."

"Mr. Mason," she interrupted, "any husband who's worth his salt can't get over the idea he's something of a devil with the women. If a woman is clever enough to capitalize on it, she can turn any man's head—but she can't turn his heart, Mr. Mason, and I think that answers your question. And now, since I've answered it, may I ask why you are here, what you are intimating, and precisely what you have in mind?"

Her eyes, which held Mason's, were frankly challenging, just a little suspicious.

"Specifically, Mrs. Greeley, I think your husband was driving an automobile on Wednesday evening of last week at about ten o'clock. He was driving over the Ridge Route.

A young woman was with him. There was an accident. Some persons were badly injured."

"You mean he was going to San Francisco?"

"No. He was coming this way."

"At what time?"

"At a little after eleven o'clock."

She thought for a moment. "That was Wednesday of last week?"

"Yes."

"Why haven't you asked Mr. Greeley?"

"Unfortunately, I haven't been able to find him."

"After all, Mr. Mason, it seems rather circuitous to come to me. . . . I think that if you have any further questions about my husband, you're going to have to ask them of him."

"That's impossible."

"Well, it won't be impossible long. He'll be in his office . . ."

"I'm afraid," Mason said, "your husband won't be in his office—not today, not tomorrow, not this week."

She was staring at him, her forehead puckered into a perplexed frown when the telephone rang.

Her eyes flashed triumph. "That," she said, "will be Irma telling me Mr. Greeley is at the office. I'm going to tell him that you're here and what you want, Mr. Mason."

She said, "Yes?" into the telephone, then frowned. "Oh, I'm sorry. Who is it, please? What is it? What's the name, please? . . . But I don't understand. You want me at the Gateview Hotel? . . . Lieutenant Tragg—of Homicide?—You mean—You mean—No! Not Adler! There's some mistake. . . . He's in San Francisco. I was talking with his office only a few minutes ago. . . . I . . . Y-y-yes, I'll be right up."

She dropped the receiver into the cradle of the telephone. Slowly, she turned to stare at Mason. She regarded him as though he had been some distorted apparition of a nightmare. Her face and eyes were filled with surprise and horror.

"You—you must have known—this."

Mason arose. "I'm sorry, Mrs. Greeley."

She might not have heard him. She got to her feet mechanically, as a reflex action brought about by the departure of a guest, followed Mason to the head of the stairs. She didn't start to cry until Mason was halfway down the treads. Then the lawyer heard one choking sob, and the sound of feet running across the living room toward the bedroom.

Mason let himself out into the bright sunshine of a cold spring day.

14

THE COURTROOM hummed with activity. Judge Cortright on the bench, disposed of half a dozen preliminary motions, listened with enforced attention to the arguments of an attorney who seemed unable to come direcly to the point, finally interrupted with a ruling, and called the next case. Lawyers came and went. The atmosphere seemed permeated with haste. These were minor matters, things which were occurring over and over, times without number, until they had lost any individuality; infractions of the law which piled up faster than they could be disposed of unless the judicial machine functioned smoothly. The only persons who thought the cases had any importance were the ones directly affected.

The white-faced wife who sat with folded hands while the attorney for her husband argued that the complaint for non-support was technically incorrect, was conscious of the fact that at last she had summoned nerve enough to make the man who sat glowering at her quit spending money on other women and help support his child. He'd always sworn that he'd kill her if she ever went to law. Would he do it? Her heart was thumping the blood through her tired arteries in pounding sequences. She felt them hammering in her ears. He'd said he'd kill her. He looked as though he wanted to. Perhaps he would. Then what about the baby? The lawyer droned on. The complaint was defective in that it failed to state the defendant had willfully withheld support.

Judge Cortright listened to the argument wearily. After all, what difference did it make? Knock out this complaint, and the man would be re-arrested. He was conscious only of the passing minutes, of his crowded calendar, of the tedious verbosity of counsel.

At length, he disposed of the preliminary matters. "People versus Stephane Claire," he called.

Harold Hanley from the district attorney's office regarded the case as a legal chore. "Your Honor, the defendant is in court represented by Perry Mason. Counsel have agreed that the preliminary may be held at this time. The defendant is on bail. By stipulation of counsel, the hearing may be had with no other notice or formalities."

"Very well," Judge Cortright said. "Your witnesses are present?"

"Yes, Your Honor."

There followed a routine of technical procedure. Attorneys whose matters had been disposed of left the courtroom, some of them still arguing heatedly, others joking, others bustling to some other department where they had matters pending. Harold Hanley called his witnesses to the stand in a quick succession. Frank Corvis, the traffic officer who had been advised of the accident, had come on the wrecked automobile in which the defendant was sitting, had lifted her out. He testified to her position. She was at the steering wheel of the car in the driver's seat. Both car doors were closed when he arrived. He had found a bottle in the glove compartment. No, he didn't have that bottle with him. He had sealed it and handed it to the head of the traffic department. Yes, he would know that bottle if he saw it again. Yes, that was the bottle. That was exactly the condition in which he had found it, about one-third filled with whiskey. Yes, he had noticed an odor on the defendant's breath. It was the odor of liquor.

"Cross-examine," Hanley said to Perry Mason.

The traffic officer turned toward Mason, squaring himself as though belligerently ready to repel any attack.

"Did you," Mason asked, "notice whether the hands of the defendant rested on the steering wheel?"

"I didn't notice *both* hands. I grabbed her right wrist to lift her up."

"Where was her right wrist?"

"On the steering wheel."

"You're certain?"

"Absolutely."

"Then, of course, her fingers were not wrapped around the steering wheel."

"What do you mean?"

"If her wrist was on the stearing wheel," Mason explained, "it would be an impossibility for her to have her fingers wrapped around the steering wheel."

Corvis frowned. He glanced at the deputy prosecutor, then away. "I think I got that wrong."

"Her wrist was not on the steering wheel?"

"Her hand was on the steering wheel."

"Now, by her hand being on the steering wheel, do you mean that her fingers were wrapped around the steering wheel?"

"Yes. I think they were."

"You gripped her right wrist when you lifted her through the car window?"

"Yes."

"You wrapped your fingers around her wrist?"

"Yes."

"Now did you notice anything peculiar about her right hand?"

"Not at the time."

"But you did later?"

"Yes."

"When was this?"

"After she had been removed from the car and was lying on the ground waiting for an ambulance. A motorist had given us an automobile robe which we had spread on the ground, and the motorist and I moved the girl over to this robe."

"Now by the girl, you mean the defendant?"

"Yes."

"And at that time, you noticed something about her right hand?"

"Yes."

"What was it?"

"There was something red on her little finger. At first, I thought it was blood. It came off and made a red smear on the back of my hand. I tried to wipe it off, and it didn't wipe off the way blood would."

"It was lipstick?"

"I think so, yes."

"Now did you notice her left hand?"

"Yes."

"There was a glove on it, was there not?"

"Yes."

"But none on her right hand?"

"No."

"Had you searched the automobile?"

"Yes."

"Did you find any lipstick in the car?"

"No. I found her purse and sent that in with her in the ambulance."

"Find any baggage?"

"No."

"Not anywhere in the automobile?"

"No."

"Now, if the defendant's right hand had been resting on the steering wheel, particularly gripping it with the force used by a person in trying to avoid an accident, there would have been lipstick on the wheel of that car?"

"Well . . ."

"Objected to as argumentative," the district attorney said.

"Sustained."

"Did you examine the steering wheel of the car to see whether there were any traces of lipstick on it?"

"Not then."

"Later?"

"Yes."

"Did you find any?"

"Just a very faint trace of lipstick in one place. . . . You see, if she'd been trying to fix her lips at the time of the accident and driving with one hand . . ."

"That will do," the judge interrupted sternly. "The court will draw its own conclusions. Simply testify to the facts."

"You looked in the trunk of the car?"

"Yes, of course."

"There was no baggage there?"

"No baggage."

"The ignition on the car was locked?"

The officer lowered his eyes. "I don't know," he said. "It was locked when the car got to the garage. You see, it was moved with a wrecking outfit. There was no reason to start the motor. I looked the car over for liquor and baggage, but I didn't notice the ignition until yesterday when it was called to my attention."

"The ignition was locked?"

"That's right."

"Did you look for fingerprints on the steering wheel of the automobile?"

"No, sir, I didn't. When we see a car go off the road into the ditch and find a person unconscious at the steering wheel with his fingers wrapped around the wheel and no one else in the car, we don't match fingerprints to see who was driving it."

A titter rustled around the courtroom. The judge looked inquiringly at Mason. "You wish a motion to strike out that last statement, Mr. Mason?"

"Oh, let it stay in," Mason said, and turned once more to face the witness.

"Now, the car doors were closed?"

"Yes."

"Both doors?"

"Yes."

"It was rather a cold night, was it not?"

"What's that got to do with it?"

"I am just asking."

"Well, it was cold up there."

"The wind was blowing?"

"Yes."

"And do you know whether the car in which the defendant was seated had a heater?"

"I believe it did. I can remember now. . . . Yes, it did."

"And the heater was on?"

"Yes, the fan was running."

"Now, you say that you lifted the defendant out through the window."

"That's right. The window in the car door."

"On what side?"

"On the right-hand side. The car was lying on its left side."

"I see. And you lifted the defendant through the right window?"

"That's what I said."

"Now, it was impossible for you to lower the glass in the window from the outside, wasn't it?"

"Naturally."

"And you didn't open the door?"

"Not then. I told you we lifted her out through the window. The door was jammed. How many more times do I have to tell you?"

Judge Cortright said sternly, "The witness will confine

himself to answering questions. However, counsel should bear in mind that the calendar is crowded with other matters, and this question has been asked and answered in one form or another several different times."

"Exactly," Mason said. "In a moment, I think Your Honor will appreciate the importance of the question. You couldn't roll this window down from the outside of the car, could you, Mr. Corvis?"

"No. I didn't say I rolled the window down. The window was open."

"Rolled all the way down?"

"I . . . Yes."

"This car was a four-passenger coupe?"

"Yes."

"There were only two doors?"

"That's right."

"And the windows were rather large—large enough to lift the defendant through?"

"We couldn't have lifted her through," Corvis said, "if they hadn't been big enough to lift her through."

The deputy district attorney let the spectators see his broad grin.

"Then," Mason said, *"another person could have made his escape from this car through this window?"*

Corvis thought for a moment. "I don't know."

"But if the defendant got through, a man could have crawled through, couldn't he?"

"I don't know."

"That question's argumentative," Hanley said.

Mason smiled. "I'll withdraw it. The facts speak for themselves. Now, Mr. Corvis, you've been a traffic officer for some time?"

"Five years."

"You've had an opportunity to observe quite a bit about the operation of motor cars?"

"Naturally."

"Did you ever," Mason asked, smilingly, "observe a car being operated at night on a mountain road with a cold wind blowing and the window in the door on the right-hand side rolled all the way down—the night being cold enough to necessitate the use of a heater in the car?"

Hanley jumped to his feet. "Your Honor, that's not proper cross-examination. We didn't qualify this man as an expert. It calls for a conclusion of the witness, a matter of opinion, it's argumentative, and . . ."

"Objection sustained," Judge Cortright said. "You didn't qualify him. It isn't proper cross-examination."

Mason, having made his point, contented himself with a smile. "That's all."

Corvis left the stand. Other witnesses told of the collision; of the four-passenger coupe being operated at a high rate of speed, swerving around a car on a three-lane pavement to find another car already occupying the third lane; of the collision; of the zigzag course taken by the car. With one exception, none of the witnesses had seen the driver of the car. It had, they explained, happened too quickly.

Edith Lions, however, who had been riding in the car which the four-passenger coupe had tried to pass, told a different story. She was about twenty-two, a red-haired girl with turned-up nose, freckles, and rapid-fire speech. She said, "I was riding with my mother and father in the car. We were sitting three in the front seat. This car was coming along behind us at a terrific rate of speed. All of a sudden it swerved out to pass us, but at that time a car coming from the other direction was passing another car which was also coming toward us."

"What happened?" Hanley asked.

"Just like the other witnesses have said."

"Never mind that. Just tell it in your own words, Miss Lions."

"Well, the person driving the car tried to cut in and scraped our fender. That caused the car to swerve back across the pavement right in front of another car that was coming toward us."

"Then what?"

"Then this other car tried to dodge, and hit a car behind us head-on."

"And what happened to the four-passenger coupe? Could you see?"

"It kept shooting right across the road, and went down the bank. Then I think it rolled over. It sounded like it."

"And what did you do?"

"As soon as my father stopped the car, I jumped out."

"Did you run back toward the cars that had collided?"

"No. I was busy dodging cars for a few minutes. Then I ran over toward the bank where this four-passenger coupe had gone over."

"What did you see?"

"It took me a little while to locate it. Then I looked down and saw the car lying on its side down at the bottom of this steep embankment."

"Did you see anyone—any person?"

"Not then."

"Later on, did you?"

"Yes, sir."

"Who?"

"That woman sitting there," pointing to Stephane Claire.

"Where was she, and how were you able to see her?"

"They turned a flashlight into the car. She was sitting in the driver's seat."

"Now, did you at any time see any other person in the four-passenger coupe?"

"No, sir."

"And could you see who was driving it when the car went past?"

"Yes, sir."

"Who?"

"Well, it was a woman. I could see that, and she was wearing the same kind of a hat the defendant was wearing."

"Cross-examine," Hanley said triumphantly.

"Your father was driving your car?" Mason asked the witness.

"Yes, sir."

"And you were sitting next to your mother?"

"Yes, sir."

"Your mother was in the middle?"

"That's right."

"Then you were on the extreme right-hand side of the car?"

"Yes, sir."

"And this four-passenger coupe passed on your left?"

"Yes."

"And then cut in?"

"Yes."

"It was dark?"

"Naturally."

"And headlights were coming toward you?"

"Yes."

"Did the four-passenger coupe at any time come directly between you and the headlights of an approaching car?"

"How do you mean?"

Mason said, "The court reporter will read the question. Please listen attentively."

The court reporter read the question.

"Do you understand it?" Mason asked.

"Yes."

"Can you answer it?"

"No," she said. "I guess not. There were lots of headlights though. They seemed to be coming from all directions at once."

"How fast was your father driving?"

"Forty miles an hour."

"And how fast was this four-passenger coupe going?"

"At least eighty or ninety miles an hour."

"And when did you first realize there was going to be an accident?"

"When this car sideswiped our fender."

"And as soon as it did that, it immediately swerved to the left?"

"Yes."

"And shot diagonally across the road?"

"Yes."

"Yet with headlights coming at you from several different directions, with your father fighting to keep your car in the road, you, sitting on the extreme right side of the seat, could look across and into the interior of that speeding four-passenger coupe?"

"Yes, sir."

"Your car did skid after the collision, did it not?"

"It was jolted around, yes."

"So that it was headed off toward the *right* side of the road?"

"Yes."

"And the four-passenger coupe also skidded toward the *left?*"

"Yes."

"And it was going forty or fifty miles an hour faster than you were?"

"Well . . . yes."

"So in order to see the coupe, you had to look across the front seat of your own car?"

"I guess so."

"And because it was going so much faster, you had only a brief glimpse?"

"Yes."

"Your father and mother were both in that front seat, and were both directly in your line of vision, were they not?"

"Well, I sort of craned my neck around."

"You mean so you could see past them?"

"Yes."

"In which direction did you crane your neck? Were you looking forward, in front of your mother and father, or backward?"

"Well, they were moving around quite a bit. Dad was trying to get the car under control, and Mother threw up her hands and screamed, and I guess I sort of looked in between them."

"And at about that time, another car was having a collision with this four-passenger coupe?"

"Yes, sir."

"And you don't think it's possible that your impressions of this brief instant are confused?"

"No, sir. She was driving that car. I saw her."

"Who was?"

"A woman that had a hat just like the one the defendant was wearing when they took her out of the car."

"Was she alone in the car?"

"I . . . she was driving."

Mason said, "Can't you do better than that, Miss Lions? If you saw the front seat of that four-passenger coupe clearly enough to see that a woman was at the steering wheel and see the type hat she was wearing . . ."

"I think there was a man in there with her."

"Where was this man seated?"

"Right beside her."

"On her left or right?"

"On her right, of course. If she was at the steering wheel, he *couldn't* have been on the left," the witness said triumphantly.

"And how was the man dressed?"

"He wasn't wearing any hat."

"And how about the window on the right-hand side of that car—the door window? Was it up or down?"

"It was down. The window was rolled down so the space was open."

"You noticed that?"

"Yes."

"You feel certain this man who was seated beside the defendant had no hat?"

"I don't think he had a hat."

"Couldn't you see plainly, or can't you remember clearly?"

"Well, I can't remember exactly."

"Then how did it happen you remembered the style and shape of the defendant's hat so clearly?"

"I just did, that's all."

"Yet there was nothing about her to make you notice *her* head more than the man's head?"

"I couldn't see his head so well."

"Was something in the way—or was it because of the light?"

"The light."

"He was in a shadow?"

"Yes."

"What was casting that shadow?"

"I don't know."

"Now, when the deputy district attorney was asking you questions, didn't you say there was no one in that car except the defendant?"

"Why . . . no."

Mason asked, "Will the court reporter please read that question and answer about whether she saw any other person in the car? It was on direct examination," Mason said.

The court reporter thumbed through the pages. "Here it is: Question, 'Now, did you at any time see any other person in the four-passenger coupe?' Answer, 'No, sir.' "

Mason smiled at her. "Did you say that?"

"Why . . . I guess I must have. I hadn't thought about this man until you asked me. Then, when you did, I could remember him. I can see him now sitting there without a hat, a man about middle age—well, maybe thirty."

"How about the cars that were coming toward you? Who was driving them?"

"Well, there was one driven by a man and one driven by a woman."

"You know that because of what some one has told you or because of what you saw?"

"Because I saw them."

"That all took place in a very short time, just a second or so, did it not?"

"I'll say so. It was the biggest mix-up you ever saw. One moment we were going along talking about a show, and the next minute we were all mixed up in a mess of smash-ups."

"Yet you saw all these things?" Mason asked.

"That's right."

"That's all," Mason said. "Only don't call thirty middle age."

"That's our case, Your Honor," Hanley said, as a ripple of laughter in the court subsided.

"May I have a five-minute recess?" Mason asked.

Judge Cortright nodded, motioned to an attorney who had been waiting, and said, "You have something you wanted to take up with me, Mr. Smith?"

Mason leaned across to whisper to Stephane Claire. "I hate to do this to you, but you've got to go on the stand and tell your story."

"Well, why shouldn't I?"

"In the first place," Mason said, "it's poor trial technique. I think that Lions girl has a vivid imagination, and is something of a liar as well, but her testimony will make a case. She probably got so excited at the time she didn't even know what she was doing. Later on, she reconstructed everything in her own mind. She's hypnotized herself. But she's positive and definite. The judge is going to bind you over. Under those circumstances, the wise thing for a lawyer to do is to make the district attorney show his hand —and quit."

"Well, if he's going to bind me over anyway, why not do that?"

"Because," Mason said, "I want to force them to put Homan on the stand. If you tell your story, they won't dare to let it go without some sort of contradiction. They'll put Homan on the stand."

Stephane Claire said, "Okay, you're the doctor."

"Don't go into too many details," Mason warned. "Just tell your story in a straightforward manner about how you were picked up by this man, about his drinking, about the accident, and about seeing this man again in the Gateview Hotel."

"You think then they'll put Homan on the stand?"

"Yes."

"Will that help us?"

"I hope it will," Mason said. "I've got to solve a murder

in order to find out what's back of the association between Homan and Greeley. I've got to find out what Greeley was doing in San Francisco, and if he hadn't gone as far as San Francisco, where he *had* gone and what he *was* doing."

"Why?"

"Because Greeley never stole that car. Greeley isn't the sort who would steal a car. If he was using that car, he was using it with Homan's permission—and that means Homan is lying in his story about the car having been stolen. Homan sent Greeley on a mission of some sort, and Greeley took Homan's car with Homan's knowledge and consent. The only reason Homan is lying now is because he simply doesn't dare to have the nature of that mission come out."

"And he's willing to sacrifice me in order to keep it from coming out?"

"That's it . . . and he saves himself a few thousand dollars as well."

"And you want me to find that key in my purse, just the way . . ."

Mason said, "No. I want you to tell it just the way it actually happened, that you found the key in your purse when I asked you about it, there in the hospital."

"And you gave it back to me?"

"Yes."

She said, "Horace Homan, the producer's younger brother, came to see me yesterday. He said he knew I hadn't stolen the car. Seems to be very much—well, interested. He wanted me to go for a moonlight cruise on his brother's yacht—and then rang me up and said his brother had changed his mind and wouldn't let him have the yacht."

"Do you like him?"

"Well, he's interesting. He told me about a lot of behind-the-scenes stuff on Hollywood. He says his brother really doesn't want to see me in any trouble, that if I should be convicted, they'd try to get probation for me."

"That's significant. Had he talked that over with his brother?"

"He said his brother was the one who told him. He's a very dynamic young man, isn't he? I can't help contrasting him with Jacks Sterne. Now . . ."

Judge Cortright finished scribbling his signature across a paper, and looked inquiringly down at Mason. Mason nodded, and the judge said, "Proceed, Mr. Mason."

"I will call the defendant, Stephane Claire," Mason said.

Stephane Claire got to her feet, walked forward, was sworn, and told her story. Hanley gave her only a perfunctory cross-examination, limited for the most part to identification of the body she had been called on to view in the Gateview Hotel as that of the man who had been driving the car.

"That's our case," Mason said.

Judge Cortright looked at Hanley. "Any rebuttal?"

"Yes, Your Honor. I have one witness here in court and one whom I'll have to summon by telephone—a man who holds an important position in a Hollywood studio. It will take him a few minutes to get here, but I think this other witness will fill in . . ."

"Very well, call this witness."

"Mrs. A. P. Greeley," Hanley said.

Mrs. Greeley, attired in black, walked slowly down the aisle of the courtroom, held up a black-gloved hand as she took the oath and settled herself in the witness chair.

"I'm going to make this as brief as possible," Hanley said. "Your name is Daphne Greeley. You are the widow of Adler Pace Greeley, a broker?"

"I am."

"On Friday of last week you were called upon by Lieutenant Tragg of the Homicide Squad to identify a body in a room in the Gateview Hotel?"

There was a moment of silence, then Mrs. Greeley said, "Yes," so faintly that the word was all but inaudible.

"And that body was that of your husband?"

"Yes."

"And the same body which Stephane Claire had previously identified as being that of the driver of the car in question?"

"Yes."

"Now, Mrs. Greeley, I want to spare your feelings as much as possible, but it's necessary that I direct your attention to Wednesday, the nineteenth of this month. Do you remember what happened on that day?"

She nodded.

"You'll have to speak up, Mrs. Greeley, so that the court reporter can write down your answer. Do you remember the date?"

"Yes."

"Is there anything in particular which fastens it upon your mind?"

"Yes. It was—it was—our wedding anniversary."

"And can you tell us generally what your husband did on that day—as far as you know?"

"Yes. We decided that we'd have a quiet day at home. Adler had been very much engrossed in business . . ."

"Now, by Adler, you're referring to your husband, Adler Greeley?"

"Yes."

"And what happened, Mrs. Greeley, on the nineteenth?"

"He said that he wouldn't go to the office at all. Several days before, he told Irma Watkins, his secretary, that he was going to be out of the office that day, and not to bother him with any matters of business, not to try and reach him, that it was his wedding anniversary, and he was going to forget business."

"And what happened?"

"The same thing which always happens whenever we tired to plan anything. Business intervened, and Adler had to go to San Francisco on the eighteenth. He promised to try and get back on the morning of the nineteenth. Then he phoned he couldn't make it. About noon he phoned again and said he'd try to take the four o'clock plane."

"When Mr. Greeley went to San Francisco, what clothes did the take?"

"He threw a few clothes into a suitcase, and jumped in the car and drove off."

"In what car?"

"In his car. He leaves it at the airport. I have my own machine."

"How was he dressed?"

"He was wearing a gray double-breasted suit."

"Any overcoat?"

"There was an overcoat over his arm, but he wasn't wearing it."

"Did he have any evening clothes in that suitcase? That is, did he take his dinner-clothes?"

"As to that I can't say. He packed the suitcase himself, but I don't think he . . ."

"The witness will refrain from stating what she thinks," Judge Cortright interrupted.

"Did you have any communication with him after he left?" the deputy district attorney asked.

"Yes, several times. He telephoned and asked me to find some papers for him in his desk."

"But when did you *see* Mr. Greeley again?"

"He came in Thursday morning, very early in the morning. I don't know just what time it was."

"You say he asked you to find some papers?"

"Yes."

"How?"

"He telephoned me."

"When?"

"About four o'clock."

"From where?"

"From San Francisco."

"How do you know it was from San Francisco?"

"I heard the operator say that San Francisco was calling, and then Adler came on the line, and said he was at San Francisco. He told me to find the papers he wanted and telephone him at a certain number what was in the papers."

"You did that?"

"Yes."

"And telephoned him?"

"That's right."

"How did you telephone him?"

"I said that I wanted to put in a call for the number he had given me."

"You remember what that number was?"

"Unfortunately I don't. I made a note of it at the time on a little pad by the telephone so I could call him back. He didn't tell me where the telephone was located, just the number of it. I've found out since. You told me . . ."

"Never mind what anyone told you," Judge Cortright interrupted. "As I understand it, he just gave you a number?"

"That's right."

"Go ahead, Counselor."

"But," Hanley insisted, "you did call long distance, tell the operator you wanted to talk with San Francisco, and give her that San Francisco number."

"That's right."

"And did you reach Mr. Greeley?"

"Almost at once. She told me to hold the line, and the call was put through at once. It was at seventeen minutes past five when he came on the line. We talked two and one-half minutes. I always hold a watch on these long-distance calls."

"Now, did you say you wanted to talk with Mr. Greeley?"

"No. It was just a station-to-station call. He told me to put it in that way."

"Since you have talked with me, you have asked for your long-distance telephone bill?"

"That's right."

"And under the date of the nineteenth, does that call show on your bill?"

"It does."

"And, using that as a reference, you can find out what this number was?"

"Yes."

"And since you have told me about it, have you made any attempt to find out where this number in San Francisco is located?"

"*You* have."

Hanley said to Mason, "It"s a public pay station at the Southern Pacific Depot at Third and Townsend Streets. You can verify it from the telephone company's records." He turned to Mrs. Greeley.

"Now, is there any possibility that it was not your husband with whom you talked?"

She smiled. "Absolutely not."

"And this call was put through at approximately five-seventeen o'clock in the afternoon?"

"That's right."

"And when did your husband come home?"

"Sometime after midnight. He told me when I talked with him over the telephone that he'd try to catch a night plane. I think he said there was a ten o'clock plane which would get him in shortly after midnight. You see, he'd taken his car and left it parked at the airport. . . . Oh, I've already told you that."

"You don't *know* where he had parked his car?" Judge Cortright asked.

"Only from what he told me."

"But you don't know of your own knowledge that the car was at the airport?"

"No, of course not. I didn't go out to look for it, but I *do* know he was in San Francisco at about four o'clock in the afternoon, and that he was still in San Francisco at quarter past five, because I talked with him on the telephone."

"You heard your husband come in?"

"Oh, yes. He wakened me, but I didn't look at the clock. I don't know just what time it was, but it was . . . Well, I went to bed at eleven. I hadn't been asleep very long. I would say it was between one and two that he returned."

Was there anything unusual in his manner or bearing when he returned?"

"No."

"Did you smell liquor on his breath?"

"No."

"Was he wearing a tuxedo when he returned?"

"No."

"Was he injured in any way?"

"No, of course not."

"You may cross-examine," Hanley said to Perry Mason.

"You don't know whether the business which took him to San Francisco was that of Mr. Jules Homan?" Mason asked.

"No. I only know it was something unexpected and important."

"Did the papers which you procured for him have anything to do with Mr. Jules Homan's business?"

"Well . . . they had to do with Mr. Homan's stock. He wanted me to get the list of Mr. Homan's holdings."

"Did he say why he wanted them?"

"No. He just asked me to get the list and then read off the stocks over the telephone."

"That's all," Mason said.

Hanley looked at his watch. "Your Honor, my next witness is one who . . ."

He turned toward the entrance to the courtroom as a man came bustling in. "Mr. Homan, will you please come forward and take the stand?"

Homan carried an alligator-skin brief case in his right hand, and walked with the quick, nervous strides of a man who is in very much of a hurry. He seemed breathless with haste. His name, he stated to the reporter, was Jules Carne Homan. His residence was in Beverly Hills, and his occupation was that of producer of motion pictures. He adjusted his glasses and frowned down at the deputy district attorney, as much as to say, "Well, well, come on. Let's get it over with."

Hanley said, "Mr. Homan, you are the owner of a certain Buick four-passenger coupe, license number 8V7243, and were such owner on the nineteenth of this month?"

"Yes, sir. That's right."

"Do you know where your automobile was on the evening of the nineteenth?"

"It was involved in a traffic accident on the Ridge Route."

"Were you driving that automobile?"

"No, sir."

"Do you know who was?"

"No, sir."

"Was anyone driving it with your permission, express or implied?"

"No, sir."

"When had you last seen the automobile prior to the time of the collision, Mr. Homan?"

"I don't know about the time of the collision—not of my own knowledge."

"Well, let's put it this way. When did *you* last see that automobile on the nineteenth of the month?"

"The last I saw of it was about noon on the nineteenth. I . . ."

"Where?"

"In front of my house on Maple Grove Street in Beverly Hills."

"Can you fix the time exactly?"

"It was shorty before noon. I don't know the exact time."

"And when did you next see it?"

"On the morning of the twentieth when I was asked to identify it."

"Do you know—or did you know in his lifetime—a broker named Adler Greeley?"

"Yes, sir. Adler Pace Greeley."

"Had you any business dealings with him?"

"He had handled a few transactions for me—stocks and bonds."

"Had you seen Mr. Greeley on the nineteenth?"

"No, sir."

"And had you given him any permission to use your car?"

"No, sir. Certainly not."

"Where is your residence on Maple Grove, Mr. Homan?"

"Twenty-five-nineteen."

"Can you describe that residence—just tell us exactly what it is?"

"It's a Spanish-type house with patio, swimming pool, and the things that go with it. I'm a bachelor. I do much of my work at home. I have this house so that when I wish to get away from the studio and avoid all interruptions, I can work there. I also do quite a bit of entertaining."

"That's what I was getting at. This is a large house?"

"It is, and it isn't. The rooms are rather large. The place is well designed. It's not—well, not what you'd call a poor man's house."

"That's the point, Mr. Homan. It's a house which requires a large staff of servants?"

"No, sir, it does not. I have a woman who comes in and does cleaning by the day. I have a combination chauffeur and general handyman who takes care of my wants. I have a Filipino houseboy who mixes drinks, does odd jobs, and keeps the place straight. The woman who does the cleaning comes in twice a week. When I am entertaining, I arrange with a caterer to take charge of everything."

"But I understand, Mr. Homan, that on the nineteenth, you were alone in your house."

"That's right."

"Can you explain how that happened?"

"I was working. I didn't want to be disturbed. I shut myself in my study. When I work, I settle down to work. I concentrate on it. I don't want anything else to disturb me. I don't even eat at regular hours. I work until I realize there's something wrong, then I stop and take stock. Usually I find I'm either hungry or tired or both. I'll get something to eat, perhaps snatch a few minutes' sleep, and go back to work. I keep an electric coffee percolator on my desk when I'm working and drink hot coffee at frequent intervals."

"But I would like to know specifically about the nineteenth, Mr. Homan. You see, the claim has been made that Mr. Greeley was driving your car at the time of the accident."

"Preposterous."

"Never mind that, Mr. Homan. I have covered Mr. Greeley's movements on that day to place him in San Francisco at five-fifteen in the evening. Now I want to show that your car couldn't have . . ."

Mason said, "This conference between counsel and witness is rather unusual, Your Honor."

Hanley said, "I'm merely trying to save time."

"No objection," Mason announced. "I only wanted to suggest you proceed in the regular manner."

Hanley said, "Mr. Homan, will you tell us just what you were doing on the nineteenth and where your car was on that day—or over such an interval of time as you know where it was?"

"I was working on a very important production. I didn't want to be disturbed. I had been working on that script almost uninterruptedly for forty-eight hours."

"At your studio or at your residence?"

"At both places. I left the studio on the afternoon of the eighteenth. I came to my house, told both the Filipino and my chauffeur to take time off, that I wanted to be completely and absolutely undisturbed. I locked myself in and went to work."

"And stayed at your bungalow?"

"No, sir. I went out for dinner about midnight on the evening of the eighteenth, and worked until about four o'clock in the morning, then I slept until seven o'clock, got up, took a shower, shaved, had coffee, and went to work. About eleven I drove to a restaurant where I had something to eat. Then I returned and went to work. It was then a little before noon."

"Did you have occasion to look for your automobile? . . ."

"Objected to as incompetent, irrelevant, and immaterial," Mason said. "It makes no difference as far as the issues in this case are concerned, and it may be an attempt to prejudice the defendant by proving another crime."

"I will stipulate that the purpose of the testimony will be limited solely for the purpose of showing the whereabouts of the car," Hanley said.

"On the strength of that stipulation, I will permit the question to be answered," Judge Cortright ruled.

"Answer the question."

"Yes, sir. About four o'clock in the afternoon I wanted to take a short drive to get some air. I had been working straight through and suddenly realized I was fatigued. I went out to get my car and drive up around Mulholland Drive. My car was gone."

"And what did you do with reference to trying to locate your car?"

"Objected to as incompetent, irrelevant, and immaterial," Mason said.

"Objection sustained."

"I think you may inquire," Hanley said with a little nod to Mason.

Homan got up and started to leave the stand.

"Just a minute," Judge Cortright said.

"Aren't you finished with me?"

"Mr. Mason has the right to cross-examine."

"Oh," Homan said and turned impatient eyes toward Mason.

"Just a few questions," Mason said, "in regard to the nature of your work, Mr. Homan. When you are concentrating, I take it that you are very irritated at interruptions."

"Very."

"You answer the telephone?"

"No. I disconnect it."

"How?"

"I have a little switch at the telephone. It was especially installed to cover my needs."

"You do, however, occasionally put through a call?"

"Very, very occasionally. The nature of my work is something that the ordinary man can hardly appreciate. It represents the very essence of concentration," and Homan glanced up at the judge.

"Now you can't recall any single instance, any isolated facts which would account for Mr. Greeley taking your car?"

"Absolutely not. I am satisfied Mr. Greeley did *not* take my car."

"And during this period that you were concentrating, can you recall having made any telephone calls?"

"No, sir. I made none."

"Now," Mason asked casually, "what was your business with L. C. Spinney in San Francisco?"

Homan stared at him.

"Can't you answer the question?" Mason asked.

"I don't understand it. I haven't any business with Mr.— what was the name?"

"Spinney, L. C. Spinney."

"I haven't any business with Mr. Spinney in San Francisco. I've never heard of the man. I remember now, you mentioned his name to me once before."

"You didn't call him on long distance on Tuesday and again on Wednesday?"

"Certainly not."

"And he didn't call you?"

"No."

Mason said, "Now, Mr. Homan, this may be exceedingly important. Please bear in mind that the records of the telephone company can be consulted and . . ."

Homan snapped his fingers, the quick gesture of a nervous man who has an idea pop into his head. "What is it?" Mason asked.

Homan said, "Mr. Mason, I don't know what you're getting at, but I can tell you this. If you can show that any long-distance call went over my telephone on either Tuesday or Wednesday, you'll be doing me a great favor, a very great favor indeed."

"Why, may I ask?" Mason said.

Homan cleared his throat, shook his head, said, "I would prefer to tell you privately, Mr. Mason."

"And," Mason said with a smile, "*I* would prefer to have you tell me in public."

"It doesn't have anything to do with the present case—that is . . ." He hesitated.

"Yes," Mason prompted.

"I don't *think* it would have anything to do with this case."

"But it might," Mason said.

"Yes."

"Perhaps then you'd better let His Honor have the information, and let him be the judge of it."

Homan compressed his lips firmly together, creased his forehead in a determined scowl, and stared at the carpet for several seconds. Then he said, "I have for some time had a suspicion that my chauffeur was putting through various long-distance calls in connection with his own business—using my phone. I would appreciate it very much if you have any information which would substantiate such a charge. I have given him notice, but—I would like to find out just the same."

"What is your chauffeur's name?" Mason asked.

"Tanner.—Ernest A. Tanner."

"Is he in court?"

A slight commotion manifested itself among the spectators. A man stood up. "I'm here," he drawled, "and I didn't . . ."

"Sit down," Judge Cortright snapped. "The course of the trial is not to be interrupted by spectators."

Homan glowered at the man who was standing, a young, broad-shouldered, loosely-knit individual who seemed grimly determined, but who wilted under the stern glare of Judge Cortright's eyes and slowly sat down.

"You do not know any L. C. Spinney?"

"No, sir. I do not. And if any long-distance calls were put through on my telephone, either on the eighteenth or the nineteenth, they are unauthorized telephone calls put through by some person who had no right to do so."

"Don't you audit your monthly long-distance bills?"

Homan shook his head impatiently. "I do not. I have no time to devote to trivial matters. I simply instruct my secretary to write checks covering all current expenses. I happen to have noticed that my telephone bills for the last few months have had numbers on them that I know nothing about, that's all. I took it for granted at first my younger brother had been calling friends. Then the other day I happened to mention it to him. Well, I suppose I can't tell about that conversation now—but—well, if you're finished with me, I have a very important matter pending. In fact, I had to . . ."

Judge Cortright said, "It is approaching the hour of adjournment, gentlemen. If the examination can be completed within a few minutes, the court will remain in session. Otherwise, the examination can be resumed tomorrow."

"Your Honor," Homan said, "I simply can't come tomorrow. I am here today only because I was forced to come. I have a matter pending . . ."

Mason interrupted to say, "I have one or two questions I would very much like to ask, Mr. Homan, tonight. About this telephone. You have said that you let both the Filipino and the chauffeur go for . . ."

"They have rooms there in the house. They come and go as they please. I meant that I released them from duty."

"Where does the chauffeur sleep?"

"Over the garage."

"And the Filipino boy?"

"In a room in the basement."

"They come and go through the front door?"

"No, sir. The chauffeur uses stairs which front on another street—a side street. The Filipino boy uses a basement door which also fronts on a side street. My house is a corner house. It takes up several lots, but it is, nevertheless, a corner house."

"Now, to get access to your telephone, would they have to come into the main part of the house?"

"No, sir. There are telephone instruments in their rooms, also in various other parts of the house. There is an intercommunicating system by which I can ring those telephones from my study. They can be plugged in on an outside line, or with any other station which may be calling."

"When you are talking on a telephone, could the others listen in?"

Homan frowned and said, "I don't think they could, Mr. Mason, but you're asking about something which is outside of my field. I know very little about the operation of the household or of the telephone. I have my house as a place to retire, a place to relax, a place to work, and a place in which to entertain. Beyond that, I care very little about it. It's . . ." He smiled and said, "As you may be aware, Mr. Mason, there's a certain amount of background which is necessary in Hollywood. A producer who . . . well, I think you understand."

Mason smiled and said, "I think I do."

Judge Cortright said impatiently, "Well, I suppose there will be more cross-examination, Mr. Mason, and some redirect. Court will adjourn until ten o'clock tomorrow. You will return then, Mr. Homan."

Homan jumped to his feet. "I can't! I simply can't. It would cost thousands of dollars to have my time disrupted tomorrow, I have . . ."

"Ten o'clock tomorrow morning," Judge Cortright said with tight-lipped finality, and walked from the courtroom into his chambers.

The loose-jointed, broad-shouldered chauffeur pushed through the swinging gate, walked over to Homan, and stood looking at him with an air of contemptuous appraisal. "What's the idea?" he asked. "Trying to make me the goat for a scrape you've got into?"

Homan said blusteringly, "I don't like your attitude."

"You're going to like it a lot less than that," the chauffeur said. "If you want me to tell where you . . ."

Homan turned away, started toward the swinging gate in the mahogany rail which separated the tables reserved for attorneys and courtroom officials from the spectators. Tanner's long right arm reached out, and his fingers clamped in Homan's collar. "Just a minute, buddy," he said, "*jus-s-st* a minute."

Homan whirled with swift agility and said in a voice harsh with rage, "Take your filthy hands off of me."

Hanley, attracted by the commotion, stepped forward quickly. "Here," he said, "none of that. Get back there. What do you think you're doing?"

"Homan knows what I'm doing," Tanner said.

Hanley's eyes narrowed. "You're Tanner?"

"Yes."

"All right, I represent the district attorney's office. Now there'll be no more of this."

Tanner's voice still held no trace of temper. There was a certain contemptuous drawl in his words. "Listen," he said, "this guy puts on a great front for the public. He's a swell showman. He's a big shot. I'm a nobody, but that's no sign he can do things to my reputation. He's going to take back what he's said, or I'm going to show *him* up. He knows damn well that if I was to talk . . ."

Hanley snapped, "This man is a witness. I consider his testimony pertinent and significant. You perhaps don't realize it, but what you are doing could well be construed as an attempt to intimidate a witness. You might find yourself in serious trouble."

"Aw, nuts," Tanner said. "I'm not intimidating any witness."

"You're trying to make him change his testimony."

"I'm trying to get the rat to tell the truth."

Homan sputtered, "I won't have any more of this. It's utterly absurd. This man is a . . ."

Hanley said, "This is neither the time nor the place for this argument. Mr. Homan, if you'll come with me, please, I want to ask you a few more questions. You, Mr. Tanner, had better get out of here—*right now!*"

Tanner stared at the deputy district attorney. For a moment it seemed as though he might express his feelings by twisting Hanley's nose. Then Hanley's attitude of being in complete command of the situation registered sufficiently so that Tanner turned on his heel.

Hortense Zitkousky came up from the back of the

courtroom to drop her hand on Stephane Claire's shoulder. "Chin up and carry on," she said.

Stephane thanked her with a smile.

Hortense said in a low voice to Mason, "That chauffeur was giving me the eye. Think it would be a good plan to . . . ?"

"Yes," Mason said, "and don't be seen with us."

Hortense moved casually away as Mason gathered up his papers and pushed them into a brief case.

Max Olger came pushing forward from the little knot of spectators who had taken time to mill around the courtroom in little gossiping groups, before departing. The twinkle of his shrewd gray eyes, seemingly intensified by the half spectacles over which they peered, appraised Mason as he grasped the lawyer's hand. "Superb," he said, "marvelous. You led the Lions girl on to absurdities. A very splendid job of cross-examination. I'm very well satisfied, very grateful."

Stephane Claire said, "And I think you did marvelously well, Mr. Mason."

Mason said, "We may get a break. Mrs. Greeley's testimony shows that her husband could very well have gone to San Francisco on Homan's business. It's just barely possible that a person could have been in San Francisco at five-fifteen and at Bakersfield at ten. It would probably mean a plane. Its two hundred and ninety-three miles. We're going to do a little checking, and we may uncover something."

"Can't you do that tonight and put on some surprise evidence tomorrow morning?" Max Olger asked.

Mason grinned. "That's why I'm stalling along tonight."

"Where's Jacks?" Stephane Claire asked her uncle.

"He was in court, but he's waiting outside. He thought perhaps it would be better for you to get out of the courtroom and away from the crowd."

Stephane said musingly, "He's a good kid, always thinking of me. Sometimes I wish he'd think of himself once in a while, just by way of variety."

"A remarkably nice boy," Olger said. "Well, we'll be at the Adirondack Hotel in case you want us, Mr. Mason."

"Be sure and be on hand tomorrow morning at ten o'clock," Mason cautioned. "Remember your bail money is forfeit if you don't show up."

Stephane Claire smiled lazily. "Do you," she asked, "caution all of your clients that way, or are you afraid I'm going to skip out?"

Mason grinned. "It's routine."

"How did I do on the stand?"

"You were good."

"Why didn't he tear into me on cross-examination? I thought he would."

"Wait until he gets you in front of a jury," Mason said. "This is just a preliminary. I'm not so certain but what Judge Cortright may turn you loose, at that. You've made a good impression."

15

Hortense Zitkousky stood in the doorway of the ladies' restroom until she heard the pound of quick steps in the corridor. She stepped out of the cross corridor just in time to confront Ernest A. Tanner as he came striding toward the elevator. She received a quick glance, and only a quick glance. He seemed very determined, very much engrossed.

Hortense followed him to the elevator, rode down in the same cage with him. Still Tanner made no effort to speak, hardly seemed to notice her.

On the ground floor, Tanner loitered near the elevators. Hortense walked as far as the door, then turned, came back, and suddenly placed her hand on Tanner's elbow.

Tanner whirled. His eyes, cold and determined, looked down into the jovial countenance of a buxom young woman who very apparently derived much enjoyment from life.

"Don't do it," she counseled. "He isn't worth it."

Tanner's eyes softened somewhat. He said, "He's got it coming."

"Oh, don't, please! I don't blame you for being mad, but I certainly wouldn't play right into his hands."

"I'm not. I'm playing right into his face."

Her good-natured laugh came welling up from her diaphragm. "Forget it. I work for a lawyer. I know what they can do."

"What's that got to do with me?"

"Homan," she said. "Why do you suppose he's staying behind? He wants a bodyguard, and protection."

Tanner said, "I can lick ten times my weight in bodyguards."

"There's no percentage in it," she said. "Come on. Let's get out of here."

"What's *your* tie-in with this?" he asked suspiciously.

"I knew a Stephane Claire in San Francisco. I read about the case in the paper and thought she might be the girl I knew. I came up here to find out."

"Was she?"

She avoided the question. "I had the afternoon off and saw no reason why I should run back to pound a typewriter. The work was all caught up anyway, and then I got interested in the case. Come on. Be a sport and get started for home. Then I can go about *my* business and forget you."

"What do you care what happens to *me?*"

She considered the question for a moment, then smiled and said, "Darned if I know. I just do. Perhaps it's a maternal instinct."

"Maternal!" he said. His eyes studied her with more interest. "Tell you what. Come on to dinner with me, and I'll call it off."

"Oh-oh," she said. "Fast like that."

"Is it a deal?"

"Come on outside, and we'll talk it over."

"You're trying to decoy me away from here and then . . ."

A descending cage came to a stop. The big door smoothly slid back, and Homan stepped out. Two broad-shouldered men were with him.

Hortense Zitkousky moved so that she was between Tanner and the elevator, raised her voice slightly, and said, ". . . and I says to her, 'That may be *your* way of doing things, but it ain't *mine*.' Well, you know Gertie, and you know how she'd take a thing like that. She . . ."

One of the men escorted Homan toward the door. The other paused belligerently. Tanner started to move around past Hortense.

Her finger traced a design on the lapel of Tanner's coat.

"Well," she said, *"that* floored her. Gertie just sat and looked at me and . . ."

The officer hesitated a moment, then followed Homan and the other plainclothes man out of the door.

Tanner let his breath go in a deep sigh. "I guess," he said, "I owe you one for that."

"Can't you see? They've got you, coming and going. There's nothing you can do with a setup like that. Come on. Forget it. If you feel that way about it, and *really* want to do something, why don't you go to the girl's lawyer?"

"Not me," Tanner said. "I don't rat."

"But there's nothing to rat about . . . is there?"

He said shortly, "Homan's a liar. It's all right by me. I'm not squealing on him, but I'm not going to be the goat."

"Oh, forget him. He's just a stuffed shirt."

"I'll say he is. Just another one of those guys who graduated from nothing into big money, and puff out like a circus balloon. Someday somebody will stick a pin into him, and he'll go *pop* and be just a fistful of limp rubber."

Hortenze Zitkousky was talking easily now. "I used to work for one of those Hollywood writers. My gosh, did *he* take *himself* seriously. And the stuff he turned out! Why, say, when he was working, he couldn't be disturbed, and he had to have coffee at just the right temperature, and a whole carton of cigarettes at his elbow, and ashtrays and matches. You'd think he was turning out the world's greatest masterpiece, and when you saw it on the screen, it made you gag. The only thing that held the audience through to the end was the dishes and groceries."

Tanner laughed. "Don't blame it on the writer," he said. "It was probably one of Homan's pictures. After it was half filmed, he pitched the script out of the window, and tried to imitate a current success over at MGM."

"Is he like that?" Hortense asked.

"Is he like that! Come on, let's eat. What do I call you besides Say?"

"My name's Hortense. My friends call me Horty. Oh, well, why not? Say, listen, you've just lost your job. You probably haven't got a heck of a lot of money, and even if you have, you've no business spending it on me. Let's go to some cheap place."

"I'll take you to the best. What do I care about dough?"

"No. I'm a working girl myself, and I hate to see a

man shell it out to some snooty waiter who wants the price of an hour's work for a cup of bum coffee, and then expects a tip on top of that. Come on. I know a swell place."

"No, you don't," Tanner said, smiling now. "Homan canned me, but I didn't need his job anyway. I've got dough, and I know where I can get more."

"Well, don't say I didn't warn you."

"All right, come on over. We'll get a taxi."

"No. A streetcar."

"A taxi."

"Say, you aren't one of the Rockefeller boys in disguise, are you? Or are you an international spy getting paid to sabotage motion pictures?"

"Oh, come on, Horty. Quit worrying about it. It's okay."

"There's a swell Chinese restaurant down here. We can walk that far."

"We can't dance there. I like to dance."

"So do I."

"Come on. You're going with me. *Taxi!* Oh *taxi!*"

The cab swung around to glide up to the curb. Tanner said, "Straight on down the street. I'll tell you where to go after a while." He assisted Hortense into the car, said, "Listen, I'm in the dumps tonight, but you're cheering me up. There's something comfortable and homey about you. What do you say we just have a sandwich and a bottle of beer now, go to a show, and then have a real dinner, and make a lot of whoopee afterwards?"

"I've got to work tomorrow."

"Forget tomorrow. I'll have you home early enough to get a little shuteye."

"Okay."

"I know a swell place that specializes in liverwurst sandwiches on rye bread, and has the best beer in the city."

Hortense settled back against the cushions of the cab. "Evidently," she observed, "you know your way around."

Tanner laughed, a laugh of masculine vanity. "If you want to *really* see the town some night—well, take a Saturday night when you don't have to get home. How about it? A date?"

"We'll see. Only promise you won't have any more trouble with Homan. I don't want to go out with a man who has a black eye."

"Homan," Tanner said, "had better leave me alone.

Once I get a chance to talk with Homan privately, he'll sing a different tune."

"Not him," Hortense said with the positive assurance of one who has some definite knowledge. "A big windbag like that always keeps up his bluff. Nothing you could say would change him."

"You don't know what I could say."

"No, but I know the sort of man Homan is. I worked for a fellow just like that one. And say, I'm going to tell *you* something. I wouldn't take Homan's word for anything. This man I used to work for—well, *I* wouldn't trust him."

"Oh, Homan's all right. But he's lying about that car."

She let her face show surprise.

"What makes you think so?"

"I don't think. I know. Look here."

Tanner took a leather-backed notebook from his pocket, opened the book to thumb through the pages. "Here we are," he said. "Homan called me on the morning of the eighteenth, said he had an important job to do and didn't want to be disturbed, that I could get out. Well, I'd just serviced the car, and filled the tank with gas. I keep track of the mileage. Here's the mileage on the speedometer. Thirteen thousand, four hundred and twenty-six miles. Now, I got the mileage after they brought the car back. They towed it in. Homan was going to junk it. He told me to get the tools out of it. Here's the mileage. Fourteen thousand one hundred and fifty-eight. Get it? Seven hundred and thirty-two miles between the morning of the eighteenth and the night of the nineteenth. I can *prove* Homan's lying."

"Well?" Hortense asked, her eyes puzzled. "What's wrong with that? That isn't too much, is it? You can drive five or six hundred miles in a day . . ."

"I'll tell you what's wrong with it. Everything's wrong with it. Sure, you can drive a bus like that seven or eight hundred miles a day if you want to, but remember Homan says he had the car sticking around until about noon on the nineteenth. You can't drive a car seven hundred and thirty-two miles between noon and ten o'clock at night, not to save your life."

"Well, for *heaven's* sake!" Horty exclaimed. "How do you figure it out, Ernest?"

"I don't figure it out . . . not right here and now," he

said, "but you can believe me, sister, I'm going to let Homan do some explaining to me—privately. And I *know* the answer."

"Say," she said with enthusiasm, "let me know how you come out. That man looks so much like the guy I used to work for that I'd sure like to see him taken down a peg or two."

"Oh, well," Tanner said, sliding his arm around her waist and drawing her close to him, "let's forget Homan—if we can. Did you notice a car has been following us? Oh, well, let him follow. Hey, driver, pull down this side street, and stop at the café in the middle of the block."

Tanner paid the cab fare, gave the driver a half-dollar tip, and piloted Hortense into a small restaurant which had a distinctly individual atmosphere. They had sandwiches and beer. Tanner kept feeding nickels into the machine which played the latest records, and they danced to the music. After an hour, he took her to one of the best picture theaters, bought loge seats, settled down beside her, and twisted his fingers around hers. "I should be grateful to you," he whispered. "If it wasn't for you, I'd probably be in the can right now. As it is, I'm feeling Jake a Million. Here's where I relax and enjoy life."

The sound tracks blared forth impressive music. On the flickering screen appeared a cast of characters, a list of names. As the cast of characters gave place to writers, technicians, and costumers, Tanner said, "They're having a big battle out in Hollywood. The manicurists for each star insist on having screen credit."

She giggled.

A blaze of light hit the screen. In huge black letters appeared the legend, "A JULES HOMAN PRODUCTION."

"Oh, cripes," Tanner said, grabbing her arm. "Let's get the hell out of *here!*"

16

MASON PACED THE FLOOR of his office, thumbs pushed up in the armholes of his vest, head thrust forward in thought. Paul Drake, sprawled crosswise in the big leather chair, smoked silently.

"Hang it, Paul. It's so near being right it almost proves itself, and then it all goes haywire, like one of those puzzles that you can almost work the obvious way. Then you run into trouble."

"I know," Drake grinned, "you think they made a mistake manufacturing the darn thing, and the wire should be bent a little bit so that other piece will slip through."

"Uh huh," Mason said. "Only in the case of a wire puzzle, it's a trap that the manufacturer made for you to walk into. In this thing—well, I don't know but what this is a trap someone made for me to walk into."

Della Street came in from the secretarial office.

"Gosh, Della," Drake said, "haven't you gone home *yet?*"

She shook her head. "I was hoping someone would buy me dinner."

"It's a swell idea," Drake told her. "They might even buy mine while they were doing it."

"News from the battle front," Della said to Perry Mason. "Latest bulletin just in over the telephone."

"What is it?"

"Hortense Zitkousky. She must be quite a gal."

"I have an idea she is," Mason said. "What about her?"

"She sounds as though she were getting just a bit high. She said it's the first time she's had a chance to get away to the telephone. She's out with the chauffeur."

"What's she found out?"

"The chauffeur isn't the least bit worried about money. Homan fired him. The chauffeur's spending dough like a drunken sailor. The automobile was driven seven hundred

130

and thirty-two miles between the morning of the eighteenth and the time of the accident on the nineteenth."

"How does he know?" Mason asked.

"He keeps a record of the speedometer figures. He has to service the car."

Drake gave a low whistle.

"Was that *all* she had?" Mason asked.

"So far. She says to tell you she's not only getting to first base with the chauffeur, but is getting ready to steal second. She's trying to find out why he isn't worried about money. And she thinks he may have something else on Homan."

Mason said, "I hope she's smart enough to try and find out about Spinney. Homan may be right about that. It *may* have been the chauffeur who was calling Spinney, and whom Spinney was calling. Know anyone out around Hollywood, Della?"

"You mean movie people?"

"Yeah."

"A couple of writers and an agent."

"You might try the agent," Mason said. "I'd like to get some of the low-down on Homan and his meteoric success. There must be some gossip in connection with him. I'd like to find out what it is. And I'd like to get the low-down on his love life. That always helps."

"I can put some men on the job," Drake said.

Mason shook his head. "A private detective in that atmosphere would stick out like a sore thumb on a waiter serving soup. The stuff I'm after is the little inside gossip that would be confined to people who are in the game."

Della said, "This agent is a card."

"Man or woman?"

"Woman. Used to be a secretary, then did a little writing, and started handling screen stuff."

"Stories or talent?"

"Stories."

"Get in touch with her. See what you can find out," Mason said. "Make it casual if you can."

"I can't."

"Then take your hair down and get her to give you the low-down. How about meeting me in a couple of hours somewhere for a report? You should be able to get what we want in that time."

"I'll get on the phone and see what I can do."

"Oh-oh," Drake said, "there goes my dinner date."

Della Street smiled. "You wouldn't be any fun. You're getting to be a wet blanket, Paul. You're worrying too darn much. Why don't you be like Homan's chauffeur?"

"I used to worry about my work," Drake admitted. "Now I'm worrying Perry will get my license revoked. If I had no more to worry about than that chauffeur, I'd be taking girls to dinner and spending money like a drunken sailor, too."

Mason winked at Della Street. "Perhaps we could get that Hortense girl to take him out some night. It might cure him of worrying.'"

"Meaning it may be the company I keep?" Drake asked.

Mason jerked his head toward Della Street's office. "Go in and see if you can locate this agent friend of yours on the phone, Della. You can trust her?"

"Asking if she's a good friend?"

"Yes."

"I'll say she is."

"Well, come right out and tell her you want the low-down on Homan. After all, this case is in the papers. You couldn't make a stall that would stick. She'd see through any attempt."

"Okay, I'll see if I can get her."

Della Street went into her office. They could hear the dial on her telephone whirring.

Drake said to Mason, "Judge Cortright may turn Stephane Claire loose tomorrow. That Lions girl didn't make a good impression on him. . . . And I'll bet Tragg's interested in what we're uncovering. I wouldn't doubt if he dropped in."

"Will you work with him, Perry?"

"It depends. I'm going to get my client out from under. He can solve his own murders. Next time I give him a tip, he'll follow it."

"What tip did he muff this time?"

"Homan."

"Be your age. Homan would have gone in to the big shot in his company, and said, 'Mr. Whosis, I can't work on that script, because this lawyer has put the police on me, and they're asking me questions about what I had for dinner last Wednesday.' Then the big shot would pick up the telephone, call the mayor. The mayor would call the chief. The chief would call the captain, and . . . you get the sketch."

Mason smiled. "Homan *has* to be lying about that car."

"Well, Tragg can't dig down into the hopper, pull out your dirty linen, and . . ."

Della Street emerged from her office to say, "I've located her, Chief. She's in her office. Still want me to run out there?"

"Yes. Take my car. I'll wait."

"Here?"

"Uh huh. Let's eat when you get back."

"Okay, I'll grab something to tide me over and meet you here."

"You, Paul?" Mason asked the detective.

"No. Della says I'm a wet blanket."

"Snap out of it," she said, smiling. "There's nothing the matter with you that four good cocktails won't cure."

Drake said, "I'll let you know later. I hate to turn down a chance to dance with Della."

She laughed. "You hate to waste a chance to eat your way through a de luxe dinner. Be seeing you. When I come back, I'll have all the inside Hollywood gossip. Give this girl a couple of drinks, and she talks a blue streak."

Drake said, "Watch her, Perry. She's getting ready to turn in an expense account consisting of a lot of bar checks. I know the symptoms."

"You should," Della Street retorted, putting on her hat and coat in front of the mirror in the cloak closet. "It's a trick I learned from auditing your swindle sheets." She drew on her gloves. "It'll take about two hours, and if I draw a blank, don't be too disappointed."

"I won't," Mason said.

Mason and Drake listened to Della Street's steps in the corridor of the deserted office building.

"One in a million," Drake said.

"Make it ten million, Paul."

They smoked in silence for several seconds. Steps approached the door. Mason frowned as knuckles beat an authoritative tattoo.

"Sounds like a cop," Drake said.

"You don't need to be a detective to tell that," Mason remarked, opening the door.

Lieutenant Tragg said, "Hello, boys. Trying to make one thought grow where two grew before?"

Mason looked at his watch. "I'll bet it's bad news."

Tragg walked in, and sat down.

"Things didn't go so well for you in court today, Mason," Tragg said.

"Oh, I don't know. I'm satisfied."

Tragg said, "I have a murder on my hands. You've got an intoxicated-driver manslaughter case. That case is in the county. I don't care a hell of a lot about it. The murder case is right down my alley. If I solve it, I get a pat on the back. If I don't, I get a kick in the pants."

Mason said, "I believe you're leading up to something."

"I am."

"Spring it."

"How would you like to be working with us for a change instead of against us?"

Mason said, "I don't know. For all I know you might be trying to pin the murder on my client before you got done."

Tragg said, "Well, we can go into that right now."

"What about it?"

"There are a couple of clues which point her way."

Mason sat rigidly erect in his chair. "For the love of Mike, Tragg! All a person needs to do is to be a client of mine, and the police immediately . . ."

"Keep your hat on," Tragg said. "I'm giving you a break."

"Go ahead. Give it to me."

"Let's talk about your client a while first."

"All right, what about her?"

"Her rich uncle showed up, plunked down a certified check for the bail, and took her out of the hospital where she was being held under detention and rushed her to the Adirondack Hotel. And where is the Adirondack Hotel with reference to the Gateview?"

Mason said, "Let's see. From Seventh and . . . it's four blocks."

"That's right. A person could walk those four blocks in less than five minutes."

"Go ahead. I presume my client had the murder gun in her handbag when you searched it?"

"No, but she had something else."

"What?"

"Well, you see she went to the hospital. It was a homicide and a county job, but they asked me to check on a couple of angles. I heard her story. She said she'd taken a key out of the ignition switch on the automobile. I checked up with the garage to which the car had been towed. The

ignition was locked, Naturally, I made an investigation of
the girl's purse."

"Without her knowledge?"

"Oh, certainly."

"Go ahead."

"Well, there was a key ring with three keys on it. Now
then, Mason, before I go any further, I want to know
whether that was a plant."

"I don't get you."

Tragg said, "Naturally, I wanted to know about those
keys. One of them looked like the key to an automobile
ignition. I thought it would be better to find out first and
ask the questions afterward. So while your client was laid
up in the hospital, I had an expert locksmith bring an
assortment of blanks. The nurse had slipped the keys out
of the purse, and the locksmith made duplicates. I took
the duplicate keys down and tried them on the car. The
automobile key fitted the ignition okay. That left me with
two other keys. I didn't know what they were for. Somehow
or other, Mason, I distrusted those keys. It looked like the
fine Italian hand of a master dramatist."

"Go ahead."

"You started beefing about Homan, so I made a quiet
trip out to Homan's place, and tried the other two keys
on his doors just to see if they'd fit."

"What was the big idea of all the secrecy?"

"Oh, I just wanted to see what little surprises you'd
thought up for the D.A."

"Well, did the keys fit?"

"No, not the door—but one of those keys is to Homan's
yacht."

"The hell you say!"

"Surprised?"

"Yes. Go on."

"Well, I didn't say anything. I just sat back on the side-
lines, waiting for the time to come when you'd explode
your bombshell."

"I'm listening."

"Well, that time came this afternoon," Tragg said. "I
naturally expected that you would build your case around
those keys, which, by the way, the girl had already accounted for and introduced in evidence. I thought, of
course, you'd say to Homan, 'Mr. Homan, is this the key
to the ignition on your automobile?' Homan would, of

course, admit that it looked as though it might be the key to his car. Then you'd ask him casually if he knew anything about the other keys or if they looked at all familiar to him. He'd then either say with some surprise that one of them was the key to his yacht, or else he'd say they didn't look at all familiar to him, and then you'd ask him to produce his keys so that you could check the . . ."

Mason pushed back his chair and got to his feet. "Hell!" he said with disgust in his voice. "And I missed doing just that! I'm going to find my client, give her back her fee, and beg her pardon."

Tragg was watching him narrowly. "Why didn't you go after Homan on those keys, Mason?"

"Lieutenant, I don't know. I was thinking about an entirely different angle of approach. I knew, of course, it was an ignition key to his car, but I . . ."

Tragg studied him for a moment as Mason ceased talking. "You had something else on your mind, something you're trying to develop, something you haven't told me about?"

"Well?"

Tragg said, "When you didn't spring that key business, I began to think that perhaps it wasn't a plant after all."

"It wasn't."

"You didn't plant them?"

"Absolutely not. What's the third key?"

"I haven't found out yet."

"It isn't Homan's?"

"No."

"How about . . . ?"

"About what?" Tragg asked as Mason hesitated.

The lawyer picked up a pencil from his desk, slid his thumb and forefinger up and down the smooth sides of the wood. "This," he said, "goes a long way toward refuting Homan's story that the car was stolen."

"Unless he left his keys in it," Tragg said.

"They'd hardly be his keys," Mason pointed out. "There are only three keys on the ring. One of them is to the ignition of the automobile. One is to Homan's yacht. Homan would have had more keys than that, keys to his house, keys to his office in the studio."

There were several seconds of silence, then Mason made a little bow to the police detective. "All right, Tragg, you win." He turned to Drake. "Tell him about the Warfield woman, Paul."

"How much?"

"Everything."

"And about this man Spinney," Tragg said. "I'm interested in Spinney."

Mason said, "Shoot the works, Paul. Begin at the beginning, about the telephone bills, and what you've done on Spinney."

Drake took a notebook from his pocket. Refreshing his recollection from that, he told Tragg the whole story. When he had finished, Tragg scowled. "And you guys were holding this out?" he asked.

"I told you," Mason said, "that if you didn't go after Homan, you'd have to ask us questions. We answered all your questions."

"Someday," Tragg said to Drake, "you're going to cut things just a little too fine."

Drake glanced at Mason.

Mason said, "When Drake works on a case under me, he follows my instructions. I'm responsible."

Tragg grinned at him. "All right, let's come down to earth. I want to clear up this murder. You want to get Stephane Claire acquitted of driving the car. You haven't closed your case. That key ring should give you something to work on. Homan told me he was very careful to lock the car up when he left it, that he had his keys with him. The idea being to prove that whoever was operating the car was operating it without his permission. All right, Homan had his keys. The chauffeur must have keys. Now then, how is Homan going to explain the fact that the man who was driving the car had a key to his yacht?"

Mason paced the floor, thumbs pushed up in the armholes of his vest, his head bent slightly forward. He said, "He isn't going to explain it. He can't. He's got to change his story."

"Well," Tragg said, "so far as I'm concerned, Mason, I'm satisfied now your client didn't steal the car, and I'm pretty well satisfied she wasn't driving it. For the sake of argument, let's say Greeley was. She hadn't known him before. She hadn't known Homan. She undoubtedly had left San Francisco that morning."

Mason said, "All right, Tragg, we'll put all the cards right on the table. From the time the chauffeur last saw the car, which was on Tuesday morning, until Wednesday, the car had been driven seven hundred and thirty-two miles. Now then, if Homan is telling the truth, that car was driven seven hundred and thirty-two miles between noon on Wednesday and around eleven o'clock, the time of the accident. Well, suppose it had been operated steadily at sixty miles an hour. That would be six hundred and sixty miles. It's an absolute impossibility."

Tragg said, "It *could* be done. That bus will do around a hundred miles an hour."

"The bus will," Mason said, "but the roads won't."

"What do you mean?"

"I don't care how fast you drive. You can pick the very fastest roads in the country, and by the time you've driven eleven hours, you'll find you can't have covered more than six hundred odd miles. Of course, you could pick a straight, fast, desert road and drive back and forth on it and average more. But a person wouldn't do that. In three or four hundred straight-road miles, you're going to encounter grades, curves, detours, cities, bottlenecks, boulevard stops. Seven hundred and thirty-two miles means that the car was driven about four hundred miles away from the city, then turned around and driven back toward the city. The accident happened about sixty miles from Los Angeles."

Tragg said, "That's interesting."

Mason said, "Paul and I have been thinking about the man who was driving the car. . . ."

"Conceding for the sake of the argument that your client is telling the truth," Tragg interrupted.

"Naturally," Mason said. "I take that for granted whenever I start in on a case."

"I can't take anything for granted."

"Well, conceding it for the sake of the argument," Mason said, "that this man either came from or went through Bakersfield around ten o'clock. He was wearing a dinner jacket. When a man puts on a tuxedo, he's usually attending something which doesn't begin before seven-thirty or eight at the very earliest. It's rather unusual for him to leave such an affair at quarter to ten. Now then, if this man didn't come from Bakersfield, we can probably stretch that time at least another hour. He must have left at quarter to nine or perhaps eight-thirty."

"Left what?"

"Whatever he was attending, dinner, dance, or whatever it was."

"It might have been a lodge."

"It might have been."

"But Greeley was in San Francisco the night of the accident."

"I'm coming to that," Mason said. "Greeley was in San Francisco at quarter past five. He hadn't taken a tuxedo to San Francisco with him, just a double-breasted gray business suit. At ten o'clock that night he was in Bakersfield wearing a tuxedo. Now stop a minute and figure what that means."

"What does it mean?"

"He couldn't have driven from San Francisco to Bakersfield in approximately four hours and forty-five minutes."

"Go ahead. You're doing fine."

"If he *had* been wearing a gray business suit at the time," Mason said, "he would hardly have taken a plane, kept a rendezvous with someone, picked up the car, changed to a tuxedo, and still been at Bakersfield at ten o'clock."

"All right. We'll pass that for the moment. He *might* have done it, but let's hear the rest of it."

"That brings us to the question of whether he was wearing the tuxedo at five o'clock. And, since he hadn't taken a tuxedo with him, it must, in that case, have been some other person's, one that Greeley had rented, or one he kept in San Francisco. But why would he have been in the Southern Pacific Depot at five-fifteen in the evening wearing a tuxedo? That's pretty early in the day for a dinner jacket."

"Keep right on," Tragg said.

"The tuxedo must have been twenty-four hours old," Mason announced. "In other words, he must have put it on for some function he was attending the night before, something from which he had been called away very suddenly and hadn't had an opportunity to change his clothes.

"If Greeley didn't have a chance to put on a tuxedo *after* he left San Francisco, he must have had it on *before*."

Tragg frowned thoughtfully. "Don't say anything for a minute. Let me think that over."

He shifted his position in the chair so that he was sitting forward on the extreme edge of the seat. He spread his knees far apart, put his elbows on his knees, raised his hands to his chin, and sat staring down at the carpet.

Abruptly, he straightened. "Mason, you should have been a detective. You're right."

"Of course," Mason said, "it's hard to back-track a man under ordinary circumstances, but a man who wears a tuxedo in daylight is very conspicuous."

Tragg said, "Give me some paper, Mason." He whipped a pencil from his pocket, braced the pad of paper which Mason gave him over his knee and started making swift notes. "We'll look up Spinney in San Francisco. Now then, we'll start checking with service stations to see if a man in a tuxedo bought gasoline for an automobile. We'll check those stations all the way down the valley route, and we'll check the air lines, and see if a man in a tuxedo didn't get aboard a plane out of San Francisco sometime on Wednesday night."

"And while you're about it, try late Tuesday night and early Wednesday morning," Mason said.

Tragg looked up from his writing. "I don't get that."

Mason said, "It's just an angle. Let's try it. You know he may have been wearing his tuxedo all Tuesday night and all day Wednesday, because his double-breasted gray suit *may* have been in Homan's house."

"What makes you think that?"

"When he left home, he was wearing a gray suit. On the Ridge Route, he was wearing a tuxedo. When he got home, Mrs. Greeley says he wasn't wearing a tuxedo. Yet he didn't take any baggage with him when he slipped out of Homan's car up on the Ridge Route."

"Well, I can't give you much on it, but it's an angle. Okay, let me phone headquarters."

"You can use Della Street's office," Mason said.

Tragg said, "I'm going to get some immediate action on this."

"You can't start the wheels grinding any too fast to suit us."

Mason and Drake sat smoking while they listened to Tragg putting through the telephone calls in Della Street's office, instructing headquarters to make a check-up, sending out inquiries to the state highway police, and asking the San Francisco police to check on what had happened at the airport.

"How about going out and grabbing a bite to eat?" Tragg asked, returning from Della's office.

Mason said, "We're waiting for Della Street. She went out to Hollywood to get a line on Homan."

"Can't you leave a note for her?"

"I could," Mason said, "but I'm watching. I thought perhaps there'd be a call from her."

Tragg said, "It'll take me an hour or so before I begin to get reports from my end, and I thought it would be a good time to eat. We may be busy afterwards."

"You folks go out, and I'll wait," Mason suggested.

Tragg said, "Oh, I'll just run down to a counter and pick up a hamburger sandwich. I . . ."

The phone on Mason's desk rang.

Mason picked up the telephone, said, "Hello," and heard a feminine voice say, with every indication of relief, "Oh, I'm so glad I caught you at your office, Mr. Mason. I must see you at once."

"Who is this?"

"Mrs. Greeley."

"What is it?" Mason asked. "No, wait a minute. Hold the phone just a moment, please."

He cupped his hand over the receiver, said to Tragg, "Mrs. Greeley on the phone. She's getting ready to tell me something, sounds rather excited. You'd better listen in on the extension—just in case."

"Where?" Tragg asked.

"Go in Della Street's office and push that left-hand button. . . ."

"I'll show him," Drake said.

Mason waited until Tragg had plugged into the line, then he said, "Yes, Mrs. Greeley."

"What was that click I just heard? Did someone else . . ."

"I thought it would be better to use another telephone," Mason said. "There were some people in my office. What is it?"

"Mr. Mason, I'm afraid I've—well, I don't know. I . . . I wanted to ask you about something."

"What?"

"I feel very guilty."

"Why?"

She said, "I may have done that young woman an injustice."

"In what way?"

"I . . . well, you perhaps know something of how I feel. Mr. Greeley and I were very close. I . . . I've been feeling so absolutely all alone and completely lost. Tonight I just felt I *had* to do something, so I started packing up some of my husband's clothes to give away. I couldn't bear walking into his room and seeing his clothes in his closet and everything, and . . ."

"Yes, go on," Mason said.

"Something happened, and I . . . well, I found something."

"What are you getting at?" Mason asked.

"I . . . well, Mr. Mason, one of my husband's dress shirts has a long red streak across the front, and the smear made by a woman's lips. I . . ."

"Where are you now?" Mason asked.

"Out at my flat."

"How long ago did you find this shirt?"

"Why, just a few minutes ago—oh, perhaps five minutes. I found it in the bag of clothes he had ready to go to the laundry. I don't think my husband could possibly have been driving that car, but . . . well, you understand, Mr. Mason, I want to be fair. I simply couldn't put that young woman in a false position. I thought you ought to know."

Mason said, "I'd like very much to see that shirt at once, Mrs. Greeley. Suppose I drive out?"

"Can't it wait until tomorrow?"

"No. I want to see that shirt at once—just as you found it."

"Well, I . . . I'll tell you what I'll do, Mr. Mason. If you'll be at your office for a little while, I'll drive by on my way to dinner and bring it in."

"All right," Mason said, "and there's something else I want you to do."

"Yes. What is it?"

"Check through your husband's clothes that are in the closet. Find his tuxedo and bring that along."

"I was just going to ask you about that, Mr. Mason, whether you wanted it."

"Yes, I do."

"It will take me half an hour to get ready. You'll be there?"

"Yes, yes, I'll be here."

"I wouldn't want to make the trip unless . . ."

"I'll be here."

"Very well, Mr. Mason."

The receiver clicked at the other end of the line.

Mason hung up the telephone, walked in to Della Street's office where Tragg was still sitting at Della Street's desk staring at the telephone.

"Well?" Mason asked.

"That's your case," Tragg said. "Put her on the stand tomorrow, and your client goes free as air."

Mason said, "That's a load off my shoulders. How do you feel?"

"I feel like hell," Tragg said.

"Why?"

"Because I don't think Greeley stole Homan's car. If Greeley was driving Homan's car, he was driving it with Homan's consent. That means *I've* got to go after Homan. And you know what that means."

"You've certainly got enough to justify you in . . ."

"It isn't a question of whether I'm justified or not, Mason. Look here, how about getting you to be the goat in this thing?"

Mason said, "When the police department needs a cat's-paw, it certainly does co-operate."

"Nuts to you," Tragg retorted. "Remember, I brought you those keys."

"You did at that. What do you want?"

"Call Homan back to the stand tomorrow. Hold this dress-shirt evidence back, and go after him. Use these keys as a basis for your cross-examination. Rip him wide open. See if you can't catch him in some contradiction, and when you do, put the screws on him."

Mason said, "I think it's all right, Tragg, but I want to think it over a bit."

Tragg said, "Well, I'll go out and grab that sandwich, Mason. You can think it over. How about it, Drake? Want to come with me?"

Drake grinned. "You're a great guy, Tragg—at times. But I can't dance with you."

"What the hell are you talking about?"

"Della Street's coming back," Drake said, "and Mason's going to buy a dinner."

Tragg smiled. "Wise guy," he said.

"Don't be too certain," Mason said. "The way things are breaking now, it looks like a busy night. We'll probably grab a hot dog and be lucky to get that."

"Just the same, Perry, I'll wait."

Tragg picked up his hat as he started for the door. "Well,

personally, I'm going to grab a sandwich while the grabbing's good. I don't want to seem to be putting any high pressure on you, Mason, but it might not be a bad idea for you to give the department a break. You might need it sometime."

"It's all right," Mason told him, "if I can work it out so it doesn't affect my client's interests."

"Shucks, she's out of it," Tragg said. "You could send Mrs. Greeley to the D.A., and he'd dismiss. You know that."

"I'll think it over, Tragg. I think it's okay, but there are a couple of angles I want to check."

"All right, be seeing you in about twenty minutes."

Tragg went out. As the automatic door-closing device clicked the latch shut, Paul Drake turned to Mason. "Why not grab at it, Perry?"

Mason said, "It's all right. I just didn't want to seem to be too eager. I don't want Tragg to get the idea he can use me as a stalking horse any old time he wants to and have me fall all over myself doing just what he wants."

"Well, you've got your client out of the mess on this one."

"As a matter of fact, Paul, I'd do just about what Tragg wants, anyway—whether he'd suggested it or not. I hate to see a man with money start putting the screws on a hitchhiker just to get himself out of a mess."

"But why is Homan doing it? Just to avoid a few thousand dollars in civil liability? You'd think that a man in his position and with his means would . . ."

"Throw money to the birdies for champagne," Mason interrupted. "When he takes a bunch down to Tiajuana or Palm Springs on a party he does, but when it comes to something of this sort, he's tight as the bark on a tree. He . . ."

The telephone rang.

Mason said, "This'll be Horty again. . . . Hello."

Hortense Zitkousky's voice sounded harsh and high-pitched. "Is this Mr. Mason?"

"Yes."

"Horty, Mr. Mason. You got a minute?"

"Why, yes."

"Listen, could you get out here right away? There's— well, I can't tell you over the phone what it is."

"I'm afraid not," Mason said after a moment. "I'm

waiting for a woman to come to my office with some evidence which will put Miss Claire entirely in the clear. I . . ."

"Listen, can't you *please* come? It's awfully important."

"Where?"

"The Adirondack Hotel, room five-twenty-eight. If you could come quick, it would help a lot."

Mason said, "It may mean a lot if I leave here. Can't you tell me something of what it is?"

"I . . . No. You've *got* to come, right away."

Mason said, "Wait for me in the lobby."

"I think I'd better wait here in the room, Mr. Mason."

"All right."

Mason slammed up the telephone.

"Who is it?" Drake asked.

"Hortense. Something's happened that's damnably important. I wouldn't go for anyone else; but that young woman has a most unusual and priceless possession—horse sense."

Drake nodded.

Mason reached the coat closet in four swift strides, jerked his coat from the hanger, struggled into it, and clapped on his hat. "Listen, Paul, you've got to hold the office. I'll be back before Mrs. Greeley gets here. Tragg may be back before she arrives. Tell him I had to talk with Stephane Claire and get her consent before I agreed to co-operate with him. Tell him it's a matter of form, just my idea of professional ethics."

"And I'll tell him you went to see her?"

"Yes."

"Wouldn't it sound a little more like it if I told him that you'd telephoned her and tried to explain it to her, and she couldn't understand so you had to go on up and see her?"

"Perhaps so. Use your own judgment. Don't be too voluble. Take it as a matter of course. I'm on my way."

Mason grabbed a taxicab from a stand in front of his office building. "Adirondack Hotel," he said, "and drive like the devil."

The cab driver said, "I can make it in five minutes."

"Try making it in four. Stop across the street if it'll save time."

The cab shot forward. Mason didn't relax against the cushions, but kept a precarious position on the edge of the seat, hanging on to the door handle, watching the traffic whiz past.

It began to sprinkle before the cab had gone a block, and was raining steadily by the time the cab driver pulled up in front of the hotel, but directly across the street.

"If you want to spring across, Captain, you can save a full minute. I'd have to go around . . ."

Mason jerked the door open.

"Want me to wait?"

"Yes."

"Okay, I'll be right in front of the place, all ready for you."

Mason ran across the wet street. Once in the hotel, he walked rapidly across the lobby, stepped into the elevator, said, "Five, please," and was whisked on up to the fifth floor. The elevator operator looked at him curiously, apparently trying to ascertain whether Mason was registered in the hotel or merely a visitor. The lawyer, turning to the left without the slightest hesitation, walked confidently down the corridor.

After he had given the elevator time to drop back to the lobby, Mason examined the numbers on the doors, and saw he was going in the wrong direction. He retraced his steps past the dark elevator shaft, found room five-twenty-eight and knocked.

A woman's voice called softly, "Who is it?"

"Mason."

The door opened. Hortense Zitkousky said, "Come in."

She looked garish below her make-up. The splotches of rouge on her cheeks, the dark red on her full lips seemed in startling contrast to the pallor of her skin where the make-up failed to cover it.

"What is it?" Mason asked.

She crossed the bedroom, placed her hand on the knob of a door, then drew back. "You do it."

Mason impatiently jerked the door open, then recoiled at what he saw.

A pillow lay crumpled on the floor of the bathroom. From the interior of this pillow, white, fluffy feathers had drifted out over the floor, over the bathroom, over the body which hung balanced over the bathtub, the head down, the arms outstretched. From the back of the head, near the base of the brain, sinister streams of red welled upward to trickle down the neck and jaw, and drop into the bathtub.

There was a faint acrid odor of burnt, smokeless powder in the room, and the ejected cartridge from a small-caliber automatic glistened in the light, the newness of the yellow brass glinting as though it had been freshly minted gold.

"I'm sorry," Horty said. "You see how it is. I couldn't tell you over the phone. Cripes, Mr. Mason, this has got me. I'm going to get sick if I stay in here."

Mason said with crisp authority, "Snap out of it." He stepped forward, bent down, and looked at the bullet hole. There were little powder marks tattooed in the skin. The rip in the pillow on the floor had a burnt discoloration around the edges.

Mason bent forward and reached for the man's wrist.

"He's dead as a herring," Hortense said.

He turned the man's head. It was Ernest Tanner, the chauffeur.

Mason stepped back. "How did it happen?" he asked.

"Let's get out of here. . . . Okay. . . . We got to feeling pretty good. He was a good egg. He knew something. He was sore at Homan. I strung him along. You know the play. After a while, he started making passes."

"What did you do?" Mason asked.

"What did you think I was going to do? Think I was going to take him out, kid him along, and then slap his face when he got fresh? Not me. I took it in my stride, and strung him along."

"Well, come on," Mason said, looking at his wrist watch. "Get down to brass tacks. Just how did *this* happen?"

"I wish I knew."

"We'll have to call the police, so let's get the facts. Get them out. Don't make statements and then wait to see how I take them."

"Well, I got this man feeling pretty good. I was trying to get him loosened up and convivial, and I guess I overdid it. I kept talking to him about how he could get even with Homan by giving Stephane a break. He was tight-lipped at first, but later on he loosened up. I saw he was getting in the mood to tell what he knew and made up my mind that I was going to have him where I could get action fast."

"You mean getting him in touch with Stephane?"

"No, with her uncle. I thought a man could . . ."

"I understand. What happened?"

"Well, I kept working him down in this direction until we finally wound up at the Adirondack Bar. And then—

well, then was when I found I'd miscalculated. He'd taken
aboard a little too much. But he was getting ready to come
through with some real information. Gosh, Mr. Mason, I
didn't know *what* to do. Under circumstances like that, a
girl has to think fast. Well, I asked him to excuse me a
minute, and telephoned up to Stephane's room. She wasn't
in. I telephoned her uncle. No answer. I wasn't going to let
him get out of my hands, so I decided to take him up to
the uncle's room, and wait for him to get feeling better and
Mr. Olger to come in."

"How did you work it?"

"It was a cinch," she said. "I simply walked up to the
desk, bold as brass, and asked for the key to five-twenty-
eight. I knew that was the suite. The room clerk was busy
talking with someone, and he just reached in the pigeon-
hole and slid the key out on the counter. I went back and
got Tanner and took him up to the room. Of course, he
got sick right away, and headed for the bathroom. I didn't
know just where I could get in touch with Stephane, so
I thought I'd better call you, tell you the whole business,
and see if you knew where Mr. Olger was, or if you
wanted to come and talk to this lad. I hated to bother you
with it, but . . ."

"Go on."

"Well, you know how it is in these hotel bedrooms. You
can hear what a person says over the telephone if you're
in the bath. Those doors are thin, and the telephone is by
the head of the bed, right near the bathroom door. I felt
Ernest would be pretty well occupied for a while. I guess
I wasn't thinking quite so clearly myself. We'd been having
quite a few. I remembered there were telephones in the
lobby in booths. So I dashed to the elevator, went down
to the lobby, and called your office. I kept getting a busy
signal. So then I came back up here to make certain Ernest
didn't walk out on me. As soon as I came down the corridor, I saw the door was slightly ajar. . . ."

"You'd locked it when you left?"

"No, I hadn't. I'd just closed it and . . ."

Mason pressed the down button, and almost instantly an
elevator cage slid to a stop.

The operator was the same one who had taken Mason
up to the fifth floor. He gave them both casual glances,
then slid the door shut, and dropped the cage to the lobby.

Mason said, "Take my arm. Don't look at the clerk.

He may think you're going to ask for information. Move up along by the desk, slide the key over on the desk very gently so it doesn't make any noise. All ready? Here we go."

"Now what?" she asked.

Mason said, "I have a taxi outside. The driver's waiting. He'll be watching for me. I don't want him to see you with me. A few minutes after I leave, go out and walk down to the corner. Take a streetcar for a few blocks, then get out, pick up a cab, and go home."

"Why not go home in a streetcar?"

"I want you to get there faster than you can in a streetcar. I want you to go home in a cab with your mad money. Do you get it? The man got insulting, and started making passes at you. You called the party off, and went home in a taxi."

"Why not on a streetcar?"

"He'd have followed you on a streetcar. You ran out and grabbed a taxi. Pick one that's in front of a bar. Come running out as though you were in a hurry, jump in, and give your address. Got it?"

"I get you."

"Got any money?"

"A little."

Mason slipped a bill into her hand. "Take this," he said, "and you'll have more. And keep your head. As soon as you get home, brew yourself a pot of strong coffee. Lay off the booze from now on."

He felt her hand squeeze his arm. "Gosh, you're a grand guy," she whispered with feeling.

Mason said, "It's our only chance to get a murderer—and it's the only way to keep Stephane out of it. The Greeley business was one thing—but this—right in her hotel room—no, they'd have us all on the grid until the clues all were lost—the ones I'm working on at any rate. Keep your head now, and don't cross me up."

"I won't."

He walked calmly out of the lobby. His taxi drew up to the loading zone. The doorman held an umbrella and opened the door with something of a flourish.

Mason stepped into the taxi and said, "All right, back to where we came from."

He settled back in the cushions, lit a cigarette, and inhaled a deep drag.

17

PAUL DRAKE had his feet on Perry's desk and was reading the sporting section of the evening paper when the lawyer latchkeyed the door of his private office.

"Well, you made a quick trip," Drake said, looking up.

"Where's Tragg?"

"Hasn't shown up yet."

Mason looked at his watch. "It's been half an hour."

"Yeah, he should be due about any time. What was the excitement?"

Mason went over to the closet, hung up his hat and coat. "I didn't think that Zitkousky woman would get as excitable."

"What's the matter?"

"Oh, the chauffeur got crocked and got to making passes at her, and she used her mad money to grab a taxi and leave him. Now, she's afraid she's made an enemy out of him, and he may not give us his testimony."

"What did you do?"

"Saw that she got some coffee to sober up on, and told her not to worry, that we'd make the chauffeur talk. And I told her never, under any circumstances, to call me again at night. I thought she had good judgment, too. You haven't heard anything more from Mrs. Greeley?"

"No."

Mason looked at his watch. "Well, she should be here. She . . ."

Drake said abruptly, "That sounds fishy as hell to me, Perry."

"What's that?"

"That story about the Zitkousky girl."

Mason grinned. "All right then, I'll change it. What sounds fishy about it?"

"About her getting so hysterical and offended at a guy

making a pass at her. She's too damned attractive and too good-natured not to have had . . ."

"All right," Mason said, "I'll change it. Thanks for the tip."

Drake looked at him with narrowed eyes. "Now what?" he asked.

Mason said, "I've got to make this sound good for Tragg."

"What's the idea? Hold it, Perry. Here's someone coming. Sounds like a woman."

Mason walked over to the door which led to the corridor. He said, "As far as you know, I haven't left the office, Paul. That may be better than telling Tragg about how Horty got sore at her boy friend." He flung open the door. Mrs. Greeley, garbed in black and carrying a light suitcase, stood in the corridor.

"Come in," Mason invited, reaching out and taking the suitcase; and when she had entered the office and he had closed the door, he went on, "Sit down, Mrs. Greeley. I'm sorry we had to intrude on your dinner."

"Oh, it's all right. To be perfectly frank, Mr. Mason, I don't suppose I should go out so soon, but I feel a lot better doing that than I would sitting home and doing nothing. It's a frightfully all-gone feeling."

"I understand."

"I guess people never realize how much they take for granted in life," she said with a little laugh. "Here it was only last week I was fussing because my husband had to work so much at nights, and now . . . and now . . . Oh, well, I'll get to feeling sorry for myself if I keep on. Wish I could get something to work on—something to sink my teeth into.

"Death is so horribly final, Mr. Mason. I—I've never been touched closely by death before. Somehow, it shakes my faith in . . . things. . . . And no one's been able to say anything that helps. Death is . . . it's cruel, it's terrible."

"It's no more terrible than birth," Mason said. "We can't understand it, any more than we can understand life —or the sky at night. If we only had the vision to see the whole pattern of life, we'd see death as something benign."

She stared up at him. "Please go on. If you can only say something practical and sensible. I've heard so much hypocritical 'all-for-the-best' business that I'm sick and tired of it. How *can* it be for the best? Bosh!"

Mason said, "Suppose you couldn't remember anything from one day to the next. You'd get up in the morning without any recollection of yesterday. You'd feel full of energy. Dew would be on the grass. The sun would be shining bright and warm. Birds would be singing, and you'd feel that nature was a wonderful thing. Then the sun would rise higher in the heavens. You'd begin to get a little fatigued.

"Along about noon you'd be tired, then clouds would blot out the sun. There'd be a thunder squall, and the heavens which had once been so friendly would be menacing. You'd see water falling out of the sky, and would wonder if you were going to be totally submerged. You'd see spurts of lightning tearing the sky apart. You'd hear roaring thunder. You'd be in terror.

"Then the clouds would drift away. The sun would come out again. The air would be pure and sparkling. You'd regain your confidence. Then you'd notice that the shadows were lengthening. The sun would disappear. There'd be darkness. You'd huddle around a light waiting to see what would happen next. You'd feel weary, more than a little frightened. You'd think that nature, which had started out to be so beautiful, had betrayed you. You'd fight hard to keep your faith, and it would be a losing battle.

"The loved ones who were sitting around the fire with you would show signs of fatigue. Their heads would nod forward. They'd lie down. Their eyes would close, and suddenly their personalities would be gone. Then you yourself would want to lie down, and yet you'd feel that as soon as you did, this awful unconsciousness would come over you. . . ."

Mason broke off, smiled and said, "My words don't carry conviction because you do know all of these symptoms as a part of life. You know that this unconsciousness is only sleep. You know that in the course of a few short hours, you'll wake up completely refreshed, that the dawn will be breaking, that the sun will be coming up, the birds singing. You know that the awful visitation of noise and flashes was only a thunder shower, part of nature's scheme to bring water from the ocean up into the mountains, to feed the streams and the rivers, to make the crops green. You'd realize that sleep is nature's means of strengthening you for a new day, that it's profitless to try to prolong the waking activities too far into the night, that nature is cooperating with you. But suppose you didn't understand these things? Suppose you could see only from day to day?"

She nodded slowly. After a moment, she heaved a deep sigh.

Mason said, "Life is like that. We can only see from birth to death. The rest of it is cut from our vision."

Drake stared up at Mason. "I'll be doggoned," he said.

"What's the matter, Paul?"

"I never knew you were a mystic."

"I'm not a mystic," Mason said, smiling. "It's simply the application of what you might call legal logic to the scheme of existence, and I don't ordinarily talk that way. I'm doing it now because I think Mrs. Greeley needs it."

Mrs. Greeley said with feeling, "Mr. Mason, I can't begin to tell you how much better you have made me feel. Your words carry conviction. I . . . I guess I'm getting my faith back."

Mason said, "I don't think you'd ever lost it, Mrs. Greeley. Now this is going to be disagreeable. Do you want to get it over with as quickly as possible?"

"I don't care," she said. "I . . . Oh, Mr. Mason, I can't tell you how much you've comforted me. After all, death *is* only a sleep. It has to be. I'm ashamed of myself, Mr. Mason. I was doubting the whole scheme of things. I was . . . Is this someone coming?"

"Should be Lieutenant Tragg," Mason said. "You know him."

"Oh, yes."

There were quick steps in the corridor, then the tapping of knuckles on the door. Mason nodded to Drake, who opened the door, and Tragg came in. "Sorry I was detained," he said. "Good evening, Mrs. Greeley. I hope you don't think we're entirely unfeeling."

"No, I understand. I want to show you these things."

She took the suitcase which Mason handed her, placed it on the floor at her feet, opened the lid, and took out a crumpled shirt. A vivid crimson streak was slashed across the front of the stiffly starched bosom, a streak perhaps five inches long. Above it was the smudged imprint of red lips, partially opened.

The men bent over the smear.

Tragg said, "Notice here. You can even see where the finger was first pressed against the shirt. Then follow the mark to the place where it vanishes. She was trying to push him away."

Mason nodded.

Tragg looked down at the suitcase. "You have some other things, Mrs. Greeley?"

She said, "After Mr. Mason asked me about his tuxedo, I looked it over. There aren't any spots on it."

Tragg took the suit to hold it under the light. After a few moments, he looked up at Mason. "Nothing I can see," he said.

"Wouldn't there have been some spots on the suit," Mrs. Greeley asked, "if—if that girl is telling the truth?"

"Perhaps," Tragg said.

"She was cut in several places, wasn't she?"

"There were some gashes, yes."

"And if my husband had been driving the car, he'd have been on the left-hand side. That would have been on the lower side. She'd have been above him. In order to have squirmed out from under the steering wheel, got past that unconscious woman, and crawled out through the window —well, it seems to me there'd have been some spots on his suit."

"Yes," Tragg said, "you'd think so. What are you getting at?"

She said simply, "I brought the shirt to you because I found it, because it was evidence. I suppose it was my duty, but—well, you'll understand. My husband and I were very close. I don't want to be sentimental. I don't want to get to feeling sorry for myself, and I don't want to impose my own private, individual grief on you people, but I would like a fair deal."

"You'll get it," Mason said.

She smiled her thanks.

Tragg said, "I don't understand, Mrs. Greeley. In the face of this evidence, do you still think that your husband wasn't driving the car?"

"Yes."

Tragg said, "I'm afraid I don't understand, Mrs. Greeley."

She said, "Adler wouldn't have done the things this man who was driving the car did."

Tragg indicated the shirt. "You mean he didn't try to kiss . . ."

"Oh, *that*," she interrupted. "That's nothing. He'd been

drinking. He was feeling good. This girl has a butter-won't-melt-in-my-mouth manner, now that she's telling about it; but in the car, she was probably kidding him along. They all do. I don't care about that. Adler was no saint. But what I mean is he wouldn't have climbed out of the car and left the girl behind the steering wheel. Adler didn't do that. That isn't his way of doing things."

"But he *must* have," Mason said.

She shook her head stubbornly. "There's something else that we don't know about, Mr. Mason. If Adler was at the wheel of that car and he got out and left the girl to take the responsibility, there was someone who forced him to do it, someone who was hidden in that car, either down on the floor in back, or in the trunk, or somewhere. Or perhaps someone who was following along behind."

"Wait a minute," Tragg said. *"That's* a theory. The evidence shows a lot of cars stopped almost at once. There was quite a mix-up."

"Someone," Mrs. Greeley said with calm sincerity, "forced Adler to get out of that car. Someone took him away from the scene of the accident, and that someone forced him to keep quiet. When you've found who that someone was, you'll have found who killed my husband, and . . . and . . ." She began to sob—after a few moments got control of herself and said, "I'm sorry. I'm pretty much unstrung."

Mason glanced at Tragg. "I don't think we need her any more, do we, Lieutenant?"

Tragg shook his head.

Mrs. Greeley gave Mason her hand. "When I first met you—well, I found myself liking you, and yet you made me very angry. I . . . I hope we understand each other better now."

She gave his hand a quick pressure, smiled at Tragg, nodded to Drake, and left the office, walking rapidly down the corridor.

Drake, listening to the sound of her diminishing footsteps said, "If I'd been Greeley, I wouldn't have been playing around. Gosh, Perry, you certainly talked a sermon."

"Did I miss something?" Tragg asked.

"Did you miss something? I'll say you did. A five-minute talk on the philosophy of life and death *I'll* never forget."

Tragg glanced at Mason, elevated his eyebrows quizzically.

Mason said apologetically, "She had had an overdose of this all-for-the-best business. I tried to give her a little of my own philosophy about life and death."

Tragg said, "Well, I've got some news. I couldn't get up here sooner because I was camped in a telephone booth down in the restaurant. I had headquarters half crazy, but I got action. A man wearing a tuxedo suit chartered a plane to go from San Francisco to Fresno early *on the morning of Wednesday the nineteenth*. Two o'clock to be exact. Get that, Mason? At two in the morning."

"What time would that have put him in Fresno?" Mason asked.

"Oh, within an hour or so."

"And then what?"

"We're tracing him from Fresno," Tragg said. "We should be able to get a line on him."

"Get the name under which the ticket was sold?" Mason asked.

Tragg grinned. "L. C. Spinney."

"How soon can you get something from Fresno?"

"It should be coming in any time now," Tragg said.

"Headquarters knows you're here? They can reach you on the telephone if anything turns up?"

"Sure."

Mason said, "Well, we're commencing to get it unscrambled. This all begins to fit into a perfect picture."

"That Warfield woman," Tragg said, "has simply disappeared into thin air. I don't like that. A simple, unsophisticated, working woman couldn't have walked out of a hotel in a city where she had no connections . . ."

Drake said, "You aren't overlooking that cafeteria friend of hers, are you?"

"No, I'm not," Tragg said. "We've interviewed her. She says she doesn't know a thing. We're going to keep a watch on her. We found out this much: after Mrs. Warfield got that cafeteria job lined up, someone came in, flashed a buzzer, and said Warfield was a convict who had escaped, that Mrs. Warfield was sending him money, and asked a lot of questions. That naturally cooked Mrs. Warfield's chance of getting the job. The cafeteria didn't want the wives of any escaped criminals . . ."

Mason interrupted, "Then that man must have known

Mrs. Warfield had the promise of that job. Only Spinney knew that."

Tragg smiled. "The man's description," he said, "fits Greeley."

Drake whistled.

Tragg said to Mason, "It's certainly beginning to look as though you were right about Homan. . . ."

He broke off as the sound of quick steps in the corridor approached the office door.

"We're having a procession tonight," Drake said.

"Probably Della," Mason assured him.

He opened the door. Della Street, walking rapidly, bustled into the room, said, "Hello, everybody. Hope I didn't keep you waiting. . . . Oh, good evening, Lieutenant."

Mason smiled and said, "For the moment, Della, Tragg is one of the bunch. There have been momentous and important developments. The police agree that Stephane Claire is innocent of the negligent homicide. She's exonerated from driving the car, and, believe it or not, *I'm* cooperating with the police."

Della Street looked down at the suitcase, then over at the shirt on Mason's desk. "How come?" she asked.

"Mrs. Greeley," Mason said. "It was her husband's. She found it in the soiled clothes after his death."

"Oh-oh," Della Street said, and then after a moment, "I presume then what *I've* found out doesn't amount to anything?"

Mason said, "On the contrary, it's more important than ever." He turned to Tragg and said, "She was getting some gossip on Homan."

"I'd like to hear it," Tragg said, studying Della Street with quite obvious approval.

"Go ahead, Della," Mason said.

She said, "La-de-dah, am I Hollywood!" She made a little gesture with her hand. "I mean *really*, you know. It's terrific. That is, I think I've got something here."

"Come on," Mason said, "unload the gossip."

"Don't we eat?"

Mason glanced uneasily toward the telephone. "Tragg has had dinner," he said, "and he's waiting for a report . . ."

"Oh, not dinner," Tragg interposed. "It was just a snack. I'm about ready for a beefsteak. I can telephone headquarters and let them know where to get in touch with me.

After all, I'm really supposed to be off duty now. Only on this job, you don't keep hours."

"Personally, I'm famished," Della Street admitted. "That is, I mean *really* famished. I think the idea of a steak would be simply terrific. Oh, definitely."

Mason picked up a law book, held it poised, and said, "Cut it before I brain you."

Her eyes were sparkling with mischief. "Don't be a dope," she said. "I mean this is the weanie of the evening."

"Come on," Drake announced, getting to his feet. "I've been waiting long enough for a chance to eat on Perry and dance with his secretary."

"In my capacity as official representative of the law," Tragg interposed sternly, "I'm afraid I'll have to preempt your claim."

"Age before beauty, my lad," Drake said.

"Don't *I* get in on this?" Mason asked.

"Go on," Drake told him. "You're the host. You're supposed to see that your guests are properly entertained."

"Socko," Della Street announced. "Colossal!"

"Come on," Mason said, getting to his feet.

"It's drizzling outside," Della Street told him.

"Uh huh," Mason said, putting on his hat and coat.

Tragg stood watching him with speculative eyes. "You know, Mason," he said, apropos of nothing, shaking a cigarette from a package, "you're damn deep."

Drake said, "You don't know the half of it."

Mason switched out the lights, shepherded them out into the corridor, saw that the door was closed and locked. They started trooping down toward the elevator.

"Good place over at the Adirondack," Della Street said.

"Oh, let's try some place that has more life," Mason said. "That's staid and stodgy."

"Suits me all right," Tragg announced. "Do I get the first dance, Miss Street?"

"That will depend," she said, "on how I feel after I've had the first steak. Right now, I'm simply caving in."

"I had the first claim," Drake warned.

Mason said, "Remember I'm painfully conscious of my duties as host, but I get the last dance, Della. Let them fight over the first."

She turned and flashed him a quick undersanding smile.

Drake sighed. "There we go, Lieutenant. Our ship's scuttled before we've even got it away from the pier. As you've remarked before, Mason is a deep one."

"Well, where are we going to eat?" Della asked.

"Oh, let's try the Tangerine," Mason said. "It's good and lively, and it has the advantage of being within three blocks of the office."

"We can walk it," Tragg said.

"Not in this drizzle," Della Street announced. "It's really commencing to rain. I mean *definitely*, I *really* do!"

Mason made a grab for her, but she laughingly eluded him, slipped around the corner, and ran the rest of the way down the corridor. As he chased after her, he had a fleeting glimpse of Tragg making silly, futile grasps at thin air. Mason caught up with her at the elevator, and his arm encircled her waist. Struggling a little, she managed to move close to him and said in a low whisper, "What's wrong with your hat, Chief?"

"Huh?" he asked, surprised.

"Tragg was looking at it when you took it out of the closet."

"Oh," Mason said, and pressed the button for the elevator. "The lid's going to blow off tonight. Keep sober."

The others came walking up. Della Street twisted away from Mason's grasp just as the elevator slid to a stop, and the quartet trooped in with much laughing and joking.

When they reached the street, it was raining hard, and they stood in the shelter of the lobby for nearly five minutes before Mason was able to get a cab. The Tangerine however, because of the rain, had plenty of vacant tables, and a deferential headwaiter escorted them to a choice location near the side of the dance floor.

Mason said, "As a perfect host, Della, I'll sit with my back to the floor show, place you between Tragg and . . . where the devil is she?"

Tragg turned around. "She was here a moment . . . Oh."

He stood looking out on the dance floor to where Paul Drake and Della Street were whirling around.

"There you are," Tragg said, seating himself. "The private detectives beat the regulars to it every time. Guess I'll have to see about getting that guy's license revoked afer all."

"Steak dinner?" Mason asked.

"Uh huh. Think I'll telephone and see if headquarters has any news."

"Cocktail?" Mason asked.

Tragg hesitated.

"You're not on duty," Mason told him.

"Well, all right, make it a martini."

"Think we'll probably have four customers on that," Mason said as Tragg threaded his way through the dancers toward the telephone booth.

A waiter approached Mason. "Four dry martinis, four de luxe steak dinners. Make the steaks medium rare except for the gentleman sitting over there, who wants his well-done, and I wish you'd keep that dinner moving right along. Will you?"

"Yes, sir."

Mason settled back in his chair, watching the dancers. Tragg returned from the telephone booth, and Mason flashed a quick glance at the officer's face. Tragg's smile indicated that as yet he had received no news of the crumpled figure which lay balanced precariously over the edge of the bathtub in the Adirondack Hotel.

"News?" Mason asked.

"I'll say. It was a cinch to pick up our man in the tuxedo at Fresno. He got off the plane, made inquiries about renting a car which he could drive himself. He couldn't get a car until about eight-thirty in the morning when one of the places opened up. He rented a car, gave the name of L. C. Spinney, drove the car one hundred and sixty-five miles, and brought it back about two o'clock. He walked out, and evaporated into thin air. We lose him from then on. The description is Greeley."

The dance music stopped. Paul Drake and Della Street came toward the table.

Mason said abruptly, "Cover the garages that rent cars *with* drivers."

"What's the angle?" Tragg asked.

"Don't you see?" Mason asked.

"No, hanged if I do."

Mason said, "Bet you the dinners that you'll find he appeared at a garage which rented cars with drivers before three o'clock in the afternoon and hired a driver to take him exactly eighty-two miles up into the mountains. He got out there."

Paul Drake and Della Street were now at the table, Drake holding Della Street's chair.

Tragg said, "I'm not going to bet you the price of the dinners because I'm a poor working man. I can't pass expenses on to a rich client the way you can. I can't make the compensation for my services sufficiently elastic to cover all the traffic will stand. And furthermore, I think you're bluffing."

"Go ahead and call me," Mason said.

Tragg said, "Well, I'll call headquarters and have them check with the Fresno police on it. If it's right, will you tell me how you reason it out?"

"Uh huh."

Tragg threaded his way once more among the tables and belated dancers who were coming off the dance floor. Della Street asked, "What is it, Chief?"

Mason said, "I think we're on the home stretch."

"Don't clean the case up too soon," Drake jokingly remarked. "I'm getting paid by the day, and I never do get these delightful dinners and a chance to dance with Della except when you're on a case and have an expense account."

Mason jerked his head toward Della. "Is she still Hollywood, Paul?"

"Oh, definitely," Della said.

"Come on, brat," Mason said. "Tell us what you found out."

"Here's Tragg coming back."

"It's all right. He's one of the family," Mason said, raising his voice just enough so that Tragg could hear as he approached the table.

"What now?" Tragg asked.

"Della's about to relay us the dirt from Hollywood."

The waiter appeared with their cocktails. "Here's to crime," Mason said, looking at Tragg across the rim of the glass.

"And the *catching* of criminals," Tragg amended before he drank.

"By fair means or foul," Della Street volunteered.

They took the first long sip from their cocktails, then, as they lowered their glasses, Tragg said, "I see you've got Miss Street educated to your outlook."

"Why not?" Mason asked. "A criminal doesn't play cricket. He accomplishes the results he wants by any means that are handy. Why shouldn't he be tripped up by the same means?"

"Because it isn't legal."

"Oh, bunk," Mason said impatiently. "You folks are either fools or hypocrites when you say that."

"No, we're not," Tragg said earnestly. "The whole structure of the law has to be a dignified, imposing edifice and built on firm foundations, if it's going to stand. Whenever you violate the law, you're tearing down a part of that structure, regardless of what goal you may want to achieve."

"All right," Mason said, grinning, "why not tear parts of it down?"

"What do you mean?"

"Well," Mason said, "suppose you're on the roof and a murderer is sneaking out through the basement. You can't stop him by yelling at him, but if you take a loose brick out of the chimney, drop it, and hit him on the head, it stops him, and why isn't it perfectly justifiable? After all, you've only taken a loose brick from that dignified structure you've been talking about and . . ."

"Well," Tragg said, "it's not exactly that way. It . . ."

"The hell it isn't," Mason interrupted. "A man has a joint where he sells liquor illegally, but he gives you all the low-down on the people that come into that joint. It's in the interests of the police to keep the place going. They know the man is selling liquor, and that the sale is unlawful, and after regular closing hours, but they wink at it."

"Well, in that case you have to admit that you're getting something which is very important in return for a very minor infraction of the law."

"Sure," Mason said, "you're taking the loose brick out of the chimney of your imposing structure and dropping it on the head of the murderer."

Tragg threw up his hands. "I should have known better than to argue with a lawyer. And, remember, Miss Street, the next dance is mine."

"Okay."

"And in the meantime, what about Homan?" Mason asked.

"My *dear*," she said to Perry, pitching her voice in the high, rapid key of a woman who is a natural-born gossip, and talking at a high rate of speed, "you've absolutely no idea about how that man has come to the front! It's been terrific. I mean really. He started in as a writer on an obscure assignment and on a play that was stinko. Then out of a clear sky he shot up into a big job, and I mean gravy."

"What's back of it?" Mason asked. "And can that Hollywood chatter before I crown you."

"A woman."

"What woman?"

"No one knows."

"How do they know it's a woman?"

"Because Homan never plays around. He lives what my informant naively describes as a monastic life. *I* wouldn't know what she meant."

"Careful," Drake warned. "That remark might be twisted."

"Yes, and you have some of the best little remark-twisters in the world gathered right around this table," Tragg interposed.

She laughed. "Well, anyway, Homan is something of a unique character around Hollywood, but doesn't always stay around Hollywood. Occasionally he vanishes, and when he vanishes—tra la tra la!"

"Where does he go?" Mason asked.

"He goes to some place where he can be all alone with his work," Della Street said with a demure manner which was purposely exaggerated. Her eyes were large and round, gazing above the heads of the diners on the far ceiling. She pursed her lips and said mincingly, "He is always trying to get away somewhere where he can *work*. He's a man who simply *can't* be disturbed. He breaks from the studio to go home and shut himself in his study where he will be free to concentrate, and then his nerves get so frayed by the environment of civilization that he has to jump in his car and go alone into the solitude."

"Alone?" Mason asked.

"Alone," she said, "definitely, positively alone. I mean really—and I *do* mean really."

The dance music struck up, and Tragg said, "We'll leave Mr. Homan's concentrational celibacy for another time, Miss Street. But right now you are in demand for another and more important matter."

He walked around to stand back of her chair. Mason said, "Don't let him pump you, Della."

"Don't be foolish. He's not the sort who would do that, are you, Lieutenant?"

"Not unless I thought I could get away with it."

Drake said, "Watch him, Perry. I think he's a viper. You'd better forbid her to dance with him at all, and let her keep on dancing with me. At least, I'm safe."

"That's right," Della said to Mason. "He's just like Homan. He wants to concentrate. All the time we were dancing, he was trying to pump me about . . ." She stopped suddenly.

"About what?" Tragg asked.

She smiled mockingly up at him. "About whether the boss could put cocktails on an expense account," she said, and, swaying slightly with the rhythm of the dance music, let Tragg take her in his arms.

Mason glanced at Drake. "Pumping her about what, Paul?"

"The little brat," Drake said. "I should have known she'd have passed it on to you."

"What?"

"Trying to find out whether she was responsible for that telephone call you got while Tragg was eating and sent you dashing out of the office."

"Why?" Mason asked.

"Oh, I don't know. I just thought that was pretty damned important, or you wouldn't have left. I somehow can't see you jeopardizing your appointment with the Greeley woman to run out to have a talk with this girl Horty."

"Now, wait a minute," Mason said, his face suddenly hard. "You told Della I went out?"

"Yes."

"And asked her if she knew where?"

"Well, not exactly that. I was trying to find out . . ."

"Now did you tell her not to mention that to Tragg?"

"What?"

"About my having gone out."

Drake's face showed sudden dismay. "Gosh, no, I didn't."

"And were you asking her seriously or just kidding along?"

"Just kidding along, Perry. It gave me something to talk about, and . . . Gosh, if she should let it out to Tragg . . ."

Mason said, "Tragg's nobody's damn fool. It wasn't raining when he came in. It started to rain right afterward. I was in taxicabs most of the way, but I had to cross a street and some raindrops spattered on my gray hat. When I took my hat out of the closet, Tragg happened to notice those damp spots. They had soaked in so they were almost invisible. You have to hand it to him for being a damn good detective, Paul. He noticed those spots, realized what they meant—and didn't say a word. What was the meaning of those silly antics of his in the corridor? Did he pick up anything?"

Drake said, "I don't know. I was watching you two. Gosh, I'm sorry, Perry."

Mason frowned down at the tablecloth. "I'd like to work with Tragg," he said, "but he's pretty fast on his feet, and after all, he's on the opposite side of the fence. Some of my methods wouldn't meet with his approval."

"What happened while you were gone?" Drake asked.

Mason said, "I went to Hortense Zitkousky's house, found her pretty high, prescribed coffee, and came back."

"Nuts," Drake said. "When you came back, you had that grim line around the corners of your mouth that—dammit, Perry, you're a gambler."

"Of course, I'm a gambler."

"You gamble for the sheer joy of risking terrific odds against your ideas of justice."

"Well, what of it?"

"Some day you're going to break through that thin ice you skate on."

"Well?"

"And when you do," Drake said, "you're going to take me with you."

"I haven't yet," Mason said.

"No. You haven't yet because you keep moving so damn fast, but . . ."

"Forget it," Mason interrupted. "They're coming back."

"What's the matter?" Mason asked.

Della Street said, "The floor's getting too crowded, and I'm getting too famished to do any more dancing until after I've had some good thick steak with mushroom sauce. Did you order mine medium rare, Chief?"

"Uh huh."

"Mine?" Drake asked.

"Well done."

"How'd you know?"

Mason said, "First and last, Paul, I've bought you enough steaks so that I should know."

"You mean your clients have. I . . ."

A bus boy approached the table, motioned to Lt. Tragg. "Telephone, Lieutenant," he said.

"Excuse me." Tragg pushed back his chair.

Mason glanced across at Della Street.

"Trying to pump me," she said tersely. "Paul was, too. I didn't mind him. He's harmless, but Tragg was deadly."

"What did he want to know?"

"Where you went while I was out."

"What did you tell him?"

"I asked him how I would know you'd been out when I wasn't there."

"Didn't say anything about Paul Drake asking you the same question?" Mason asked.

She said, "Don't be silly. Then he'd *know* you'd gone out. As it is, he only surmised it from seeing the raindrops on your hatbrim."

Drake heaved a sigh. "Good girl," he said. "Gosh, I was worried over that."

"What's in the wind?" Della Street asked.

Mason said, "Nothing, only we're gradually closing the net."

"Did Homan kill Greeley?"

"That," Mason said, "is going to keep for a while. What I'm concerned with right now is finding out how I can prove that Adler Greeley was operating that automobile as Homan's agent and in accordance with specific instructions by Homan. Then Tragg will have enough to force him to go after Homan."

"Why?" Drake asked. "If you can prove that *she* wasn't driving the car, that lets you out, doesn't it?"

Mason said, "Homan's been so willing to let her take the rap that I want to see him get his. And it'd be a good thing for her to stick him for damages. She might be able to use the money."

Drake gave a low whistle.

"There's no question but that it was Greeley who was driving the automobile?" Della Street asked.

"Not unless someone planted a smeared shirt in his soiled-linen bag," Drake said and looked significantly at Mason.

Mason shook his head. "Don't blame that on me."

"You *would* have done it though," Drake charged. "And that red mouth print looked like Della's lips."

The waiter appeared with seafood cocktails, said deferentially to Mason, "And I'll keep the dinner moving right along, sir."

Tragg was back before the waiter had finished serving the cocktails. He waited until the waiter had left, then sat down, and pushed the plate with the cocktail glass away from him so that he could lean across the table and look directly at Mason.

"Find out anything?" Mason asked, holding a fork over his cocktail.

Tragg said, "Mason, I have to hand it to you. You have a touch of—well, more than a touch of the genius."

"What now?"

"Spinney showed up at a garage just as you had predicted, took the automobile and the driver, was driven exactly eighty-two miles, stopped the car in the middle of a mountain road, said he would get out there, and the last the driver saw of him he was sauntering along the mountain grade, just a harmless nut attired in a tuxedo, light dress shoes, and a topcoat, strolling casually in the deep dust of a dirt road among the pines. Now then, that's one thing I learned."

"And the other?" Drake asked.

"And the other," Tragg said, keeping his eyes fastened on Mason, "was that the body of Ernest Tanner has been found doubled over the bathtub in the bathroom which communicates between the rooms of Stephane Claire and her uncle, Max Olger, in the Adirondack Hotel. And in case you don't remember, Mr. Mason, Ernest Tanner is the chauffeur for Jules Homan, the man Homan virtually accused of using his telephone to place unauthorized long-distance calls to Mr. L. C. Spinney in San Francisco."

Mason straightened. His fork clattered against his plate. "You're not kidding?" he asked.

"I'm not kidding," Lieutenant Tragg said in a calm, level voice, "and for your information, Mason, the murder was apparently committed at just about the time when you left your office while I was eating my hamburger sandwich."

Mason said suavely, "Can't resist the spectacular, can you, Lieutenant? If you'd asked me about those wet spots on my hatbrim . . ."

"That," Tragg interrupted, "was simply my starting point. What the hell do you think I've been doing all the time

I've been telephoning? I've had headquarters get in touch with the taxi drivers who stand around your office building. The time I have reference to, Mason, was when you dashed out, jumped in a cab, went to the Adirondack Hotel, stayed about twelve minutes, and then tore back to the office."

18

PAUL DRAKE'S FACE showed surprise and consternation, but Lieutenant Tragg wasn't watching him. He was studying Mason with the concentration of a surgeon making a diagnosis.

Della Street said casually, "Chief, don't tell me you've committed *another* murder?"

Tragg, still looking at Mason, said, "He didn't commit a murder, but Stephane Claire did, or else found the body in her room and telephoned Mason, and he told her to go out and concoct an alibi."

Mason said, "Come, come, Lieutenant. You jump at the most absurd conclusions. How do you know that I didn't go to the Adirondack Hotel while you were eating your sandwich to find out from Miss Claire whether it would be all right for me to take you into my confidence?"

"And what did she say?" Tragg asked.

Mason laughed. "Rather obvious, Lieutenant. I'm afraid I can't help you there. I didn't see her at the Adirondack."

"Why did you go there?"

"I could have gone to see her, and yet not seen her."

"You could have, but did you?"

Mason said, "I see no reason why I should account to you for *all* my moves."

Tragg said, "Mason, you're a delightful host. Personally, I like you. Officially, we're opposed. And I'm asking these questions in my official capacity."

Mason said, "All right, I'll answer you in *my* official capacity. I'm an attorney at law. I protect my clients to the best of my ability. I don't have to disclose anything that a client has told me. A client could tell me he had committed a cold-blooded, deliberate murder, and that communication is absolutely confidential."

"The communication might be," Tragg said, "but there are other things which aren't."

"Such, for instance, as what?"

Tragg inserted his thumb and forefinger in his vest pocket, took out a small piece of paper, unfolded it, and disclosed a small white feather, the tip of which was still moist. The lower half of the feather, however, was a dark, sinister crimson.

Tragg, keeping his eyes steadily on Mason, said, "I have been advised Tanner was killed with a shot in the base of the brain, fired at close range from a small caliber revolver. A pillow had been used to muffle the report of the weapon, and a fold of the pillow got in the way of the bullet, ripping the pillow open and scattering feathers pretty much over the bathroom. It had started to rain. When you went in, there was moisture on your shoes, between the heel and the sole of the shoe. One of these feathers stuck to your heel without your knowing it, and it wasn't until you returned that the feather dried enough to drop from your shoe to the floor."

"Are you trying to tell me you picked that up in *my* office?" Mason asked.

"Not in your office. I noticed your hat when you took it from the cloak closet. Then when you were chasing Della Street down the corridor, this feather was swirling around on the floor in the air currents generated by Miss Street's skirts."

Della Street said quickly, "I think that's being *very* chivalrous of you, Lieutenant. Another man would have suspected *me*."

Tragg's eyes suddenly shifted to hers. "By George!" he said.

She raised her eyebrows.

"Why the devil didn't I think of it sooner? *You* were out. You *said* you were in Hollywood. Someone telephoned Mason. The message was important enough so that he left his office while he was waiting for Mrs. Greeley to bring in some evidence which would exonerate his client. It had to be you who telephoned."

He stopped talking to study her intently. She met his

eyes with a level gaze. "Go on, Lieutenant. It's fascinating to see a keen mind at work."

He said slowly, "You found the body, and Mason didn't want you mixed into it. He wouldn't have risked so much to protect Miss Claire. It was you he was trying to keep out of a mess. But the feather fell from *his* shoe. He'd been over there in that room with the corpse."

He ceased talking.

"Well?" she asked.

"What have you to say to that?"

She said, "As they say in Hollywood, you really have something there. It's terrific. I mean definitely."

Tragg pushed back his chair. "Nuts! I'm going up to the Adirondack," he said.

"Why not have your dinner first?" Mason asked. "You'll have men up there who can take care of the routine work."

Tragg paid no attention to the invitation. He leaned forward, putting his clenched fists on the table. "Mason," he said, "I like you. Sometimes I think you like me. But I'm just as good a fighter as you are, and just as bitter a fighter and just as ruthless a fighter. Have I made that plain?"

"Perfectly," Mason said.

"You represent people who have committed crimes," Tragg continued, "and I don't want you to leave this restaurant until I tell you you can. If you do, the results may be unfortunate. If you don't hear from me within the next thirty minutes, call me at the Adirondack Hotel or at headquarters. Tell me when you're going and where you're going."

Mason said, "I'll do nothing of the sort. I report to no man. The only way you can control my activities is to put me under arrest."

"And I might even do that."

Mason got to his feet. "No hard feelings in case you do, Lieutenant. But I'll have your hide if you try it. I enjoyed our little visit very much. It was a pleasure to co-operate with the police, even for so brief an interval. You understand my position, and I understand yours. I hope you'll do me the honor of continuing our interrupted dinner at some later date."

There was a trace of a grim smile at the corner of Tragg's lips. "Mason, I may have to put you in jail one of these days."

"That's swell. Then I might have to get myself out, and make a monkey of you in the process."

"That's fine *if* you can do it; but I might *keep* you in jail."

Mason pushed out his hand. "That's fine," he said, "*if* you can do it."

They shook hands.

Tragg said, "I'm going up to look over that homicide. Remember what I told you about keeping in touch with me and not leaving here until you ask my permission. Good night."

Mason watched him stride across the corner of the dance floor, thread his way among the tables.

"Any use to tail him?" Drake asked.

"Certainly not," Mason said. "He's already made arrangements for plainclothes men to sew this place up, and it's a ten-to-one bet that he's tapped the line out of that telephone booth, hoping that I'll call someone. And," he added with a grin, "I'm damned if I don't."

"Watch your step, Chief," Della Street cautioned.

Mason glanced at his wrist watch. "I'll give him ten minutes," he said, "to make certain he's got all of his preparations made."

"Then what?"

Mason chuckled.

Drake said, "Perry, he *did* pick up that feather in the hall. There was no fake about that. How did it get there if you weren't in the room with the body?"

"Just the way he says it did, Paul."

"Good God, Perry! Don't admit you *were* there—not to me."

Mason picked up his fork and started eating his cocktail again. "Tragg is a very dangerous adversary."

Drake sighed. "If I only had nerves like that," he said to Della Street.

The dance music struck up. Della Street's foot sought Mason's ankle under the table, give it a slight nudge. He pushed back from the table, moved over to Della Street's chair. A moment later they glided out onto the floor.

"What was it?" she asked.

Mason said, "Hortense Zitkousky telephoned. She was in a panic. I decided it would take a lot to get her in a panic, that I'd better go see what it was. It was Tanner lying across the bathtub just as Tragg described it. Someone had pushed a pillow up against the back of his head, stuck a gun into the pillow, and pulled the trigger."

"What was he doing while all that was going on?"

"Apparently being very ill from having absorbed too much alcohol."

"Who did it?"

"Horty says she has no idea. She got him up to Stephane's room because she wanted to have some central place to park him until Max Olger could get his story. He was getting talkative. She thought he was going to spill something important. She went downstairs to telephone me. The phone was busy. She went back up to the room and found what had happened. The second time, she called me from the room. She was wearing gloves."

Della Street followed Mason's leads mechanically while she digested that information.

"Knowing Horty," Mason said, "you can believe her. If you didn't know Horty, you wouldn't."

"But they'll find out she was out with him."

"How?"

"Well . . . don't you suppose someone saw them? Her appearance is rather—well, distinctive."

"It is if you connect her with Stephane Claire. Otherwise it isn't. She's not so heavy. It's the way she carries herself. She's one of the few women I've known who stand out in my mind as really justifying the adjective voluptuous."

"But after all, you weren't responsible. Why not simply have notified the police and . . ."

"Because I'm a hunter, Della. Some men get their thrills in life out of standing up to a charging lion or tiger. Some like to shoot small birds; some just like to hunt, not for what they kill, but for the thrill of hunting. . . . Well, I hunt murderers. I think I know who killed Greeley. It's the only solution which fits in with the facts. And, Della, *I* want to bag that murderer. I don't want Tragg to do it. I'm willing he should have the credit, but *I* want to be the one to do the hunting, and finding."

"Well, why mix into Tanner's case so deep that you . . ."

"Tragg wouldn't have let me be free to work. He'd have had me all sewed up."

"You mean just because you reported a murder?"

Mason laughed. "Sure. Look at it from Tragg's viewpoint. He leaves me to go get a sandwich, and I run out and turn up another corpse."

"Well, he knows you were there now."

"Thanks to that telltale feather," Mason said. "That was an unforeseen break which went against me."

"Then you're in hot water now?"

"Well, I can feel it getting warm," he admitted. "Come on, let's get back to the table and hold Drake in line. He may get ideas of his own if we leave him alone too long, and I want to put through a couple of telephone calls."

"To whom?"

"Oh, to some people I think Tragg should check up on."

They circled the dance floor until they were near their table, then Mason escorted her back to her chair. "Hold the fort," he said to Drake, "I'm going to telephone."

Drake said, "The waiter was here. He told me you said you wanted the dinner served right along."

"Yes. We might even skip the soup and get busy on the steaks. It may be quite a while, Paul, before we get nice tender filet mignon again."

Drake winced. "I wish you wouldn't kid about it. Tragg really means business this time."

"Uh huh," Mason agreed.

He skirted the dance floor, picked his way between the tables to the telephone booth, and dialed Homan's unlisted telephone number. A few moments later, he heard the voice of the Filipino boy on the line.

"Is Mr. Homan there?" Mason asked.

"Who is this talking please?"

"This is Mr. Mason, the lawyer."

"Oh, I am sorry, sah. He is very busy. He leave a message that no one is to disturb, no matter who. But perhaps . . ."

"Okay, Felipe, tell Mr. Homan to remember that you didn't go out tonight. Do you understand? You didn't go out."

The boy's voice showed surprise. "But I have *not* gone out, Mr. Mason. I am here all evening."

"That's the stuff," Mason said, and hung up the telephone.

Mason consulted his notebook, found the telephone number of Mona Carlyle, the employee at Rigley's Cafeteria, and called her.

"Miss Carlyle," he said, when he had her on the telephone, "this is Mr. Mason. I'm speaking on behalf of Mr. Drake. Mr. Drake offered Mrs. Warfield a position. For some reason best known to herself she decided not to take that position and left the hotel where she was to stay until Mr. Drake told her where and when to report."

"I'm sorry, Mr. Mason," the voice at the other end of the line said. "I simply can't help you at all. I don't know a thing about her."

"I understand that is the case," Mason said, "but it occurs to me that she may get in touch with you within the next few hours."

"Why? What makes you think so?"

"I don't know," Mason said. "Perhaps it's just a hunch. When she does, would you mind telling her that I've verified my information about her husband, and that if she wants complete information about him, I'll be only too glad to give it to her. But she must get in touch with me personally. Will you tell her that in case she communicates with you?"

"Why, yes," dubiously. "I'll tell her, but really, Mr. Mason, I haven't the faintest idea that she'll get in touch with me. . . ."

"I think she will," Mason said. "And thank you very much." He dropped the receiver into place.

He returned to the table where Drake and Della Street were conversing in low tones. Della looked up, smiled, and said, "I'm glad you're back. Every time they get me alone, it's the same old story."

"Trying to pump you?" Mason asked as he sat down.

"Uh huh. I'm afraid I'm losing my sex appeal. He used to try kidding me along. Now he's changed his objectives."

Drake said, "Dammit, Perry, you're always dragging me into some mess, and then making me go at it blind."

"I know," Mason said soothingly, "but it's better that way, Paul. It keeps you from getting gray."

"Well," Drake said, "couldn't you satisfy my curiosity? Just off the record?"

"There isn't any such thing as off the record, Paul. You're too conscientious. *You* wouldn't take a brick out of the chimney to drop it on an escaping murderer."

"That was a swell illustration you gave Tragg," Drake said, "but you couldn't have made it stick with me. I know you too well. You pull the house down and leave only the loose brick in the chimney standing."

"But," Mason smiled, "I put it all back together again."

"You have so far. This time you'll be like all the king's

horses and all the king's men who couldn't put Humpty Dumpty together again."

"Only in this case," Mason said, "Humpty Dumpty hasn't fallen off the wall."

"What were your telephone calls?" Della Street asked.

"Oh, just something to keep Tragg out of mischief. He's been afraid to go after Homan, knowing Homan will pin his ears back through some political pull. Well, this time I've put him in such a position he'll have to either fish or cut bait. And the second call is insurance. He'll let me stay in circulation now. We may as well settle down to enjoy our dinners."

"You aren't going to try to leave here?"

"Not until after Tragg comes back to ask me about the young woman with whom I was seen in the elevator. I . . ."

A bus boy approached the table. "Are you Mr. Mason?"

"Yes."

"Lieutenant Tragg wants to talk with you on the telephone."

Mason said, "The lieutenant is saving time. I guess you folks will have to excuse me once more. Oh, waiter. Just go ahead and serve the dinner. We'll have to hurry."

Mason went to the telephone. Tragg's voice said, "Mason, one of the elevator operators recognizes your photograph."

"*My* photograph."

"Yes."

"Where in the world did you get one of my photographs?"

Tragg said, "If you think I'm going to play around in your back yard without having a photograph of you all ready for emergencies, you're badly mistaken."

"Well, that's a commendable piece of foresight. What about the elevator boy?"

"He picked you up on the third floor. There was a young woman with you. Now what were you doing on the third floor, and who was the young woman?"

"The bellboy's identified my picture?" Mason asked.

"That's right."

"The identification is positive?"

"Absolute."

"Then," Mason said, "the young woman must have been my client. Don't you think that's a reasonable deduction, Tragg?"

Tragg's voice held an edge. "Mason, this is murder. I'm

not going to play horse. I know you usually have an ace in the hole, but this time I'm calling for a showdown."

"I can't answer any questions about any young woman with whom I was ever seen by an elevator boy in any downtown hotel at any time when any murder was committed," Mason said. "It's a policy of the office. I think that covers the situation, Lieutenant?"

Tragg said, "Mason, I'm going to let you stay out of jail until eleven o'clock tomorrow morning."

"Why the generosity?" Mason asked.

"Because," Tragg said, "I'm going to put you on the spot. I'm going to turn you loose on Homan. You've been trying to get *me* to stick *my* neck out. Now I'm going to let *you* pull some of *my* chestnuts out of the fire."

Mason said, "I don't have to ask him a single question. Mrs. Greeley's testimony will take care of everything."

"Did you think that crude trick was going to fool me?" Tragg asked.

"What was crude about it?"

Tragg said, "Mrs. Greeley, you'll remember, was very positive her husband wouldn't have ducked out on the girl. She was, however, conscientious enough to produce the shirt as soon as she found it. You'd have been in a spot if she'd simply ditched it."

"What are you talking about?"

"About that little alibi you fixed up for your client, Mason. When you planted that shirt, you overlooked one thing."

"I haven't the faintest idea what you're talking about, Tragg."

"You know what I'm talking about, Mason. It was a nice trick, but it didn't work. I suppose your charming secretary furnished the lipstick—and the imprint of the transferred lips?"

"All right, you're one up on me. Tell me what's wrong."

"The laundry mark on the shirt. You overlooked that, didn't you, Mason?"

"What about the laundry mark?"

"Unfortunately," Tragg said, "the laundry mark on the shirt is one of the corroborating bits of evidence that I decided should be checked. I checked on it, and it isn't Greeley's laundry mark. That shirt was planted in that bag after Greeley's death so Mrs. Greeley would find it. It was planted by some shrewd opportunist who knew that dead men can tell no tales, who knew that Mrs. Greeley, on finding that shirt, would communicate with you. And it was timed beautifully, Mason."

"Wait a minute," Mason said, his voice showing his concern. "Whose laundry mark is it?"

"We haven't been able to find out whose it is," Tragg said, "only whose it isn't. It isn't Greeley's laundry mark."

"Perhaps he had it done in San Francisco."

"No. It isn't Greeley's shirt. The sleeves are an inch and a half shorter than Greeley wears them, and, above all, the collar is sixteen and a quarter. Greeley wore fifteen and three-quarters. So I think, Mr. Mason, that we'll let you cross-examine Mr. Homan about the keys in the morning. And now you're free to leave the Tangerine at any time you want. But whenever you get ready to tell me the name of the young woman who was in the elevator with you this evening, you know where to reach me. And, by the way, I won't be back to eat my steak, so you'd better eat both steaks. Tomorrow night your diet will be much less elaborate. It will probably be some time before you have a good thick steak again."

"Listen, Tragg, about that shirt. I . . ."

"I've told you all I'm going to tell you, Mason. Miss Claire isn't out in the clear, not by a long ways. You've got to go to work on Homan in order to get anywhere, and immediately after the court disposes of the Case of the People versus Claire, you're going to tell me who that young woman was who came down in the elevator with you, *or* you're going to be placed in custody as a material witness. And if that should be Paul Drake's shirt, tell him *he'd* better eat two steaks as well. Because I'm eventually going to trace that laundry mark."

And the receiver clicked at the other end of the line.

Mason hung up the telephone, walked slowly back to the table where Della Street and Paul Drake were seated, their faces turned toward the floor show which had just started. Other patrons of the establishment were showing the mellowing effects of good liqour, good food, and a good show. Drake and Della Street looked as though they had been sitting at a funeral.

Mason slid into his chair, pulled his steak over toward him, picked up knife and fork, and attacked the meat with extreme relish.

"Doesn't seem to affect your appetite any," Drake said.

"It doesn't," Mason admitted. "You've always said I'd skate on thin ice, and break through, Paul. Well, get ready to smile. I've fallen in!"

"What is it?" Della asked.

"That wasn't Greeley's shirt. Someone planted it in the laundry bag for Mrs. Greeley to find."

"Good God!" Drake exclaimed. "That means we're elected."

Mason said, "Watch the floor show and quit worrying, Paul. Tragg says he won't arrest us until after I've cross-examined Homan."

19

THERE WAS a tense atmosphere of excitement permeating the courtroom as Judge Cortright called the Case of the People versus Stephane Claire, and Homan once more took the stand.

"Just one or two further questions, Mr. Homan," Mason said.

"Very well. Will you try and be as brief as possible?"

"If you will answer my questions," Mason said, "without equivocation, I think we can finish with you very shortly. Lieutenant Tragg is in court, I believe?"

Mason turned to look at Tragg. Tragg returned the stare. His forehead puckered into a slightly perplexed frown.

Mason said, "Lieutenant Tragg, you have, I believe, in your possession a white starched shirt with some red stains on the bosom. May I ask you to show that shirt to this witness?"

"What is the idea?" Harold Hanley asked.

Mason said, "You will remember that according to the testimony of the witnesses, there was a smear of lipstick on the little finger of the right hand of the defendant in this case. I . . ."

"I think that question is proper," Judge Cortright ruled.

"Do you have such a shirt in your possession, Lieutenant Tragg?"

Tragg nodded.

"Here in court?" Mason asked.

Tragg hesitated a moment, then reached under the counsel table, and picked up a black handbag. He opened it while spectators craned curious necks to see the shirt with its telltale smear, then Tragg handed it to Mason.

"Thank you," Mason said. "Now, Mr. Homan, will you examine this shirt carefully and tell me whether it's yours."

"*My* shirt?" Homan exclaimed.

"Yes."

"Great Heavens, man, *I* wasn't driving that car! I was here . . ."

But please examine it just the same, Mr. Homan, and then answer my question."

He spread the shirt out across Homan's knees.

Homan looked at the shirt with its crimson smear. "I don't know," he said promptly. "How could I tell whose shirt it is?"

Mason said, "Come, come, Mr. Homan. We can do better than that. Do you know your own laundry mark?"

"No, sir. I don't."

Mason said, "Well, perhaps I can help you. I'm sorry to bother you, but will you loosen your tie so I can see the inside of your neckband?"

Homan complied and leaned forward. Mason read the laundry mark, "W. 362."

"Now then," Mason said, indicating a mark on the inside of the neckband of the shirt, "you will see *this* shirt has the same laundry mark."

Homan regarded the shirt with narrowed eyes, took it in his hands, turned it over, looked at the smear of lipstick, then broke into bitter expostulation. "That's a frame-up. I never saw the defendant in this case in my life. I didn't give her any ride. I . . ."

"That will do," Judge Cortright interrupted. "You will confine your answers to questions."

"The question, Mr. Homan," Mason said, "is whether that is your shirt."

"I don't know."

"But it is your laundry mark?"

"I guess so, yes."

"And you wear a sixteen and a quarter shirt?"

"Yes."

"Do you see anything about it which indicates it is *not* your shirt?"

"No. I guess not."

Mason said, "Very well, I am now going to call your attention to the keys which the defendant found in her purse, and ask you if this key is a key to the ignition switch of your automobile."

"It looks like it. I presume so, yes."

"And do you know what this one is a key to?"

"No, sir."

"Doesn't it look at all familiar?"

"No. It . . . wait a minute. . . . No, I thought for a moment it looked like one of my keys, but it isn't."

"These are not your keys?"

"No, sir. Absolutely not."

"Do you happen to have your keys in your pocket?"

"Why . . . yes."

"May I see them, please?"

"I don't see what that has to do with it."

"The witness will produce his keys," Judge Cortright ordered. Homan reluctantly took a leather-covered key container from his pocket.

Mason said, "Let's compare these keys and see if we can find any that check. Why, yes, here are two that are identical. Can you tell me what this key in your key container is to, Mr. Homan?"

"My yacht."

"A lock on the cabin?"

"Yes."

"Now this other key. Do you have one that's identical with that key?"

"I wouldn't know. I can't remember what all my keys look like."

Mason checked through the key container. "No," he said, "you don't seem to have one."

Homan shifted his position.

"Now you don't think these are *your* keys?"

"No."

"You didn't leave your keys in the car by mistake when you parked it—the day it was stolen?"

"No."

"You're certain?"

"Yes."

Mason jingled the key ring. "This third key—the one you haven't been able to identify—you haven't any idea what lock this key fits?"

"No."

Mason regarded him steadily for several seconds. "Eventually, Mr. Homan," he said at length, "the police are going to find the lock this key fits. It would be unfortunate if that should prove to be . . ."

"Wait a minute," Homan interrupted. "I'm very absentminded when I'm working. I *may* have left my keys in the car when I parked it."

"Then these may be your keys?"

Judge Cortright said sternly, "Do you want this court to understand you don't know your own keys?"

"Yes, Your Honor, I have so many keys . . . I'm afraid that . . . well, you see, I'm always giving keys to servants and chauffeurs, and then getting them back. These may have been some old keys I'd left in the glove compartment. Yes, that must be it, some keys I'd inadvertently left in the glove compartment."

Judge Cortright looked down at the witness for several contemptuous seconds, then said to Perry Mason, "Go ahead with your questions, Counselor."

Mason smiled. "I'm finished."

"What!" Hanley exclaimed in surprise.

"I have no further questions," Mason announced.

Tragg and Hanley whispered, then Hanley got up and crossed over to Mason. "What's the idea?" he whispered. "You've got him on the run."

Mason said, "You can question him if you want to."

"Not me," Hanley said. "I can't ride him with spurs. His studio would be gunning for my job before noon."

Judge Cortright looked down at Mason. "Counsel will understand," he said, "that the court is interested in this phase of the testimony. There have been enough facts adduced to cast some doubt in the court's mind, but not enough as yet to overcome all of the evidence introduced by the prosecution."

Mason said, "I'm sorry, Your Honor, but I have no further questions."

Judge Cortright hesitated, then turned to Homan. "Mr. Homan, were you driving that car on Wednesday the nineteenth?"

"No, sir. Absolutely not."

"Do you know who was?"

"No, sir."

"Where were you on Wednesday the nineteenth?"

"On Wednesday the nineteenth," Homan said, "I was at my residence in Beverly Hills. As soon as I missed the car, and verified the fact that my younger brother was out in my yacht, fishing, so that there was no possibility *he* could have unlocked it with his keys, and taken it without consulting me, I reported the car as being stolen to the city police at Beverly Hills. A representative of the police called on me to ask me the details. That can be verified."

"That was Wednesday the nineteenth," Judge Cortright asked.

"Yes, Your Honor."

"At what time?"

"I would say about five or six o'clock in the afternoon."

"Have you any explanation as to how this stain of lipstick got on your shirt?"

"No, Your Honor."

Judge Cortright looked down at Lieutenant Tragg. "Is there," he asked, "any reason to doubt this evidence? In other words, is there anything to indicate it has been fabricated?"

"I hadn't thought so," Lieutenant Tragg said, his voice showing that he was badly perplexed. "But apparently— well, something must be wrong. Of course, if Mr. Homan can account for his whereabouts at the time of the accident . . ."

"I can," Homan said calmly. "I was at my home in Beverly Hills. I reported the car as being stolen as I have said. I had a conference with a representative of the police of Beverly Hills, and then I went to the studio, taking the script on which I had been working and had a conference with a certain department head."

"What time did that conference start?" Judge Cortright asked.

"At about nine o'clock in the evening, and continued through until nearly midnight."

Cortright and Tragg exchanged glances, then Tragg and Hanley went into a whispered conference.

Mason said suavely, "These, gentlemen, were *your* questions, not mine."

Judge Cortright looked down at Mason. "Evidently,

Counselor," he said with some acerbity, "you knew *exactly* where to stop in your examination."

Mason smiled serenely at the baffled judge. "Quite evidently I did, Your Honor.

Hanley got slowly to his feet. "Your Honor," he said, "some of this evidence comes as a distinct surprise to us. We had anticipated that the examination of the witness would be more complete, that there would be some effort to show the identity of all the keys on this key ring. It might even be the police could furnish Mr. Mason with an opportunity to get this evidence, or at any rate to see if this witness . . . well, we'll cooperate with Mr. Mason in any and every way." He stopped and looked across at Mason, but Mason returned his gaze with eyes which showed only bland disinterest.

Hanley turned back to Judge Cortright. "The situation is one which is very peculiar, Your Honor. The district attorney's office doesn't wish to be a party to any injustice. As the court may well know, further developments in this case have become exceedingly grave and somewhat complicated. We feel that in justice to all concerned, the hearing should be continued while we check Mr. Homan's testimony carefully."

"Does that mean I've got to come back here again?" Homan demanded indignantly.

Judge Cortright studied the indignant picture producer for several thoughtful seconds, then said quietly, "It does. The court will continue this case until Monday morning at ten o'clock at which time the witnesses will return to court."

"But, Your Honor, I can't keep trotting back and forth here to court . . ."

"You're a witness," Judge Cortright said. "Furthermore, Mr. Homan, there are some matters in your testimony which have not been explained to the court's satisfaction. The case is continued until Monday morning at ten o'clock. The defendant remains on bail, Mr. Deputy District Attorney?"

"She is on bail at the present time."

"Is there any motion to have that bail increased?"

Hanley said, "No, Your Honor, I guess not," and then added, "The defendant seems to have a perfect and complete alibi for all of yesterday evening when the second murder was committed."

"Very well," Judge Cortright said, "the court will take a recess for ten minutes, and then take up the Case of People versus Sampson."

As Judge Cortright left the bench, Tragg came over to Mason. "What's the idea, Mason?" he asked.

Mason said, "It's your move, Tragg. You said you'd give me until this morning, and unless I could make some satisfactory explanation, you'd arrest me after I had cross-examined Homan. Well, here I am."

Tragg said, "Mason, you knew about that murder last night."

Mason smiled and said nothing.

"I have enough circumstantial evidence to hold you—at least as a material witness."

"Do it," Mason said, "and you'll regret it as long as you live."

Tragg sighed. "I wish," he said to Mason, "we could get along. After all, we should be working together on this case."

"We could if you weren't always trying to get something on me," Mason said.

"Get something on you! Good Lord, you play tag with corpses, violate half of the laws in the penal code, and then expect me to tag along with a happy smile. How the hell did you know it was Homan's shirt?"

Homan, who had marched from the witness stand and was standing on the outskirts of the group, pressed forward and said, "Gentlemen, I dislike to interrupt, but I simply want to tell Mr. Mason I think his questions are impertinent."

Mason merely smiled.

Tragg said, "Mr. Homan, I don't want to bother you, but it's imperative that we check up on your statements as to what you were doing on Wednesday. Will you kindly sit down over there and write the names of every person with whom you talked on Wednesday afternoon?"

"Gladly, sir," Homan snapped. "I'll do everything in my power to contribute to a solution of this case. I know I wasn't driving that automobile, and I don't believe Adler Greeley was driving it. What I object to is the manner in which my private affairs are being pried into."

"I understand your position perfectly," Mason said. "You object. You've made your objection—and it's overruled." He turned his shoulder.

Homan glowered indignantly, then strode over to the table which Tragg had indicated, whipped some paper from his brief case, adjusted his horned-rimmed spectacles, and started to scribble.

Mrs. Greeley came walking toward them from the back of the courtroom. She said, "Mr. Mason, I had no idea that was not my husband's shirt when I brought it to you last night. But I knew Adler wouldn't have been guilty of the things they claim the driver of this car did. And I most certainly had no idea that shirt belonged to Mr. Homan. You evidently know something I don't. Apparently, there is some mysterious connection between my husband and Mr. Homan. Can you tell me what it is?"

Mason shook his head. "Not right now, Mrs. Greeley. But if you can wait a few hours, I think I'll have a lot more information."

She said, "You were so helpful last night, Mr. Mason, so—so encouraging. You made things so much easier for me."

"I'm glad I did. And here's one way you can help. In going over your husband's correspondence, did you find anything that would connect him with a Mrs. Warfield?"

She frowned. "There's nothing at the house. Perhaps his secretary at the office could tell you."

"I'd prefer to have you try to dig it up, Mrs. Greeley." He turned to Tragg and said, "After all, Lieutenant, Della Street is the one who really called my attention to the key clue in the entire case."

"What's that?" Tragg asked as Jackson Sterne came up to stand diffidently on the edge of the group.

"Mrs. Warfield. She didn't leave the Gateview Hotel that night. On the other hand, she certainly didn't sleep in her room."

Tragg said, "I don't get you, Mason."

Mason smiled. "I'm going to the Gateview Hotel. I'm going to take a room, and I'm going to question the various employees in detail concerning a theory I have. Any objections?"

Tragg's eyes narrowed. "No objections right at the moment, but until you've accounted for that feather, Mason . . ."

"Really, Lieutenant, you mustn't attach too much importance to these inanimate clues. It's much more satisfactory to analyze motivations and opportunities, and de-

duce what must have happened. Well, I'll be seeing you."
He picked up his brief case and calmly walked away.

Jackson Sterne stood watching him, blinking slowly.
Mrs. Greeley watched Mason's back with eyes in which
there were quick tears. "He's going to clear Adler of
getting out of that car and leaving Miss Claire to take the
blame," she said in a voice which carried conviction.

Hanley said with feeling, "There never was a more
clever outlaw. Essentially, the man is nonsocial, nonconven-
tional, a nonconformist. He may respect justice, but he
certainly has no regard for the letter of the law!"

"But," Tragg pointed out, "he's done more to solve
murders than any man on the force . . . but . . . well, *damn
him!*"

20

MASON SAT in his room in the Gateview Hotel. From time
to time he looked at his watch. The pile of cigarette stubs
in the ash tray mounted higher. Toward noon, Mason
called his office. "Anything new, Della?"

"Everything quiet and serene at this end."

Mason sighed. "I'm afraid Tragg's interference has
wrecked my little scheme. If you don't hear from me in
half an hour, call Tragg and ask him to come up here, will
you?"

"Okay. Anything else?"

"That's all. Be seeing you, Della."

Mason clicked the receiver into place, took another
cigarette from his hammered silver case, and heard a knock
at the door.

"Come in," he called.

The door opened. Mrs. Greeley entered.

Mason jumped to his feet. "Why, Mrs. Greeley, I had
no idea *you* were coming!"

"I hope I haven't disturbed you, Mr. Mason, but I've
found something . . ."

Mason glanced at his wrist watch. "Can't it wait, Mrs. Greeley? I'm expecting someone else."

"It will only take a minute."

Mason hesitated, then quickly closed the door, and placed a chair for her. "I don't want to seem inhospitable," he said, "but I'm expecting someone who may come at any minute."

"Mrs. Warfield?" she asked.

"What makes you think of her?"

"Because I've found that correspondence you were asking about."

"Where is it?"

"Here." She indicated a brief case. "Do you want to look at it now?"

Mason once more consulted his watch, hesitated, said, "Could you leave it with me?"

"Yes."

"I'm sorry," he apologized, "but seconds are precious. I'm trying to . . ."

"I understand," she interrupted. "I'll just put these over on the bed. I'm frightfully nervous, Mr. Mason. I'm wondering if my own life isn't in danger."

"Frankly," Mason said, "I think it is."

"Mr. Mason, did you know what was in these letters?"

"I had an idea."

"Do you know who the man was my husband was protecting?"

"I think I do."

"Can you tell me?"

"I'd prefer not to—not right now."

She said, "There's something in that first letter, the one on top, I'd like to have you read now."

Mason reached for the letter. "This one?" he asked.

"Yes. That . . ."

Mason whirled. His hand clamped on her wrist.

An involuntary half scream left her lips. Something heavy dropped from her right hand, struck the edge of the bed, thudded to the floor. The fingers of her left hand continued to clutch at the pillow. Her right hand sought his arm, gripped it until her fingers dug into his muscles.

Mason said, "You're perfectly safe here, Mrs. Greeley, but you're not going to be safe if you carry that gun and draw it at the slightest noise."

"There's someone at the door! Someone turned the knob!"

Mason strode quickly to the door, and jerked it open. There was no one in the corridor.

"I heard someone," she said. "Someone was turning the knob, very slowly and stealthily. The door was sliding open."

Mason frowned. "I'm afraid you've ruined everything."

"I'm sorry."

"It's as much my fault as yours. And as for carrying that gun—you're foolish. Your life is in danger; but it's nothing you can ward off with a gun. The persons who are after you are far too clever to be disposed of that way.

"Now, look here, you're nervous, unstrung, and hysterical. Go to your family physician and ask him to give you a narcotic which will make you sleep for at least twenty-four hours. How long since you've slept?"

The corners of her mouth twitched. "Not more than an hour or two since . . ." Her face was distorted by a spasm. "I can't get it out of my mind! I can't. I can't! I'm going to be next. I know it. I've been followed. I've been . . ."

Mason said, "Mrs. Greeley, I want you to go see a doctor right now. I can't give you any more time now. Promise me you'll go to your doctor at once. Will you do that?"

His hand patted her shoulder.

Her eyes blinked up at him through tears. "Mr. Mason, you're absolutely wonderful. I'll go at once."

She took a deep breath, and tried to smile. "I'm sorry I lost control," she said. "Good-by, Mr. Mason."

"Good-by."

Mason closed and locked the door. Some thirty minutes later, in response to another knock, he tiptoed to stand on one side of the door so that a bullet sent crashing through the panels would miss him. "Who is it?" he asked.

"Tragg."

"I don't recognize your voice."

"What's the idea?" Tragg asked. "Can't you . . ."

Mason unlocked the door. "I just wanted to be sure."

"Why all the caution?"

"I'm expecting the murderer to call on me."

"So I gathered. What's the idea?"

Mason dropped into a chair, lit a cigarette. "Mrs. Warfield came to this hotel. She didn't stay in her room that night."

"Certainly not. She went to Greeley's room. I found her baggage there."

"Where did she go after that?" Mason asked.

"She stayed right there."

"After shooting Greeley?"

"Yes. Why not?"

"She couldn't be certain someone hadn't heard the shot."

"No, of course not," Tragg admitted, "but it didn't sound like a shot. Two or three people heard the noise, but thought it was a car exhaust."

"She, of course, had no way of knowing that."

"What are you getting at?"

"She didn't leave the hotel until the next morning."

"She stayed there in the room."

"With Greeley's body?"

"Why not?"

"The bed wasn't slept in."

"She'd hardly lie down with a corpse and go to sleep."

"And she'd hardly sit up all night in the room with a dead man. Grant that she has a pretty strong stomach. It's sitll asking too much."

"What *did* she do?" Tragg asked.

"Spent the night in another room."

"Whose?"

Mason shrugged. "There are a lot of things about this case that can't be proved—yet. But, Tragg, we know what the answer is, and if there's anything wrong with my reasoning, point it out."

"All right, go ahead."

"When I realized what must have happened here at the hotel, I had Drake look up the registrations. Two single rooms were rented within fifteen minutes of the time Mrs. Warfield registered. One was to a man who answered the description of the driver of the car. So I didn't bother with the other.—I realize now I should have."

"Who was the other?"

"A woman. Don't you get it?"

"No. I don't."

"Mrs. Warfield must have spent the night with that woman."

"But her baggage was in Greeley's room. . . ."

"Certainly," Mason said. "Mrs. Warfield registered and went to her room, then she went back to the lobby to try and pick up some back numbers of *Photoplay Magazine*.

I'd shown her a photograph of Homan. I asked her if it wasn't her husband—or Spinney. She had been trying to locate Spinney—to find out who he really was. She thought this was Spinney's picture.—Through him, she thought she could reach her husband. When she found she couldn't get the magazine she wanted, she returned to her room. Greeley was probably there waiting for her."

"You think Greeley was Spinney?"

"Yes."

"Then who was her husband?"

"Greeley."

"I don't get you."

"Greeley created Spinney out of thin air to give himself a go-between."

"Go ahead," Tragg said.

"Now Greeley takes Mrs. Warfield down to his room. Naturally, he takes her baggage along. Remember he is her husband, and she's crazy about him."

"You think he was waiting for her when she got back from the lobby?"

"Sure. Otherwise she would have at least washed up and used the soap and a towel. All right, now we've got Mrs. Warfield in Greeley's room. He makes the mistake of trying to confess and ask her forgiveness. In place of that, he gets a bullet in his brain. Mrs. Warfield has been through too much to do any forgiving. She's been working to the limit of her endurance, and sending every cent she could possibly spare to a man whom she loved. When she finds out he has been deliberately milking her of money so she wouldn't have enough carfare to come to the Coast and investigate . . ."

"All right, she shot him," Tragg interrupted. "Then what?"

"She goes back to her room, prepares to make an escape. That's when the woman found her."

"Who was the woman?"

"Mrs. Greeley."

"*What?*"

"Yes. It must have been."

"And what did Mrs. Greeley want?"

"Mrs. Greeley was suspicious. She didn't have proof—not then. She wanted to pump Mrs. Warfield."

"What happened?"

"Mrs. Warfield recognized a marvelous opportunity to

escape. She strung Mrs. Greeley along, stayed with her that night, and calmly walked out in the morning."

"That's a pretty fancy story."

"It checks with the evidence. Mrs. Greeley is in love with Jules Homan. In Hollywood, they handle those things very nicely. The husband steps aside. There's a quiet divorce, and the parties marry. But Greeley wasn't of the Hollywood crowd. He became suspicious and wanted to hook Homan for big damages for alienation of affections. Homan couldn't stand that. It would hurt his business career."

"How do you get all this?" Tragg asked.

Mason said, "Homan must have been driving that car Tuesday. Mrs. Greeley must have been with him on Tuesday night and Wednesday morning. That's the only way you can put the evidence together so it fits. They left Beverly Hills Tuesday, went to a mountain cabin which Homan owns in the mountains back of Fresno. You'll probably find the third key on that ring fits the lock on that cabin. Those were Homan's keys, an extra set he kept for his expeditions with Mrs. Greeley when he could get away—sometimes on the yacht, sometimes up to this mountain cabin."

Tragg said, "I think it's cuckoo, but I'll hear the rest of it."

"Tanner, the chauffeur, had been bribed by Greeley to act as his spy. Greeley was in San Francisco taking the identity of Spinney for the purpose of keeping Mrs. Warfield where he wanted her. He knew, of course, that it must be during his trips to San Francisco that Homan was taking advantage of his absence. Tanner telephoned Greeley in San Francisco twice. The first time, he told Greeley that Homan had taken the car and left. The second time that Homan hadn't gone to the yacht, and, therefore, must be in the cabin back of Fresno. And at least once Greeley telephoned Tanner at Homan's residence."

"The calls charged to Homan's phone?" Tragg asked.

Mason smiled. "That's poetic justice."

"Go ahead."

"It was sometime late Tuesday night when Tanner definitely found out they were at Homan's mountain cabin. Greeley took a plane to Fresno, hired a car, investigated, found Homan and his wife were there. He couldn't steal Homan's car without leaving his hired car for them to get away in. So he drove back, hired a car with a driver, got out on the highway somewhere within a mile or so of Homan's mountain hide-out, took Homan's car, so as to leave the lovers abandoned in their love nest."

"Why didn't he bust in on them and call for a showdown?" Tragg asked.

"For one reason, he wasn't ready for a showdown. For another, they weren't there."

"I don't get you."

"They were back *in* town Wednesday afternoon. There's only one answer. They must have spotted him snooping around on his first visit, telephoned for a plane, and rushed back here. It's less than two hundred miles in an air line. I don't *know*, mind you, but I'll bet twenty to one that there's some sort of landing field near that cabin. There has to be."

"Why the hell didn't they take Homan's car? Why leave it and take a plane?"

"Time, for one thing. Then they knew Greeley had actually seen the car. The best way to establish an alibi was to rush back by plane, and report the car as stolen."

"Why wasn't Greeley ready for a showdown?"

"Because of Mrs. Warfield. He already had a wife. It would be rather embarrassing for him to sue for a couple of hundred thousand dollars, and then have some smart lawyer bring Mrs. Warfield into court. This way, he steals the car and thinks he's leaving them marooned in the mountains. Back in Los Angeles, he'll abandon Homan's car and go home. His wife won't be there. She'll show up after a while, very much alarmed, and with some plausible lie that he'll certainly be able to disprove when the time comes. But as it turned out, it was he who did the hitch-hiking."

"He wanted Mrs. Warfield to get a divorce?" Tragg asked.

"At first," Mason said. "Later on, I think he decided to kill her."

Tragg snorted. "Next thing I know you'll be trying to prove self-defense."

"Well . . . let's say she beat him to the punch, if that's what you mean. Understand, Tragg, I'm not a mind reader. I'm only giving you a solution which fits the evidence. If you can punch any holes in it, go ahead."

Tragg scratched his head and thought things over. Then

he said suddenly, "But Mrs. Greeley talked with her husband in San Francisco."

"No. After Greeley died, she *said* she did."

"She talked with *someone*."

"Sure. Part of her alibi. She telephones some friend from a pay station and arranges for the *second* station-to-station call. That way, she establishes the fact, by the telephone company records, she was in Los Angeles, and doesn't have to drag her friend's name into it."

"How do you know all this?" Tragg asked.

Mason said, "I don't, but it's the only way the evidence fits together."

Tragg pushed his hands down deep into his pockets, stood staring down at the tips of his shoes. "Anything else?"

"A lot of minor corroborating facts," Mason said. Greeley, of course, was having detectives keep an eye on Mrs. Warfield. When they reported she was coming to Los Angeles to take a job with a Mr. Drake, Greeley was waiting for her at the bus depot—keeping out of sight of course."

"And he followed you folks to the hotel?"

"Yes."

"And how about Mrs. Greeley?"

"She must have followed Greeley. Maybe she even saw the wire reporting Mrs. Warfield's arrival. Remember, she was watching her husband like a hawk on those days because she suspected he knew of her affair."

"How about that stained shirt?"

Mason smiled. "Now comes the touch of real comedy. You'll remember, Homan and Mrs. Greeley rushed off to their love nest at night after Mrs. Greeley found her husband was going to be detained in San Francisco. Homan didn't stop to change his dinner jacket, but just threw some other clothes in a bag. Now, when they were getting out of the cabin, they must have been in a panic, grabbing things right and left. In the confusion of packing, Homan's stiff shirt got put in Mrs. Greeley's bag. When Mrs. Greeley found that shirt, the logical place to hide it was in her husband's laundry bag. She dropped it in there, intending to dispose of it later.

"After her husband's death, she realized that I was working on the Warfield angle, and checking up pretty closely on Homan. She and Homan were both in a panic for fear I'd bring out the evidence of their little affair. The best way to head all that off was to get Stephane Claire acquitted. One way to do that was to prove that Greeley had been driving the car. So she went to his laundry bag, grabbed the first stiff shirt she came to, smeared lipstick on it, and brought it to my office. Poor girl, it was a last desperate attempt. By that time her mind must have been going around in circles, or she would have remembered Homan's shirt."

"Why did you come here, Mason?" Tragg asked.

"To check on the identity of the woman who had registered immediately after Greeley."

"But evidently you knew that already."

"I surmised it."

"Any idea where Mrs. Warfield is?"

"She might be on Homan's yacht. Remember, his brother Horace wanted to use it, but Jules suddenly refused to let him."

Tragg studied him thoughtfully. "What's that stuff on the bed?"

"Some papers Mrs. Greeley brought—correspondence between her husband and Mrs. Warfield, stuff she found after his death."

"Well, I guess . . . hello, what's this?"

Tragg's eyes had come to rest on the gun lying on the floor.

"Mrs. Greeley dropped it."

"Dropped it?"

"Yes. She's hysterical. Now has the idea someone's trying to kill her. I made her promise she'd go to her doctor and get him to give her some sleeping stuff."

Tragg picked up the gun. "A small caliber automatic."

"Yes. It fits nicely in her bag. Do you want it?"

Tragg studied it for a moment, then dropped it into his hip pocket. "Mason, I congratulate you."

"I haven't done anything," Mason said, "except put the evidence together."

"That's enough, isn't it? It's a triumph for you."

"I don't want any of it, Tragg. You take the credit. All *I* want is to have Stephane Claire acquitted of that negligent homicide."

Tragg's face flushed. "Gosh, Mason, that's damned white."

Mason said, "I'm an amateur. You're the professional. You turn up the murderer. I'll get my client off."

Tragg turned toward the telephone. "I'll get headquarters and . . ."

"Wait a minute."

"What's the idea?" Tragg asked.

"There's no hurry."

"The devil there isn't! We've really got something on Mrs. Warfield now—if she *is* on Homan's yacht—"

Mason broke in, "There are a couple of angles I want to check, and I've been hoping something would turn up here in the hotel. Let's go have a drink, Tragg, and check the evidence over carefully."

Tragg's eyes narrowed. "What's the idea?" he asked.

"Nothing," Mason said, "only before you talk to the . . ."

Tragg suddenly snatched up the telephone. "Get me through to headquarters," he said. "Yes, police headquarters. This is Lieutenant Tragg. Rush that call!"

Mason said, "Don't do that, Tragg."

Tragg looked at him over the top of the telephone. "Damn you, Mason! You had me sold. The only thing that tipped me off was the way you tried to keep me from sticking my neck out just now. . . . Hello, headquarters. This is Tragg. Get the dispatcher to throw out a dragnet for Mrs. Adler Greeley. We have her description and photograph. . . . Yes, first-degree murder. . . . Her husband and Ernest Tanner. And cover all drugstores in the vicinity of the Gateview Hotel, and see if a woman answering her description has tried to buy poison. Get that started at once. I'll call back later with details."

Tragg dropped the receiver into place. "You could have fooled me," he said to Mason, "if you hadn't been such a softie. You knew that if I called headquarters and gave them that line on Mrs. Warfield, it would sound like a logical solution. The newspaper boys would make me out a regular Sherlock Holmes—and tomorrow morning when they found Mrs. Greeley's body and her confession, I'd be the laughingstock of the town. I presume you told her to commit suicide."

Mason sighed. "I only told her to see her doctor, Tragg."

21

DELLA STREET came through the door from the outer office. Mason, tilted back in his swivel chair, his feet crossed on the corner of the desk, was staring in frowning concentration at the tips of his shoes.

"What is it, Della?"

She didn't answer at once, but walked around the desk to place a sympathetic hand on his shoulder. "Lieutenant Tragg just telephoned, Chief."

Mason looked up with a quick glance, then at what he saw in Della Street's face, turned away once more.

"They've found her."

"Where?" Mason asked.

"In the place no one would ever have thought of looking."

"The Gateview Hotel?" Mason asked.

Her eyes were wide. "How did you know?"

Mason said, "My guess would be she never checked out of that room she took. She didn't want to attract any attention to herself, so it's very possible she paid a week's rent on the room when she registered."

"Then she must have intended to kill him at that time."

Mason nodded.

"Why?"

"To protect the reputation of the man she loved."

"Homan?"

"Yes."

"And your idea was to throw Tragg off the scent just long enough to give her an opportunity to . . . you *are* a softie."

Mason said, "She's intensely emotional, Della. She's a woman. She loved Homan, madly, passionately. She did what she did in order to save Homan's reputation. And then Tanner started blackmailing her. And when she knew Tanner knew, she had to silence his lips in the same way she had silenced her husband's. And the tragic part of it was, if she'd only waited, it wouldn't have been necessary. If she'd only talked with Mrs. Warfield before she went down to her husband's room. Oh, well," Mason said with a sigh, "you can't reverse the hands of the clock."

"Chief, what did actually happen?"

"A great deal of it was just the way I outlined it to Tragg," Mason said, a note of weariness creeping into his voice. "But there were one or two important variations. When Mrs. Greeley learned her husband was corresponding with a detective agency over a Mrs. Warfield, she probably thought Mrs. Warfield was a witness in the case Greeley was planning to file for alienation of affections against Homan.

"She followed her husband to the hotel. Of course, she didn't go to Mrs. Warfield's room first. She went to *his* room—and killed him. We can only surmise what happened next, but under the evidence, it's not taking much of a chance. Greeley probably had some of Mrs. Warfield's correspondence to Spinney in his pocket when he was murdered, and it wouldn't have taken Mrs. Greeley long to realize that here was a marvelous opportunity for framing Greeley's murder on Mrs. Warfield. She goes to Mrs. Warfield's room, gets Mrs. Warfield down to her room, and worms the whole story out of her. Mrs. Warfield is afraid of the law, believing her husband to be a convict, and she is already suspicious of Drake and me, so it's easy to persuade her to ditch us and disappear so Drake and I can't find her. Mrs. Greeley has to put her some place where she won't see the newspapers. The answer is Homan's yacht."

"And Mrs. Warfield's baggage?"

"Mrs. Greeley put it in Greeley's room, of course—probably telling Mrs. Warfield she was going to spirit it out of the hotel."

There was a long pause. Then Della frowned. "Greeley wasn't wearing his dinner jacket when he got home."

"Sure he was, but he changed his clothes before awakening his wife."

"How much did Homan know of what Mrs. Greeley had done?"

Mason shook his head. "I don't know. That's up to Tragg. But my best guess is he didn't know a thing."

"Not even if he was keeping Mrs. Warfield on his yacht?"

"No. I don't think he knows she's on the yacht. Only

that Mrs. Greeley said he wanted to borrow it to keep some witness concealed. In any event, that's Tragg's headache. I'm not going to worry about it. Dammit, Della, I sent a woman to her death. I don't want to talk about it any more."

Della picked up an ash tray, emptied it, and replaced it on the lawyer's desk.

"What about your beautiful blonde, Chief?"

"She's in the clear."

"Sure. I mean——"

"Oh, that uncle of hers will come around after I've talked with him."

"Uncle!" Della's nose wrinkled in disdain. "I mean her love life."

"Well—there's the Romeo from home—but I'm betting on young Homan. He's not a bad kid, and if I know the signs——"

The telephone rang. Della Street picked up the receiver, said, "Hello? . . . Hold the line a minute," and turned to Mason. "It's Tragg." Mason took the phone.

"Hello, Perry," Tragg said. "I just wanted to thank you. The newspaper boys think I'm some detective."

"That's fine."

"When did you first know, Mason?" Tragg asked.

Mason said, "I *should* have known some time before I did, but when you found that white feather in my hallway, Tragg, I realized at once what had happened. When Mrs. Greeley telephoned about the shirt she wasn't calling from her house. She was telephoning from the Adirondack Hotel or some place near by, but said she was at home so that she'd have an alibi."

"And she'd already committed the murder?"

"Yes. She'd followed Tanner ever since he left the courtroom. By that time she was desperate. She'd tried to protect Homan and herself and she was going to see it through. She realized Tanner held the whip hand. Remember, when she called she said she couldn't leave right away, so she had time to dash by and pick up the shirt and tuxedo. You should have known as soon as you found that feather, Tragg."

"You mean she was the one who dropped the feather?"

"Of course," Mason said.

"How did you know *you* didn't?" Tragg asked.

Mason grinned. "I wouldn't want to make any admissions to you in your official capacity, Tragg, but *if* I had been in that room in the Adirondack Hotel, I certainly hope you don't think I'd be so confoundedly negligent as not to look over my shoes very carefully while I was returning to the office in the taxicab. A man of ordinary intelligence would know that loose feathers would stick to wet shoes—and take proper precautions."

And Mason gently slid the receiver onto its hook before Tragg could make any reply—or ask any questions.

Perry Mason mysteries by
ERLE STANLEY GARDNER

Published by Ballantine Books.
Available in your local bookstore.